FUTURE PERFECT
A Collection of Fantastic Erotica

by Helen E. H. Madden

ISBN: 978-1905091-20-1
Published by Logical-Lust Publications © 2009

Cover image © 2009 Helen E. H. Madden, pixelarcana.com

Acknowledgements

Books do not happen on their own. *This* book would never have happened without the help and encouragement of several people. Many thanks go to Adrienne Benedicks and the staff of the *Erotica Readers and Writers Association* for giving me a forum to post these stories and for encouraging me to write more. Thanks also to the members of the ERWA Story Time group for their invaluable critiques. Good writing does not happen without good critiquing.

I owe a huge debt of thanks to Jim and Zetta Brown and Rachel McIntyre of *Logical Lust Publications*, for giving me the opportunity to see these stories in print. It takes a special kind of publisher to put out something that doesn't fit the standard definition of erotica, and these guys specialize in defying the standards.

Some of the stories in this book originally appeared on the *Heat Flash* erotica podcast. There never would have been a *Heat Flash* erotica podcast if it were not for Tee Morris, Paul Fischer, Martha Holloway, and podcasting's Rich Sigfrit. These four people delivered an eye-opening workshop at RavenCon 2007 that forever changed my writing career. Thanks, guys, for showing me the light.

Finally, the biggest thanks of all go to my husband, Michael. Honey, for every weekend you took the kids so that I could work, for every evening you let me lock myself in the office to wrestle with a story, and for all the software you bought and the computers you built and fixed at all hours of the night, I say thank you. I never could have done this without you.

Dedication

To Michael, because you can't buy good tech support,
you gotta sleep with it and bear its children

Table of Contents

Circus! Circus!

In the Circus Noir sat an audience of one.

"Entertain me," she demanded. The ringmaster cracked his whip. Naked acrobats tumbled into her lap. Contortionists twined pretzel-like to felate each other at her feet. Cossack riders galloped bareback, flogging their cocks and their fiery steeds.

"More!" she cried.

In marched the freaks—Siamese twins, bearded ladies, the Crocodile Boy of Nairobi. An act for every fetish. Surely one would please?

No. She writhed in her seat, panting. "Isn't there anything else?"

"Of course, madame."

The ringmaster drew himself up to his full height and thundered...

"Send in the clowns!"

Event Horizon

"Some people say the universe was created by the gods in a moment of cataclysmic orgasm. Do you believe that?"

The question came from a woman wrapped in a clingy black gown that covered her from neck to toes, yet managed to reveal every detail of her voluptuous figure. Although her face shone bright as a star, it was her nipples that caught my attention. I couldn't tear my eyes away from those two points standing out like twin beacons against that night-colored fabric.

"Orgasm," I said, tracing the curve of her breast with my eyes. "Yeah, that sounds good."

We stood on the main terrace of the Perihelion Restaurant, the crowning jewel of the Ganymede Space Station and Tourist Resort. While the Perihelion was known for its interstellar cuisine, most sentient beings came here for the view. Transparent opti-screens covering the restaurant's walls and ceiling displayed the nearby Pleiades cluster. Patrons *ooh*-ed and *ah*-ed at the glittering star nursery floating in a web of cobalt filaments of light. Only the floor remained opaque, as most customers became too queasy to eat if they couldn't tell up from down.

But no one was eating this evening. Instead, the patrons of the Perihelion had formed a nebulous cluster of their own. On the main floor below us, a group of Gr'avlox, Oonorns, humans, and other sentient beings convulsed together in a writhing orgy of arms, legs, and other limbs. Sweat and semen glistened on skin, scales, and feathers alike beneath the glow of the Seven Sisters. They all seemed to be enjoying themselves and I would have joined them, but I personally found the Oonorns a bit off-putting. Some people rave about the pleasures of tentacled genitalia, but I wouldn't fuck something like that even if the universe were about to end.

Which, unfortunately, it was.

I looked up as a star—Alcyone, I think—pulsed and flared on the opti-screen wall. Two sister stars had already collapsed, unable to bear the strain of the gravitational forces emanating from a nearby rift in space. After countless eons, the universe had finally worn itself out, stretched so

10

thin by its own constant expansion that its very fabric began to unravel, and then tear. Rifts had appeared in the space-time continuum. The smaller ones destroyed planets and swallowed suns. The larger rifts shredded galaxies. A midsize one had appeared in the center of the Milky Way two days earlier. Half the galaxy was gone now, including Earth. Ganymede Station hovered only a few light years from its frayed edge, just waiting to be sucked in. And in the midst of all this destruction, I stood in some damned restaurant, looking for one last bit of human tail. Wasn't there anything more important I could be doing with my final moments of existence?

Apparently not. I looked at the woman again, this time seeing her face. She smiled, and my cock stiffened.

"Do you believe in the Big Bang?" she asked.

"Well, the theory is sound," I replied, wondering if her question might be a come-on.

She tossed her jet-black hair and laughed. "Theory shmeory! We're talking about the creation of the universe here. We're talking acts of God!"

I held up a hand and backed away. The last thing I wanted to do before the universe ended was listen to some nutcase proselytize about the Almighty and the sinful state of my immortal soul.

"Look," I said, "I'm glad you've got religion—"

"Oh, forget religion!" She held out her arms to me and I gravitated toward her without thinking. "Religion is the pox of the sentient mind. It is fakery and deceit. It distorts true vision and interferes with our experience of the great Divine. And you know," she murmured slyly, "there's really only one way to experience the Divine."

She reached up and touched the throat of her gown. The clingy black fabric split open in the front and slipped away from her body. She stood before me, beautiful and naked. Her breasts were round and full, not the starlit points of a young girl but the twin moons of a goddess in her prime. I reached out and touched one. It burned with a cold fire.

"Oh yeah," I said, dumbfounded by this last bit of good luck at the end of all things. "I'm getting laid."

"Oh, not just laid," she replied. "You're about to experience procreation on a cosmic scale."

I stared at her. "Um, maybe you hadn't noticed, but now is not the best time to procreate. The universe is dying!"

As if to emphasize my point, Alcyone flared up again, bathing the restaurant in a wash of crimson light. Then the light contracted, suddenly seized back into the core of the star as it collapsed in on itself.

The station shuddered, pulled closer to death by the nearby implosion. I shuddered too as I noticed how few stars were left on the opti-screens.

The woman held out her hand to me. "Life and death are all the same, you know."

I flinched. "Look, we don't have much time left. So can we dispense with the philosophy and just get on with the fucking?"

She raised an eyebrow and I blushed.

"I'm sorry. I didn't mean to be rude. It's just that I really want to go out on a high note."

"You will," she said as she caressed my face. The touch of her hand burned with the same cold fire I had felt in her breast. "But there's no need to rush. We have all the time in the universe to make love."

Even I had to laugh at that. "Lady, you're crazy! What's your name?"

"Shiva," she said.

Another star collapsed on the opti-screen, casting a blazing halo around Shiva with its dying light. I blinked, trying to clear my eyes of the dazzling effect, and then blinked again. Either I had been mistaken about her species, or Shiva had suddenly acquired an extra pair of arms.

"Shiva, god of destruction," I murmured, transfixed by four graceful, swaying limbs. "I thought he was male."

"Shiva is what Shiva is," she replied.

One of her hands snaked around my waist and pulled me closer. Another unfastened my clothing while the remaining pair pinched my nipples in time with the pulsing of the few stars remaining on the screens.

"Lovemaking is the penultimate art," she explained. "A part of the never-ending choreography of creation and destruction. The individual dancers cease to exist as their essences merge to create something new and wonderful."

As Shiva spoke, her skin darkened, first becoming the grey of ashes and then the ebon color of death. On her forehead, a third eye appeared. It opened like a rift in space.

"Dance with me!" Shiva tore away the last of my clothing and twirled me around in her arms. "Be lingam to my yoni!"

I swayed as she stroked my body. Every touch left a trail of fire. Her fingers continued teasing my nipples, tracing endless spirals around the hardened nubs. A hand combed my pubic hair, the gentle rhythmic movement coaxing my cock to its fullest length and girth.

Another implosion and the station shuddered again. My fear of extinction overwhelmed all reason. In that moment, I desperately wanted Shiva, extra arms and all. I grabbed her by the waist and thrust my hips toward her. But when she spread her sable thighs to receive me, I faltered. Nesting beneath the curls of her pubic hair was a ravenous darkness.

"What the hell is that?"

"The end of all things, beloved."

The restaurant began to spin. At first I thought the last implosion had knocked the station off its axis and sent it tumbling through space. The orgy soared off the floor. The opti-screens cracked and peeled away from the walls. Everything in the restaurant was caught up in a maelstrom. But though the Perihelion swirled around us, Shiva and I stayed fixed in place, like the eye at the center of a terrestrial storm. I tried to break free, but Shiva wrapped all four arms around me and held fast. My naked flesh pressed against hers and everywhere she touched me, I burned.

"Don't go yet," she said. "Dance with me some more."

I looked down and gaped. The darkness between her legs had spread, twisting down and out of her like an inverted whirlpool. Bewildered, I could only watch as the orgy swung past us, caught in the gravitational pull of the black hole I had mistaken for a lover. Shiva opened her legs wider and the twisting blackness expanded. The orgy reached the periphery of that celestial tempest and disintegrated, the participants too busy fucking to notice their own demise. The rest of the Perihelion Restaurant followed suit.

In the blink of an eye, we were left floating in the cobalt light of the nebulous gas. All the while, Shiva smiled and caressed me. I writhed in her arms, tormented by the burning pleasure of her touch. Her hands were everywhere, massaging my thighs and balls, sliding down my back to grab at my ass. As I stood there on the brink of destruction, Shiva grabbed my cock and stroked it. It was the beginning of the end for me. Not even light could escape her grasp.

"I hold infinity in the palm of my hand," she said as she brought me to the verge of orgasm and kept me there.

I moaned, but the void swallowed the sound even as it left my lips.

"Do not fear!" Shiva commanded. "Look at me. Feel me. Know me!"

We kissed. Shockwaves coursed through my body and out into the cosmos. The remains of the Pleiades nebula disintegrated beneath their force. We floated in the vacuum of space while the last of the Seven Sisters winked out of existence.

Shiva's hands continued teasing me. A single drop of semen welled up from the tip of my cock. It glowed like a seed of light.

"Shiva! I'm going to come!"

"Yes, come to me," she murmured. "All things do in the end."

She let go and I felt myself swept away by the tides of gravity that emanated from deep inside her. Those fatal currents pulled me, like Shiva's caress, bringing me closer to ecstasy even as they threatened to sunder my very being. I collapsed into a pinprick of matter, my senses expanding as my body contracted. Life and death, creation and destruction, implosion and explosion—I felt the universe turn itself inside out around me.

As I rushed toward the void between Shiva's legs, words came unbidden to my mind. This is the way the world ends; this is the way the world ends...

"This is the way the world ends," Shiva intoned. "Not with a whimper, but a bang!"

And with that, I came. The orgasm exploded from me in a final burst of cosmic fury as I passed through the event horizon. My seed sprayed into the void, a blazing comet tail issuing from my cock. It took with it the last shreds of my physical being.

"Shiva!"

"Beloved!" Her voice came from everywhere, soothing my scattered particles. "Look at what we have created!"

I opened eyes that no longer existed and peered beyond the event horizon, beyond the end of the universe. I looked into the void that was Shiva and cried out with joy.

Inside her, there were stars.

The Voting Booth

"Name?"

"Selma Marie Shoop."

"Address?"

"667 Cherry Street, Homersville, Maryland."

The voting official, a frowsy, grey-haired woman, studied the picture on Selma's ID and then looked at Selma. Selma smiled back nervously.

"Okay. Selma Marie Shoop, 667 Cherry Street, Homersville, Maryland," the woman told her partner.

"Got her." He stifled a yawn as he checked the voter registration log. "You're number 643," he said to Selma. "Go line up with the others."

He handed her a numbered chit and pointed to the line of voters waiting for a booth. Selma went to join them, her stomach twisting into knots. Every year it was the same—the nerves, the anxiety, the doubts. What if she didn't like any of the candidates? What if she picked the wrong one? This was a presidential election, for god's sake. She was supposed to help choose the leader of the free world. What if her vote fucked it all up?

Selma had done her best to study up on all the candidates. She'd visited their websites and read all the flyers that appeared in her mailbox. It didn't help. All those glossy, seductive images designed to fool her into thinking each candidate was the right one for her ... it left her even more confused than before.

Desperate to sort things out before Election Day, she'd watched the big debate, doing her best to follow each candidate's position. Unfortunately, the whole thing quickly devolved into an orgy of sound bites and mudslinging. It made for entertaining television, but afterwards she couldn't remember who was who. There were just too many naked bodies slipping and sliding against each other, squelching mud between them as they mouthed tantalizing campaign promises. Had the impressive eight-inch cock that orgasmed over tax cuts belonged to Governor Romero or Vice President Capra? Or maybe that had been the ultra-realistic strap-on frequently sported by House Speaker Sarah Silvertongue? It certainly hadn't belonged to Senator Bedford. That man was known for screwing people, but not in the right way.

"Number 643?" the booth attendant called out.

Selma stepped forward, hands shaking as she handed over her number.

"First time voting?" the attendant, an elderly lady, asked with a smile.

"Oh no, I vote at every election. It's just..." Selma sighed. "Whoever I vote for, I never know if I'm making the right choice."

The attendant nodded. "It's tough. I voted this morning and it took me forever to decide. So many candidates! But don't worry. You'll figure it out."

She ushered Selma into the booth. "Now don't forget. Take off *all* your clothes, underwear too. And no vibrators. The candidates have to *earn* your vote!"

The door clicked shut. Selma stripped off her clothes and set them aside. The booth came equipped with all the standard furnishings—a brass bed, a leather arm chair, a pillory with fur-lined leather cuffs, and a voting console. She went to the console. There were nineteen candidates listed on its glowing display panel. None of their names sparked any inspiration in her.

"I'll just have to try them all, I guess."

Selma hit the first button. A door slid open in the back of the booth and in strode a naked man.

"Hi, I'm Jerry Johnson, candidate for the New Liberal Democratic Party, and I'd like you to vote for me."

Jerry—or rather, his carefully programmed simulacrum—dropped to his knees in front of Selma and started to beg. He whined and pawed at her, all the while rubbing his hard cock against her leg.

"Please vote for me! I'll do whatever you want! I'll be your whipping boy, your political bitch, just PLEASE vote for me!"

"Forget it."

Selma hit the reject button on the console. The candidate stood up, said "Thanks for your time!" and marched back out through the door.

"Okay, who's next?" Selma said, pouring over the console.

One by one, she went through all the candidates. Some were good. Others were simply dreadful. The Green Party candidate, Alvin Menkin, stomped around the voting booth, shrieking about how global warming was

16

to blame for his limp dick. The Evangelical candidate, Reverend Moral Godly, demanded to know if Selma was gay before he would do anything.

"Ah refuse, Ah say, Ah simply refuse to court the gay vote!"

"Why?" Selma asked the bloated, naked figure. "Gays and lesbians make up 12% of the voting population. Can you really afford to ignore the—"

At which point the good reverend cut her off with a sermon about the sins of sodomy and oral sex.

"To hell with that," she said, hitting the reject button once again. "Any candidate who's opposed to anal sex is just too big an asshole for me."

On it went. It turned out that Governor Romero was indeed the owner of the eight-inch cock she'd seen in the debate. Unfortunately, he had no idea how to handle it. Every time he thrust into Selma, he banged an ovary. On the other hand, Sarah Silvertongue, the House Speaker, was determined to live up to her name. She never said a word about her platform, just buried her face between Selma's thighs and licked enthusiastically. It felt very nice, but Selma couldn't quite get off on the idea of yet another lesbian president. They'd had three in a row, and the last one had been so touchy-feely. Wasn't it time for something different?

At last, she came to the final candidate on the list—Ahnold Schwartzenator, leader of the Mega-Ultra Conservative Bodybuilders' party.

"Here goes nothing."

Selma pushed the button. In marched an over-muscled man wearing a drill instructor's hat and wielding a leather paddle.

"I am your next president," he growled. "Bend over and accept your master!"

"Oh my!" Selma's heart skipped a beat at the sight of his brawny arms and massive chest. His cock wasn't nearly as large as the rest of him, but the way it pointed at her aggressively sent chills up and down her spine.

"What are you doing?" he barked at her. "When I say move, you move!"

Ahnold grabbed the startled Selma by the arm and hauled her over his lap. *WHAP!* Selma squealed as the leather paddle came down hard on her ass.

"I am a candidate of traditional values," Ahnold thundered. "You will accept those values as your own!"

WHAP! The paddle hit her again. "Oh my god!" Selma cried out.

"That is right! I am your god! I will make the laws and you will obey them!"

WHAP! Selma's bottom grew hotter with every strike. She shrieked and she struggled, but she couldn't get away. The more she fought, the hotter she got. With each blow, Ahnold beat yet another plank of his party's political platform into her buttocks. He walloped it into her until Selma could recite it by heart.

"I am your next president! You will respect my authority!"

WHAM! The last strike sent Selma over the edge, tossing her into a furious orgasm of scarlet heat and stinging pain. She came all over Ahnold's massive thigh, screaming his name over and over again until the voting console registered her vote.

When it was over, Ahnold stood up, dumping her unceremoniously on the floor. He was about to leave when she called out to him.

"Hey! Aren't you forgetting something, pal?"

"Oh, right." He leaned over and gave her a quick kiss on the cheek. "Thank you for your vote."

Then he was gone.

Minutes later, Selma stepped outside the booth. The attendant handed her a sticker that read "I voted!" and waved her good-bye. On her way out, Selma passed a young man standing in the line of voters.

"Any good candidates this year?" he asked nervously.

"Yeah," she nodded wearily. "Just make sure you get a kiss after they screw you."

THE MESSENGER

The Morning Star appeared at dawn.

Gabriel didn't notice the Fallen One's arrival as he made his morning rounds, strolling along the sleepy streets on his way to the small villa on the outskirts of town. The Prince of Lies could be frighteningly quiet when it suited him. Not that Gabriel was looking for evil on a quiet Sabbath morning. His mind was fixed on his current charge, a pious young maiden about to dedicate her life to the service of God. She didn't know it yet, though. Her fate would be revealed to her in three days time. Gabriel would announce it himself.

"How should I tell her?" he murmured as he walked. Sunlight bounced off his golden hair, creating a pale echo of his exalted halo. "Hail, anointed one, blessed by the Lord ... no, that's not right. I come to thee, daughter of God, with momentous news? No, no, too pompous. *Ave*, holy child? Too Roman..."

He stepped lightly along the winding byways, each syllable of speech sounding like a note of liquid honey falling from his tongue. The words had to be just right. He was God's messenger, after all, and this was one of the most important missives he would ever deliver. Would the maiden be ready to hear it, though?

He thought of the girl, so slight and demure, with eyes like a dove's. Her heart-shaped face peeked out at him from behind the veil of her long, dark hair. She was barely a woman, too young to comprehend what was about to be asked of her. Yet Gabriel knew the Lord would not ask if she was not ready, and he felt certain that this one was indeed ready. The archangel had watched over her since before her birth, had seen her grow from a suckling babe to a paragon of grace and virtue. Obedient to God, mindful of her parents, modest and pure—the maiden would rise to the occasion. Gabriel was confident of that.

His confidence evaporated the moment he turned the corner. Stepping onto the maiden's street, he pulled up short at the sight of Lucifer perched on a stone bench outside the villa's front gate. The Morning Star sat there in his carmine robes whistling an off-key tune.

"Asleep on the job again, brother?"

Wings fluttering in confusion, Gabriel whirled around to meet his accuser. Another archangel, dark and brooding, stepped out of the shadows, hefting a golden sword in his right hand.

"Michael." Gabriel struggled to compose himself, but couldn't stop the slight blush that crept across his face. "I'm not asleep. The safeguards are in place. Lucifer doesn't dare approach the girl."

"Certainly not while *I'm* here," the warrior replied. He stabbed his sword into the ground. "What does he want?"

"I don't know. I've just arrived. I haven't asked him yet."

"Then maybe I should."

"Wait. Don't!"

With a scowl, Michael pushed past the sputtering seraphim and strode toward the rogue idling at the gate. Gabriel hurried to catch up. The Fallen One rose to his feet and smiled brightly as they closed in.

"Good morning, brothers. Having a nice walk? I envy you. This is such a beautiful town, especially at dawn with the sunlight shining down on all that stately Roman architecture. Good old Romans. You know, I think they've done more to corrupt the Yehudi than I ever could. I mean really, have you seen the statues they put up around the main temple? I especially like the one of Helios, the heathen sun god. It looks a bit like me, I think. Absolutely stunning piece of artwork!"

"What do you want?" Michael demanded. His alabaster wings flared behind him and his sword cut through the air in a deadly arc.

Lucifer nimbly sidestepped the blade. "Just the pleasure of your company."

"Liar." Michael sliced at the intruder again, only to be eluded once more.

"The best lies are hidden in truths, dear brother."

"You wouldn't know the truth if it—"

"Let me handle this." Gabriel pushed between the two celestial beings, deftly catching Michael's sword blade between his bare hands. "If you don't mind, that is? This is *my* responsibility."

The warrior glowered but backed down. Gabriel turned to Lucifer.

"What are you doing here, Satan? You can't tempt this one."

"If you're so sure about that, why are you guarding her?"

"To protect her from harm," Gabriel said tersely.

20

"You don't honestly think that *I* would hurt her?" The fallen angel reached for the handle of the gate only to be rebuffed by a violent flash of light. "Oh! I guess you do. That stings, Gabe," he said and sucked on his fingers.

"It's supposed to. Now why are you here?"

Lucifer grinned. "I just want to check out His little project. See what I'm going up against. I'm allowed to look, you know. He's never stopped me from doing that."

"Well you've had your look," Gabriel replied. "Now you can leave."

"But that's just it." The Deceiver spread his hands wide. "I haven't seen the girl at all. I would have thought a young, virtuous maid such as herself would have been up at dawn, feeding the chickens, weeding the garden, breaking fast with her doddering old parents. But she hasn't shown her pretty face. What gives? Did she stay out too late with her betrothed last night?"

Michael shot an anxious look at Gabriel, who fumbled for an answer.

"She didn't go anywhere last night..."

"Well, maybe he came to her," Lucifer drawled. "After all, I can't tempt her, but I can tempt him."

"He wouldn't dare!" Gabriel snapped, but inside he cringed. Could the maiden's betrothed have paid a late-night visit? Suddenly, he wasn't sure.

Michael grabbed Gabriel by the sleeve and pulled him away from the gate. "What's going on? Don't you know where the girl was last night?"

"Of course I know!" Gabriel whispered back. "She was right here, all night."

"Alone?"

"Yes."

"Are you sure of that? You stayed and watched her all night?"

"Not all night. I didn't..."

He dropped his gaze, unable to face the look of fury twisting Michael's face. "I didn't stay all night. I have the message to work on. I needed to take a walk. But the girl is safe, I tell you."

"Idiot!" Michael pushed him away. "I'm going to check on her now. If something's happened, if she's been hurt or spoiled—"

21

"She hasn't. She couldn't be," Gabriel insisted, but Michael was already gone.

"Problems, brother?"

Gabriel turned and smiled wanly at Lucifer. They could have been twins were it not for the Morning Star's reptilian eyes and scabrous wings.

"No problems, *brother*. The girl is fine."

"Michael has his doubts."

"Michael is simply doing his duty. You've put him on his guard."

The fallen angel gave a knowing grin that twisted Gabriel's guts into knots. A moment later, Michael reappeared.

"The maiden is safe," he declared. "She's inside with her family, preparing for the Sabbath."

Gabriel let out a sigh of relief. "The Sabbath, of course. She'll be inside all morning, until they leave for the temple."

"Well then," Lucifer said with a lazy stretch, "I suppose I'll have to come back another time to see her. Until then, brothers." With a flap of his leathery wings, he soared up into the sky.

As the Morning Star disappeared from view, Michael let out a hiss. "You should have known. I shouldn't have had to check. Why our Lord gave this job to you instead of me, I'll never understand."

"Maybe it's because you said you were too busy to play nursemaid to a bothersome slip of a girl," Gabriel shot back.

"Now it seems I must play nursemaid to you both." Michael spread his wings. "Stay awake from now on. We're too close to the end of this for you to fail." Then he took to the sky as well, passing over the town in the form of a thundering cloud. Gabriel ducked his head beneath his wings to escape the coming storm.

*   *   *

The maiden and her parents spent the morning inside, only leaving the house to attend evening services just as the storm lifted. Gabriel walked with them, shadowing the girl's every step. Satan had caught him napping once. It wouldn't happen again.

At the temple, he followed the girl and her mother inside to the women's area. He nodded with approval when the maiden averted her eyes from the Roman's blasphemous statue of a half-naked Helios that sprawled opposite the temple door. Then he frowned as she scanned the incoming congregation. Her eyes lit up when she spotted her betrothed entering the

22

main door. As though summoned, the man looked up and smiled back, too eagerly for Gabriel's comfort. The angel gritted his teeth. It was good that the man loved her so much, but he was vulnerable to Lucifer's machinations. In fact, no mortal man could resist this girl. She was perfect, flawless...

"Beautiful," a voice at his shoulder breathed. "She's simply beautiful. Her future husband is a lucky man."

Gabriel's stomach gave a sickening lurch. "Lucifer, this is a holy place. Have you no shame?"

"My sin was pride, remember? I'm not ashamed of anything I do." The Prince of Lies chuckled. "Don't worry. I'm not here to cause trouble. I just came to see the girl now that she's left the safety of her house."

"She's still safe, even here," Gabriel bristled.

"Of course she is." The fallen angel held up his hands in a placating gesture. "I didn't mean to imply that she wouldn't be. You've done an excellent job protecting her, in spite of what Michael thinks."

"Michael is just—"

"Doing his job?" Lucifer interrupted. "How is insulting you part of his job? No, forget I asked. You'll stand up for him no matter what, faithful and loyal to the very end. Those are good qualities for a guardian angel to have."

The rabbi began the service and Lucifer mercifully ceased talking. For the rest of the liturgy, the two angels stood side by side behind the maiden. Gabriel fought the urge to put himself between Satan and the girl. She was safe. The rogue couldn't corrupt her, nor would he dare harm her, at least not as long as another archangel was around. But his presence still left Gabriel ill at ease. Why was Lucifer showing up now? Michael was right. He would have to watch the maiden every second until he completed his task.

Which reminded him, he still had to compose the message. In less than three days, Gabriel was expected to speak to her, and he still had no idea what to say. As the rabbi droned through a reading from the Torah, the archangel wrestled with his upcoming speech. His lips moved silently, phrasing and rejecting salutations and proclamations. This announcement was to be his gift to the maiden, the ultimate revelation of her role in God's plan. She was special, more so than any other mortal he had spoken to before. The words needed to be perfect, just as she was perfect.

By the end of the service, however, Gabriel was no closer to knowing what he would say. As the rabbi uttered the closing benediction, the weary angel gave up his struggle with a sigh. The words would come to him soon, he decided. For now, he had more pressing matters to attend to.

With the end of the service, the maiden and her family wandered out into the town square. Her father stopped briefly to speak with her betrothed. The girl herself said nothing, merely stayed by her mother's side a few yards away, face modestly hidden behind the veil of her hair. But her eyes never left her betrothed's face as the two men talked, and long after they parted ways, she kept peering over her shoulder, watching him as he walked away through the crowd. Then Gabriel did give into temptation and placed himself between the girl and her future husband, obscuring her vision like a cloud of dust until she looked away.

"I expect it will be hard for you to give her up," Lucifer said as they followed the maiden home.

"What do you mean?"

"Well, you must feel some attachment to her. You've watched over her from birth, kept her safe from all harm. No one will be able to offer her that kind of security again, not even her husband, assuming he still wants her after the Almighty is done with her. Once you leave, that poor creature is going to suffer terribly. I'm amazed you're going to stand by and let it happen."

"It's the lot of all mortals to suffer," Gabriel answered.

"Yes, but her suffering is going to be so much worse. I know exactly what's in store for her. Me, for starters, and all the misery I can throw at her. Granted, she'll suffer piously and never curse God the way Job did, but I wonder. Will she be able to bear her burden or will she break beneath her sorrows?"

"She's strong. She'll endure."

"How do you know that?" Lucifer caught Gabriel by the arm. "She's a child still, one you've coddled and protected since birth. She's never even had so much as a stubbed toe, thanks to you. Face it. You've done your job too well. This girl has never been tested and she isn't prepared for what God wants of her. Do you really think you can just drop this awful destiny in her lap, say 'toodle-oo,' and expect her to carry on?"

Gabriel didn't answer. He knew what the maiden faced, and it was terrible enough to make him weep. She was so small and innocent, yet she was foreordained to bear witness to such incredible pain. How could he thrust her onto the course of misery?

"Well?" the fallen angel prodded. "Say something, Gabe."

"Go away, Satan. Leave her alone before I smite you."

"Ha!" His laugh was the bark of a jackal. "You sound like Michael now. I'll go, but you know I'll be back. Just as soon as you condemn this girl to her fate, I'll be back."

*   *   *

Night came and an uneasy quiet descended upon the villa where the maiden lived. Gabriel paced in the yard, still struggling to frame his message to the girl. He would have preferred to walk the streets again, as he had the past few months, to clear his head, but he didn't dare leave the maiden alone. Instead, he watched and waited for Lucifer to return. When Michael showed up, Gabriel let out a bone-weary sigh.

"He came back," the warrior complained, as though the rogue's return were Gabriel's fault.

Gabriel continued to pace. "He's allowed to look. You know that. God has never hidden anything from him."

"He followed her into the temple." Michael fell in beside him, dogging his steps.

"So?"

"You should have chased him out."

"How was I supposed to do that? I can't keep him out. Even you can't keep him out. As long as men are weak and willing to give into temptation, he has a way into wherever he wants."

"So you're just going to let him hound the girl until he finds a way into her, as well?"

"He can't touch her!" Gabriel stopped so suddenly that Michael stumbled into him. The warrior drew back in astonishment as Gabriel rounded on him, his beatific face twisted by fury. "She's immune to his vile effects. The bastard can't touch her, can't tempt her, and I've made certain he can't harm her. So why don't you just fly off and trust me to do my job?"

Michael eyed his brother warily. "I cry your pardon. I only want the same thing you want, to see this to completion, to further His plan."

Gabriel snarled. "Well you don't have to ride my back to make that happen."

"Fine." Michael drew himself up. "I'll leave you to it then. If you need help—"

"I won't be calling you."

Gabriel turned on his heel and stalked away. He refused to look back. He focused instead on his message. The words were there, hiding inside him, but try as he might he couldn't find them.

*   *   *

"It's good to see you stand up for yourself," Lucifer remarked. He stepped out of the shadows and approached the window where Gabriel sat.

"Hush, Satan. She's asleep."

The fallen angel peered through the window to see the slumbering form of the maiden. "Ah, the sleep of the innocent. How peaceful. You don't see that very often these days."

"Why are you here?" Gabriel asked. His voice, weary from hours of fruitless rehearsal, cracked on the question.

"Truthfully? To talk with you."

"About what?"

Lucifer settled into the window beside Gabriel. "How long have you been arguing with Michael over this girl?"

"Forever, it seems," he said with a sigh.

"More like the last six months. I know. I've been watching you both. Ever since this girl was betrothed, Michael has been at your throat. You know what I think?"

Gabriel shook his head.

"I think your pugilist brother is in love with her."

Gabriel snorted. "Ridiculous. He's God's warrior. He's not disposed to such tender feelings."

"Are you sure?" Lucifer shifted against the window. His wings hissed and whispered like half-truths spoken on a moonless night. "Even angels have their weaknesses. Mine was pride. Michael's is love, or maybe just lust. The girl is beautiful, made special by God for a special purpose. Don't you see how he could be tempted?"

Gabriel jumped up from the window as though he'd been stung. "No, I don't. Michael can barely stand to spend time around her. When he was asked to guard her, he turned the job down. He said the task was beneath an angel of his stature."

"So he said," Lucifer continued. "But maybe he refused the job because he was afraid of getting too close to her. And now he's afraid of losing her, to her husband and to God. That's why he keeps attacking you. He's jealous. You took up what he threw away—the chance to guard and guide the woman he loves. You get to spend these last few days of precious tranquility with her while he can only flap about on the sidelines and watch in impotent rage."

"Why are you telling me this? You're the Prince of Lies. What game are you playing?"

The Fallen One answered with a lazy chuckle. "It's called revenge. Michael will try to take the maiden for himself, in spite of the Almighty's plans for her. If I can prevent him from doing that, he'll suffer a great humiliation. Imagine me, the ultimate evil, working to save God's plan while His greatest warrior succumbs to the temptations of the flesh. What a lark!"

Gabriel stumbled, shocked by Lucifer's words. "Impossible. Never, never would it happen."

"Oh admit it," Lucifer hissed. His eyes glowed red in the deepening night. "You knew all along. You knew that pompous prick was watching in secret, lusting after the girl. Tell me, how often do you think he takes the form of a man, just so he can relieve himself when his desires grow too strong?"

"No, no, no!" Gabriel dropped to his knees, eyes shut tight, hands clapped over his ears. Satan slithered closer.

"He wantssss her," came the sibilant whisper. "He dreams of touching her, tearing away her homespun gown to feast on the sweet flesh beneath. And if he takes her, if he pierces her maidenhead with that mighty sword of his, he'll ruin her and all of God's plans too."

Tears streamed down Gabriel's face. "Michael wouldn't do this. He's not like you!"

"Don't play stupid. You can stand by and pretend nothing's wrong, and then explain to your Lord what happened, or you can take steps to prevent this catastrophe. Which will it be, Gabe? It's all up to you."

The Serpent coiled around Gabriel, closer than a lover, whispering into the archangel's ear. Try as he might, he couldn't shut out the Devil's voice. The foul creature spoke the truth, a truth Gabriel had held secret in his heart these past few months. The maiden was in danger. Only he could save her.

"Keep close to her, Gabe, close as you can. Don't let her out of your sight, not even for a moment. Michael's just waiting for his chance. Don't let him have it."

The Serpent disappeared, leaving the angel kneeling alone in the dust. He wept openly, frightened by the possibility of his brother's

27

downfall. It was a lie, he knew it. He was talking to the Father of Lies, for God's sake! But there was a ring of truth about it that shook Gabriel to the very core of his being. If only he could separate the truth from the lies, pull the light out of the shadows. If only he could do that.

Still weeping, he slipped inside the villa and found the maiden in her bed. He spent the rest of the night there, standing guard against friend and foe. He tried to chase away his fears by composing his message to her.

The words, however, still refused to come.

*   *   *

The night dragged on, becoming an endless pit of darkness through which Gabriel fell into despair. The angel muttered as he stood at the foot of the maiden's bed. Useless syllables tumbled from his mouth while the message he sought so desperately flitted through his brain, elusive as all the hopes of mortal men. Lost in a reverie of words and nonsense, he drifted away.

A sound, like the restless murmur of feathered wings, snapped him back to the present. In the darkness, the maiden's bed lay empty. Sick with fear, Gabriel lurched out of the room, searching. He stumbled through the too-quiet house until he came to the bath. In the corner, he spied a shadow. He rushed forward, ready to fight, only to find the maiden crouching by a basin, staring at him in astonishment.

He stared back. She was not supposed to see him, not until the appointed time, yet her wide grey eyes plainly locked with his. Her clothes lay in a neat pile on the floor. Water dripped from her naked body. One hand still rested in the basin, clutching the sponge she used to bathe herself. He stepped toward her. She shivered, whether from the night's chill or from fear he didn't know, but Gabriel felt a heat growing inside him that would burn them both.

"Do not fear," he whispered, as much to himself as to her. He held out his hand and after a long moment, she reached for it. Slender white fingers brushed against his and Gabriel felt himself tumble to the ground, felled by a single touch.

The maiden fell with him, the curtain of her hair spilling over his face as she collapsed in his arms. He cradled her against his chest, lifting her off the rough stone floor. When she trembled, he opened his robes and drew her in. Her small breasts pressed against his chest. Her heart beat like a frightened bird trapped in a cage.

"Do not fear," he whispered into her hair, and he kissed her.

Her mouth pressed against his, soft and sweet. Her hands traced the muscles of his stomach in a tentative exploration. As they delved lower, the angel transformed into a man. Gabriel tossed aside his robes and pulled the girl upright until she straddled his aching groin. Moaning, he held her tight and savored the feel of her body rocking against his.

Then her kiss twisted into a sneer. Her soft sighs became a wicked chuckle. Her breasts hardened and flattened into the muscular chest of a beast.

"I see Michael's not the only one who desires this girl."

With an anguished cry, Gabriel shoved Lucifer away. The fiend fell backwards, roaring with laughter. "Oh, you should see yourself, Gabe—your cock rampant and ready to defile such a sweet thing. You dirty dog!"

"Liar!" Gabriel shouted. "You filthy deceiver!"

He grabbed the stone basin and hurled it at his fallen brother. Lucifer easily dodged the missile and it shattered against the floor. "Now, now, how can you call me a liar when I've worked so hard to show you the truth?"

"This isn't the truth!"

"Oh, but it is."

Gabriel threw on his robes and raced out of the bath. His breath came in hard, ragged gasps as he stumbled through the darkened villa. Lucifer followed, laughing as he chased down the distraught angel.

"You can't escape it," he said as they ran into the courtyard. "You love the girl. You lust for her!"

"No, I don't!"

"Now who's the liar?" Satan roared.

He grabbed Gabriel by the wings and threw him to the ground. Leaping atop his prey, he tore open the archangel's robes and seized his swollen member. As he stroked it, he hissed, "In two days' time, you're supposed to deliver a message to your little lovebird that will send her down the path of pain and misery. But you don't want to do it. That's why you're fighting against Michael. That's why you keep letting me in. You know that if you can foil God's plans, the girl might yet escape what's in store for her."

"Lies. Lies!" Gabriel thrashed beneath him, tormented by the demon's words and his touch.

"If I lie, then tell me what you plan to say to her when the time comes. Give me the message, Gabe."

29

Gabriel opened his mouth to speak, to utter even a single word, but nothing came out. God's message wasn't there, he realized. It had never been there.

Because he had deliberately blocked it out.

"Oh my God," he whimpered. "What have I come to?"

Lucifer kept stroking him. "A moment of decision, my brother. Deliver your message or save the girl. Love your God or love her. That's what you've come to."

The Deceiver's hand sped up, drawing fire into Gabriel's loins. "Listen to me, brother. When you take the girl, bring her to Hell. I'll give you sanctuary from His wrath. You and she will be safe there for all eternity, and I will never ask anything of you. Just come to me and save your beloved."

The archangel bucked and moaned beneath his adversary until his entire body was consumed by the blaze. He erupted in liquid flames, crying out wordlessly into the night before blacking out. When he came to, the night had faded. Dawn touched the horizon. Satan was gone, and Gabriel despaired.

*　　*　　*

"He's been back twice more."

"I told you to leave me alone."

"What has he said to you? What's he done? It isn't the girl he's after anymore, is it?"

"Go to Hell, Michael."

Gabriel sat in an olive tree in the courtyard, his face buried in his hands. He couldn't meet his brother's eyes. How neatly Lucifer had trapped him with his lies. Michael had never wanted the girl. That had merely been the Devil's trick, a means to ferret out Gabriel's secret weakness and torment him with it.

But how can love be a weakness? he asked himself. The question went unanswered as Michael grabbed him by the shoulder and gave him a fierce shake.

"He's after you, isn't he? What's he offered you? Power? A seat at his right hand? Rule over all the mortal world?"

"No!" Snarling, Gabriel shoved his brother away. "I don't want any of those things."

30

"Then what do you want? What's your price for betraying our Lord?"

Just then, a door swung open and the girl entered the courtyard. Gabriel sat up, his eyes fixed on her. Her beauty was like a spear thrust to his heart.

Michael sucked in a razor-sharp breath. "Oh, you fool," he whispered.

"Go away."

The girl sat on the stone bench beneath the olive tree and pulled out a length of fine linen cloth. Her wedding veil, Gabriel realized as the spear point dug deeper into him. She smoothed the garment over her lap and, humming, picked up a needle and thread. As she stitched, a delicate flower bloomed beneath her hands.

"How could you let this happen?" Michael asked. "You're His messenger. You're supposed to deliver His Word to her, not hand her your heart."

The maiden embroidered another blossom, linking it to the first.

"His Word will destroy her," Gabriel replied.

"His Word will lift her up. She'll become a queen among her people."

"Not until centuries after she dies. While she lives, she'll have nothing but anguish and grief."

"She's His chosen one."

"And look at what happened to His other precious chosen ones!" Gabriel swung round. "Remember what happened to Moses after I spoke to him? The Lord let the man wander in the desert for forty years until he died, and never once allowed him to set foot in the Promised Land. And what about Abraham? I spoke to him, foretold that he would father nations. Then God demanded his son's life as a sacrifice. That poor, broken old man wept as he tied up his son and held a knife to the boy's throat, but his God asked and he had to deliver. He would have died of grief if the Lord hadn't let me intervene at the last moment. These were grown men and look how they suffered for Him. She's just a girl, and He wants so much more from her. It isn't right!"

Beneath them, the maiden continued to stitch. The flowers now formed a chain along the hem of the veil. Gabriel's heated words raised a strong breeze that scattered a pall of dust over her handiwork.

"This isn't about what's right or wrong," Michael shot back. "You've delivered countless messages, sent thousands to their fates, and never once did you question His plans. But now Satan's tempted you with his lies and you're ready to take the Fall."

"Maybe you should fall instead!"

Gabriel spun round on his perch and kicked out with both feet. He caught the other angel square in the chest and toppled him from the tree. Without pause, he leapt after Michael. He knotted his fingers in the warrior's hair and took off again, dragging the archangel with him. Shrieking, Michael clawed at Gabriel, rending robes and angelic flesh as he fought to get free. They whirled around the courtyard, the frantic beating of their wings churning up a furious storm. The olive tree bent and bowed beneath their onslaught; the girl cried out in fear. As the two angels crashed together in a tempest of snowy feathers and scarlet-streaked robes, a thunderclap tore the veil from the maiden's hands and knocked her to the ground.

"Stop it. Stop!" Michael shouted as he pinned Gabriel beneath him. "Don't you see we're hurting her?"

He hauled the archangel up to show him the limp form sprawled in the center of the courtyard. With an anguished wail, Gabriel tried to fly to her but Michael held him back.

"No, don't." He locked his arms around his brother. "This is Lucifer's plan. If you touch her, you're lost."

"She's hurt!"

"Let her family tend to her." Michael dragged Gabriel away as the girl's parents rushed into the courtyard. Her aged mother clasped shaking hands together in fearful prayer while her father lifted her up and whisked her back inside.

Gabriel sagged against Michael, weeping. The warrior half-carried him to the bench and propped him up against the olive tree.

"How has it come to this?" Michael asked.

"You know how." Gabriel wiped at his face with a wounded hand. Tears mingled with blood. "Of all His creations, mankind is the frailest, weakest, and most flawed. In spirit, they succumb to every temptation. In the flesh, they sicken, age, and die. You could snuff them out like a candle flame, yet while they live they burn more brightly than the sun. They're His ultimate creation, made in His likeness, and she's closer to Him than all the rest. To love her is to love Him. Isn't that what I was made to do?"

Michael soothed back the hair from Gabriel's brow. "Yes, but not like this. You can't keep this girl for yourself. If you love her, deliver the message. Tell her what God intends for her. Otherwise, she'll serve no purpose and you will have loved an empty, meaningless thing."

"I have no message. The words won't come." Gabriel turned his face to the cloud-scudded sky. "Can you offer me no other comfort?"

"Only this." Michael pressed his lips to Gabriel's. His wings curled around them both and sheltered them from the coming night.

*   *   *

In the morning, Gabriel awoke beneath the olive tree to find Michael curled up at his right side, an arm wrapped protectively around his waist. Lucifer dallied next to him on his left.

"My, aren't we cozy?" The Prince of Darkness leered. "Sleep well, boys?"

"Be gone, Serpent," Michael commanded, reaching for his sword.

"Give it up, I'm not going anywhere. Today is the big day, remember? We finally get to see what our boy Gabe is going to do. Obey God or follow his heart? I know what I'm betting on." To Gabriel he whispered, "Remember whom you love."

He pointed to the villa door as it opened and the maiden emerged. In the early dawn, she glowed with a dazzling light. Gabriel stood on shaking legs, his immortal heart pounding against his ribs.

Michael gripped his arm. "Remember *why* you love," he echoed.

With a faltering gait, Gabriel stepped away from them both. On the far side of the courtyard, the maiden stooped over the well to draw water. What should he do? If he delivered the message, he would lose her to God's will. If he didn't, she would cease to be special and the reason for his love would disappear. His mind reeled, trapped by such a cruel paradox. If only he could stop time and hold the maiden forever in the current moment. If only he didn't have to choose.

Halfway across the courtyard, he shed his wings and halo and assumed the form of a man. The fire in his brain descended to his loins, heightening his torment. He groaned. The girl looked up, startled. The pitcher of water slipped from her hands and shattered on the ground. The dam in Gabriel's brain broke with it and the words ran like a river overflowing its banks. With a breaking heart, he realized he could never have her. He knelt and looked into her wide grey eyes, at last speaking the words of his message.

"Hail Mary, full of grace, the Lord is with thee..."

A Fish Tale

In my dream, the ocean is crystal blue, capped by silver-crested waves. Shimmering lancelets of sunlight pierce the surface, illuminating the aquatic fairyland beneath where I swim. The dancing light ripples over my arms, breasts, and belly, and makes the scales of my lower half gleam like precious gems. My tail ends in a pair of gauzy fins unfurled in the current. I used to have legs, but I gave them up when I came to live in the sea.

My scales are sapphire dark. Diane's are gold, to match her flaxen hair and sun-kissed body. They glitter as she races past, laughing and calling my name, singing a siren song to entice me into chasing her. It's the same tune she sang on the day we first met. Come away, come away. Come swim with me, my love.

Diane said I belonged in the water, not on dry land like other mortals. Even my name, Marnie, meant "of the sea". She said if I just followed her into the waves, I could be a mermaid too. I couldn't resist her then, just like I can't resist her now.

Eager to chase, I take off after Diane. My tail whips back and forth, propelling me through the water. I almost catch her, she's just a finger's length away, but then she darts into a reef and disappears. I speed after her through a maze of coral and stone until we come upon a dead end. Trapped by a wall of black rock that reaches all the way up to the surface, Diane turns. Her fingers trace delicate spirals around her swelling nipples and she gives me a wicked grin. I rush in to take the bait, but before I can grab her Diane shoots to the surface. I see a flash of gold as she leaps out of the water and over the rock wall. I swim up after her and shatter the waves. My long sleek form hangs suspended in the air before I dive down … and smash into the wall of stone.

Something in my back goes *snap* as I hit the rocks. My body slumps across the wall. I'm still trying to figure out how I misjudged the dive when the waves roll me back into the sea. The water changes from crystal blue to an indigo abyss as I plummet down, down, down. I try to swim because I don't want to go that deep, but the cold creep of death washes over my lower half. My fins hang limp and a frightening numbness laps at my waist. Above me, Diane swims in circles, watching me sink like a stone. Her eyes are cold, distant. I scream for help. All that comes out is a torrent of bubbles quickly swallowed by the briny deep. Salt water pumps into my lungs to replace my last breath and suddenly I realize I'm drowning.

I scream again, inhaling more salt water. The sea turns pitch black and clutches at me like a living thing. Just before it pulls me to the bottom, Diane dives down and grabs me by the wrist. As she hauls me up to the surface, I feel my vertebrae grind together like broken stones. Fire spreads through my upper half while everything below the waist is cold, numb, dead. I look down and see the fishtail peel away from my body, the skin of gleaming scales sloughing away to reveal a pair of useless, shriveled legs.

When we reach the surface, I gulp at the air, shrieking. Silent, Diane drags me to the shore.

She shakes her head at me. "A real mermaid would have made that jump," she chastises. Then she points to my legs and says, "Those will never work in the water."

They'll never work on land again either, I want to add. But she already knows that, which is why she kisses me goodbye. With a flip of her tale, Diane rushes away with the receding tide, and I'm left behind on the beach to cry.

*   *   *

"And I'm still crying for her even after I wake up." I clunked my beer down on the table. "Can you believe that? It's been over a year, and I'm still having the same nightmare, still calling after that bitch. God, I can't believe Diane left me."

The waiter, a gangly fellow with thinning hair and a nameplate that read "George", shuffled from foot to foot. It was Tuesday evening and business at Ray's Raw Bar was slow. I sat outside on the dock, watching the spectacular Florida sunset stain the sky coral red. The rows of tables around us stood empty. The slips along the dock were devoid of boats. A busboy made the rounds in the building behind us, cranking open the windows to let in the evening breeze. A couple of beach bums dozed inside at the bar. There was no one else around to rescue the waiter from my bitter ramblings, so he stood there fidgeting beneath the deluge of my sob story. He did his best to listen politely, but his eyes kept straying to the water as I ranted about Diane.

"You say you two were mermaids?" he asked, swallowing hard.

"Yeah, we practically swam our way around the world. Diving in Belize, spear fishing in Australia, body surfing at Oahu..." I paused to remember my life before the accident. "We were a couple of real adrenaline junkies. Spent almost four years together doing crazy shit like that. Tonight would have been our five-year anniversary."

The waiter twitched. "Uh, you planning on meeting her here tonight to celebrate?"

I almost laughed. "Haven't you heard a damn thing I've said? The bitch walked out and never looked back."

"She walked?" His narrow chest heaved with a sigh of relief. "Oh thank god. She had legs then!"

"Excuse me?" I leaned back in my wheelchair to stare at him.

"You know, it's just like in your dream. If she had legs, she wasn't really a mermaid."

"Of course she wasn't really a mermaid! It was a metaphor, okay? It means we liked to swim. A lot."

"Oh." The waiter twisted his apron into knots. "I guess I'm confused. I thought you meant the two of you were the real thing."

I picked up my beer and scowled. "Trust me, pal. Mermaids are like faithful lovers. They don't really exist."

"Of course not." He gave a nervous laugh that sounded like he was choking. "Say, would you like to sit inside? It's a lot cooler in there."

A salty breeze ruffled my hair and I sighed. I'd deliberately chosen a table on the dock outside to be as close to the ocean as I could get. "No, I'm fine right here."

"Are you sure? When you sit this close to the water, the smell of fish can be pretty bad..."

Again, his eyes strayed to the waves.

"What?" I asked. "You see something down there?"

"No! I was just thinking you'd be—"

"More comfortable inside," I finished for him. "I heard you the first time, and the answer is still no. I'm fine right here."

Before the waiter could argue, a battered van pulled up in the parking lot and disgorged a gaggle of surfers. Tanned and laughing, they strutted down the pier toward the bar. Casting another wary glance at the water, the waiter hurried off to greet them at the door.

As soon as he disappeared inside, I tucked my half-empty beer in the side pocket of my chair and rolled away from my table to the edge of

36

the dock. What the hell was he looking for, I wondered. Three feet below me, the incoming tide lapped at the wooden piles. A school of fish darted beneath the glassy surface. Other than that, there was nothing to see.

More cars pulled up, and customers began trickling into Ray's. The waiter seated some of the new arrivals outside, apparently no longer worried about the weather or the smell of fish. Then he noticed me sitting at the edge of the dock and frowned. My blood began to boil as I figured out what was going on.

"What's the matter, asshole?" I muttered. "You afraid I'm going to roll off the pier and drown?"

Fuming, I gripped the wheels of my chair and rolled down the dock. If the waiter wanted to be uptight, then I'd give him a reason to be. When I reached the nearest slip, I aimed myself at the far end and started pumping the wheels of my chair fast. In a perverse game of chicken, I raced to the end of the gray planks and then coasted back. Stupid, I know, especially since I couldn't swim anymore, but I was pissed.

Just because I was in a wheelchair, that didn't mean I was some fucking invalid. I knew how to handle myself and I didn't need to be protected from accidents that weren't going to happen.

On my last run down the slip, I brought my chair almost to the very edge and stopped. "Just a few more inches, Marnie, and you'll drown for sure," I said.

As if he heard me, the waiter came running.

"Miss, please don't sit there!"

I grinned and eased the chair forward to see what he would do. He screeched to a halt, mouth agape.

"Don't! That's not a good idea."

"Really?" I wheeled back and he sighed. I scooted forward and he nearly croaked.

"What?" I asked, all wide-eyed and innocent. "You afraid I'll fall in?"

He wrung his hands. "No, it's not that. Just please, come away from the edge of the pier. If she sees you—"

Boy if that didn't light the fuse to my temper. I spun my chair around and snarled. "Is that the problem? Someone might notice the poor cripple sitting out here on the pier?" My words split the air like a gunshot. "Listen, you stupid jerk, there's a goddam law that says you can't discriminate against people with disabilities!"

"That's not what I meant!" George backed away so fast he tripped over his own feet. "I only meant there was someone specific who might see you, and uh ... uh..."

He glanced at the water again and groaned. I followed his line of sight but saw nothing.

"What?" I snapped. "Why do you keep looking at the damned water? You think the creature from the Black Lagoon is down there waiting to jump out and grab me? Well let him!"

I hit the parking brakes on my chair and flipped up the footrests. It took me a second to scoot forward and slide out. My butt landed on the deck with a heavy thump that told me I'd have bruises the next day.

"You want me to move?" I snarled at the waiter. "Then you come move me. Otherwise, I'm parking my ass right here!"

He opened his mouth to say something and then snapped it shut. He hung his head, defeated. "Ah, forget it, lady. You can sit any damn place you please. It's probably too late now anyway."

"What the hell is that supposed to mean?" I yelled, but I got no answer. Crablike, George scuttled away.

A bitter tide of anger washed over me. I turned my attention to my legs, running my hands over them to make sure I hadn't hurt myself with my stupid show of bravado. My legs were fine, but I felt lousy. I knew the waiter hadn't meant to insult me. He just didn't know how to deal with a girl with a broken back. Neither did I.

I rescued my beer from the pocket of my wheelchair then shoved the contraption away. Carefully setting the bottle aside, I pulled myself over to the end of the slip to gaze down on the waves. I hated being stuck in a wheelchair. I wanted to be in the water, playing with the fish, but I hadn't been swimming since the accident. The closest I'd come was in the pool at the rehab center, where my body turned to lead every time I went in. My therapist swore I could float if I'd just try, but I knew better. I could drive, get dressed, and do everything else I needed to get by, but swimming? Forget it. I was doomed to be a fish out of water for the rest of my life.

Sighing, I hauled my legs over the end of the slip and picked up my beer. I decided to forget about therapists, ex-girlfriends, and ignorant waiters for a while and just enjoy the view. I had a moment of peace while I sipped from the bottle. Then I spied a long sleek shadow glide beneath the water.

"What the hell?"

I set the beer down and craned my neck, trying to catch another glimpse of whatever had just swum by. Was it a shark? Impossible. Sharks never came this close to the shore. Then the shadow passed by again, swift and sleek, just inches beneath my toes. If it was a shark, it was at least nine feet long, big enough to take a chunk out of me.

Heart racing, I scrambled to get my legs back onto the dock. The waiter had been right. This wasn't a good place to sit, after all. I pulled my right leg up, snagging my jeans on a nail. Before I could free myself, the shadow glided right up to the slip. I stifled a shriek as a pair of muscular arms shot out of the water and grabbed the pier beside me.

"Ahoy there, matie!" the newcomer crowed as she hauled herself up. "I'm Salty Sal, the queer mer-gal! How the hell are you?"

I gaped at the creature sitting beside me. From the top of her violet buzz-cut down to her rippling abs, she was human—a regular butch dyke complete with nose ring and bulging biceps. On one arm, she wore a tattoo of a naked woman riding a bucking blue dolphin. On the other, she had a pair of pirates going down on each other sixty-nine style. The sodden t-shirt plastered over her breasts proclaimed, "If it tastes like fish, eat all you wish!" Her nipples stood out clearly beneath the wet black cotton. They looked pierced and happy.

From the waist up, she was a strange-looking gal. From the waist down, things only got stranger. A few inches below her navel, her pink human flesh faded into a slick gray and white dolphin tail that stretched down into the water below us. Submerged beneath the waves, a pair of broad, tapered flukes swayed back and forth in lazy strokes.

"Holy shit!" I stammered. "You're—you're a—"

"A lesbian!" she cried out. "I know!"

"No, no. You're a mermaid! This can't be real."

Dumbfounded, I leaned forward to get a better look at the tail. Bad idea. I overbalanced and began to topple forward. For one harrowing moment, I hung suspended over the water. Then the mermaid thrust her arm in front of me and pulled me back in.

"Hold on, doll face! I want you wet, but not that wet. At least not yet."

I clung to her, my heart pounding so hard I thought it'd break my ribs. "Don't let go! Don't let me fall in!"

"Whoa, honey! It's okay. I've got you. You're safe with Sal."

I buried my face in her wet t-shirt and started shaking. The mermaid stroked my hair and held me tight. Her arms felt strong and safe.

Salt water perfumed her skin. Caught in a stranger's embrace, I recalled bittersweet memories of Diane and me making love on the beach. Moaning with longing and despair, I felt the swell of the mermaid's breast beneath my cheek and her hardened nipple protruding below my lips. I had the sudden wild urge to suckle it like an infant, but before I could do that a shout came up from the bar.

"Sal! Don't you harass my customers!"

George the waiter hurried toward us, flapping his hands at the mermaid. "Shoo! Go away! Bad mermaid! Miss, I'm terribly sorry. I tried to warn you. This wretched creature shows up all the time to scare away my customers—"

The mermaid scowled. "Oh shut your pie hole, George. I'm not bothering the lady. We're just talking."

As the waiter sputtered to a halt, she reached across my lap and snagged my half-empty beer bottle. She took a swig and spit it right back out. "Man, I can't believe you serve this piss-water to your customers! George, go back to the bar and get this nice young woman a real drink. Put it on my tab. Say, doll face, how'd you like to have 'Sex On The Beach?'"

George ignored her. "Ma'am, if this *person* is bothering you—"

"No, it's okay," I interrupted, carefully freeing myself from Sal's embrace. "I'd like her to stay."

"Miss, I don't think—"

"She stays."

I glared at him. After a few moments, he slunk off to get our drinks. Sal leaned back on her elbows and chuckled.

"Thanks, doll face. Ol' George always tries to run me off the moment I show up." Her voice dropped to a conspiratorial whisper. "He says I cause him too much trouble."

She winked at me and I giggled. "He does seem like an easy target," I agreed.

"Too easy! So what's your name?"

"Marnie." I looked around to see if anybody else noticed the bizarre creature chatting me up. The beach bums inside the bar waved and smiled. A few of the other customers rolled their eyes at us then went back to their drinks like nothing strange was happening. I decided to go with the flow. "Are you really a ... a mermaid?"

Sal flipped her tale, sending up a spray of foam. "Nah, I've been around the dock too often to be any kind of *maid*. I prefer *mer-gal* or *mer-dyke*, if you really want to give me a label."

40

"Oh. Aren't you supposed to have a scaly tail and wear a clam shell bra?"

She threw her head back and howled. "Doll face, scales are for cold-blooded creatures. I'm hot-blooded—very hot-blooded, if you catch my drift. As for the clam shells, have you ever tried stuffing your titties into a pair of those things? Not a comfortable fashion statement. Hell, I usually go topless. I'm only wearing a shirt right now because of that stupid sign George posted over there."

She nodded toward the sign at the bar's entrance that read, "No shirt, no shoes, no service."

"I don't worry about the shoes part," Sal added, "seeing as how I don't have feet. Speaking of feet, are yours tired? Because you've been running through my mind all evening, sweet cheeks."

I winced. "I don't do any running these days."

"Really? With a hot bod like yours, I'd have thought you were a real jock." Sal reached up and squeezed the back of my arm before sliding a finger under the strap of my tank top. I shivered as the strap slipped down my shoulder, suddenly aware of how wet my shirt was from hugging Sal. My nipples tightened to hard knots beneath the cold damp fabric, making plain to anyone who cared to look that I wasn't wearing a bra. Sal obviously cared to look. She smiled and squeezed my arm again. "You got a lot of muscle, doll face. I like that. You ever go scuba diving?"

"Not lately, I'm afraid."

"How about pearl diving?" she asked with a smirk. "That's a mer-gal's favorite sport, you know."

George came back with a couple of drinks. "So is drinking without paying," he grumbled. "Fork it over, Sal."

Sal made a show of fishing a gold doubloon out of her cleavage and handed it to the less-than-thrilled George. "There are more in my 'treasure chest' if you care to dig them out," she offered.

He shuddered and promptly ran off. We laughed as he made his getaway.

"So," I said, turning back to Sal, "is 'Sex On The Beach' a mer-gal's favorite drink?"

She leered at me. "Of course! You know what our favorite food is, don't you?"

I shook my head. "Tell me."

"Bearded clam!"

I cracked up so hard I spilled half my drink down the front of my shirt. My nipples stood up even more as Sal slapped my back.

"Doll face, the wet look is definitely you!"

We spent the next couple of hours sitting on the pier, swapping dirty jokes. We kept George hopping as we called for more drinks. Twice, he came out and told us to keep it down. We just laughed even louder. With Sal around, I forgot about my earlier bad mood. She kept reaching out to touch me, squeezing my arm, stroking my shoulder. Each time her fingers brushed against my skin, I felt a heady sort of jolt. If I could have felt my clit, I'm sure it would have been buzzing. Instead, all that electricity settled into my breasts until my nipples fairly ached from want.

Before long, I was touching Sal back, running my fingers along the cutout neck of her t-shirt. I eased the frayed neckline lower and lower, trying to get a peek at what she had underneath. When my fingertips brushed the tops of her bare breasts, Sal started singing.

"Oh, what do you do with a drunken waiter, what do you do with a drunken waiter, what do you do with a drunken waiter … earl-eye in the morning?"

"Sal, don't you dare!" George shouted at her from inside the bar, but she kept singing.

"Fuck him with a strap-on 'til he's sober, fuck him with a strap-on 'til he's sober—"

"Sal!"

George popped his head out a window, his face purple with outrage. A ripple of laughter went up inside the bar. Sal broke off, snorting and slapping her tail as he glared at her then disappeared back inside.

"Man, did you see the look on George's face?"

"Yeah, he's about ready to piss himself." I bent over laughing. Then I straightened up, reminded of something I'd forgotten.

"Aw shit!" I reached down to feel the crotch of my jeans. I was damp, and not in a good way. Face burning, I reached for the wheelchair that had somehow stayed invisible throughout Sal's visit. I had to get to a bathroom and quick.

"Holy crap! Is that yours?"

Startled, my head snapped back to Sal. She pushed past me and snagged the chair.

"This is so fucking cool!" she exclaimed, running her hands over the wheels. "Can I try it?"

Sal didn't wait for an answer. Before I could stop her, she grabbed the arms of the chair and hauled herself up into it. She twisted around until she sat facing forward with three feet of tail still lying on the deck.

"Hey everybody, look at me. I'm Bette Midler!" She flipped up her tail and popped a wheelie in the chair, shouting, "'The question before us is where's her clitoris!'"

"Sal! Don't!" I hissed as she took off down the pier.

My body felt overfull, like a water balloon ready to burst. I didn't even have the safety net of an adult diaper. The damned things made me feel like an infant. Pissing myself in public, though, would feel even worse. If I didn't get my chair back and get out of there fast, I'd be sitting in a puddle. I waved frantically to Sal as she raced up and down the pier, belting out one-liners to the customers inside the bar. But by the time she finally wheeled her way back to me, it was too late. The water balloon had burst.

Sal parked the chair and slid out to sit beside me. "Hey Marnie, what's wrong?"

Humiliated, I grabbed the chair and tried to drag myself up into it, but Sal had parked it at the wrong angle. I swore as I shoved the thing into position. Before I could pull myself up, Sal's arm snaked around my waist to hold me back.

"What's wrong?" she demanded.

I pushed her away before she could notice my sodden jeans.

"Nothing. I have to go."

I climbed into the chair and rolled away as quickly as I could. Behind me, I heard a loud splash and then just before I reached the ramp to the parking lot, Sal rose up out of the water and landed on the dock before me.

"That's far enough, doll face!" She stretched her entire length across the pier to form a living speed bump. "What the hell's going on?"

"Get out of my way, Sal. I have to leave!"

"Fuck that. I thought we had something going on back there. Why are you trying to ditch me now?"

She reached toward me and I shrank back. "Don't. I can't. I just... I just..."

I started blubbering then, great big choking sobs that racked my entire body. Sal pulled herself closer.

"Doll face, whatever's wrong, just tell me." She stroked my legs as she crooned to me. The scent of urine filled my nostrils and I cried even harder. I knew Sal could smell it too.

43

"I just pissed myself, okay!" I wailed. "I lost track of how much I had to drink and I couldn't hold it!"

"Hey, it's okay."

"No it isn't! I hate this fucking chair and I hate having a broken back! I can't do a goddam thing, not even make it to the stupid bathroom in time!"

Then I really began to bawl. Sal wrapped her arms tight around my shins. I had to double over to cry on her shoulder as customers filtered in and out of Ray's. They gave us a wide berth as they went past, but left us alone.

I don't know how long we sat there, maybe fifteen minutes, maybe more. When I finally got control of myself, I tried to pull away, but Sal wouldn't let go.

"Don't," she said. "You had one little accident. Don't let that ruin the rest of tonight."

"I'm soaked in piss," I protested.

"We'll get you cleaned up. Just don't walk away, okay?"

"Fuck you. I can't walk away. I've got a broken back."

She rolled her eyes. "Well then, don't wheel away."

"What if I have another accident?"

Sal shrugged. "Don't worry about it. Do what I do instead."

"What's that?" I asked, still sniffling.

"Piss in the ocean and swim away real fast."

My snort of laughter caught me by surprise. Giggling and crying, I sat up and wiped my face. Sensing she had me on the ropes, Sal kept going.

"Hey, I'm serious. I mean can you imagine me sitting on the john? We don't have toilets down on the ocean floor. Even if we did, how would I use one? It's not like I can squat down, spread my legs, and aim my pussy at the bowl. I'd probably piss in my face if I tried it!"

The image of Sal on a toilet was too much. I started to howl. Sal grinned from ear to ear.

"Hey," she whispered when I'd quieted down a bit. "You want to see it?"

"See what?"

"You know, the fish taco."

She pointed to her pelvis and I blinked. One moment Sal's tail was a smooth, uninterrupted surface from her waist to her flukes. The next, a small slit appeared at her hips, revealing a pair of swollen labia with a flowery bud of dark pink cunt nestled between them.

44

"Go ahead, have a taste!" Sal cackled as I ogled her pussy.

"Sal!"

Sal's pussy snapped shut as George came stomping down the pier, shaking a finger at her. "This is a public place! I told you last time, if you can't keep it zipped—"

"Then I have to leave," Sal chimed in. She tossed her head at the outraged waiter. "Don't get your knickers in a knot, George. We were headed out anyway."

She let go of my legs and pushed off the pier. A tremendous splash went up as she hit the water.

"At least I can get rid of this stupid thing now," she hollered. George let out a squawk as her wet shirt came flying back and landed smack in his face.

"As for you..."

I looked down and saw Sal bobbing in the waves, smiling up at me.

"Let's go for a swim," she said.

In a flash, Sal sprang up out of the water. Her arms wrapped tight around me, pulling me out of my chair. We hung in the air for a moment, then plummeted down.

Cold salt water closed over our heads as we dove. Panicked, I struggled in her arms, but it was like moving in slow motion. A stream of silver bubbles escaped from my mouth. Sal plunged onward, pulling me further under and away from the pier. Just when I thought my lungs would burst, we surfaced. I came up sputtering and shrieking.

"I can't swim! I can't swim!"

"Yes you can." Sal kept a firm grip on me while I flailed about, panic-stricken. Ray's Raw Bar and the pier were several hundred yards away.

"Fuck you! My back is broken and my legs don't work. I can't swim!"

"Doll face, who the hell needs legs to swim?"

Her tail broke the surface and came crashing back down, dousing me. I quit struggling long enough to punch Sal in the chest.

"*I* need them. I'm not a damn mer-dyke, okay?"

"Ouch! Yeah, you are," she said and laughed. "You just don't know it yet."

She held onto me, floating effortlessly while I wore myself out screaming at her. When I finally drooped against her, Sal relaxed her grip.

"You can swim, okay? You just need to learn how. Now don't fight me. Let's try floating first."

She tipped me back in the water. Terrified, but seeing no other choice, I did as she said. Suddenly, I was a five-year-old kid again, taking swim classes at the Y. Sal kept one hand under my shoulders, the other somewhere below my waist where I couldn't feel it.

Without control of my legs, I couldn't figure out what to do. Every time Sal pulled her hands out from under me, I bent at the waist and sank, unable to hold my pelvis straight. She caught me each time, though, and after a while I started to relax.

"You're focusing on the wrong area," she told me when I sank for the fifth time. "If you can't control your hips and legs, you need to start thinking up here." She tapped my chest. "Your breasts are big enough to act as floatation devices anyway, so push those babies up out of the water and let them do the work for you."

I complied, thrusting my chest above the waves and trying to hold the rest of my body steady around that point. I sank twice more, but then something finally clicked. As the moon sailed high overhead, I stretched out my arms and let the ocean carry me. Sal pulled her hands away and I floated.

"I knew you could do it."

She stroked my chest, the spot where I had placed all my concentration, and drew slow spirals around my breasts that ended at my nipples. The hard nubs rose up beneath my wet tank top. Sal kissed them, her lips closing over my wet shirt to suck on each one.

"You ready for some more?" she challenged.

"Hell yeah."

"Take a deep breath," she said, and then we dove.

We hurtled along beneath the waves. Every so often, Sal and I porpoised to the surface to catch a quick breath. Her body rocked against mine as she held me, her dolphin tail propelling us to even faster speeds. The waves became a blur. The ocean roared in my ears. We didn't slow down until we neared land.

We let the surf wash us up onto the shore. A narrow strip of beach glistened silver beneath the moonlight. The black silhouettes of palm trees swayed in the cool night breeze. The sound of traffic was a distant whisper over the *shush, shush* of the breakers.

Sal rolled me over onto my back and kissed me. She slid a hand beneath my shirt and squeezed my breast, sliding her thumb over the nipple. I groaned. Then she reached for the zipper of my jeans and I froze.

"Stop." I batted her hand away.

In the bright moonlight, I saw Sal frown. "Why?"

"I told you, I'm dead from the waist down. I can't feel anything. So just don't, please."

She put her forehead to mine. "Doll face, who lied to you? Who told you, you were dead down there? "

I swallowed hard. "Diane, my ex. But she didn't lie. It's true."

"Really? She the one who said you couldn't swim anymore either?"

That hit me like a sucker punch. "She said my broken back was crippling us both. We couldn't do stuff like we used to. We couldn't go swimming, couldn't go sailing or surfing. Then she said there wasn't any point in making love to me if I couldn't feel it."

"What a goddam cunt!" Anger radiated off of Sal in palpable waves of heat. "Don't listen to her, Marnie. She was wrong!"

"But she wasn't!" I cried. "I can't walk. I can't figure out when I need to take a piss. And you saw how hard it was for me to even float."

"Did a doctor say you couldn't make love anymore?"

"No. But everything's so goddam hard now, Sal." I broke down crying. Sal just squeezed me tight.

"Hon, your problem isn't your broken back. It's your broken heart. I'm sorry your fucked-up ex couldn't deal with what happened to you, and I know things are hard, but that doesn't mean you should give up. A dead fish can float ashore, but it takes a live one to swim against the tide."

"What the hell does that mean?" I asked, sniffling.

"Let me show you." Sal eased my wet shirt up over my chest until my breasts lay bare to the cool night air. She thumbed my nipples until I groaned, then slowly stripped away the rest of my wet clothing. When I lay naked on the sand, she came back to my breasts, taking a nipple in her mouth. The pull of her sucking was persistent and powerful. I twined my arms around her neck, swimming in ecstasy, more helpless now than I'd been out in the ocean.

"Let's play a game," Sal suggested, coming back up for another kiss. "I'm going to explore every inch of your body and find every sensitive spot you've got. Each time I find one below the waist, you have to play with your tits while I watch. If I make you come, then you have to go down on me."

"Like I don't already want to do that," I breathed. Still, I hesitated. "But what if I don't feel anything down there?"

"Then just watch me enjoy your beautiful pussy. Don't you want to see me go down on you?"

I could only nod. I did want to see that, and badly. I wanted to watch her back muscles ripple beneath the moonlight as she lapped at my cunt. I wanted her fingers inside me, fucking me hard even though I knew I'd never feel it. I wanted to be loved and I knew Sal would do it right.

She started at the top of my head and slowly worked her way down my body. Inch by inch, she tasted me, mindless of the sand that coated my skin. All the while, her hands stayed busy with my breasts as her mouth set my upper body on fire. Then she reached my waist, the grey area between feeling and numbness, living and dead. I stiffened.

"Easy now," she murmured. Still pinching my nipples, she continued down. She placed one slow kiss after another on my belly. Enthralled, I watched as one hand left my breasts to caress my hip. I felt nothing, but I couldn't look away. Then a shock of heat hit my body, making me cry out. Sal leaned back and grinned.

"Look what I found! Sensitive spot number one, right here on the inside of your left hip." She stroked the spot again and I quivered. The touch of her hand felt distant, but it was definitely there.

"More!" I begged.

"Not so fast." She waggled a finger at me. "Let me see you play with yourself first."

Trembling, I touched my breasts. I slowly rolled the tips of my nipples between my fingers until I began to moan. Sal stroked my hip again, sending fireworks shooting through me.

"Don't stop," she said. "Keep playing with yourself while I explore some more."

She moved from my hips to my thighs, brushing her lips over my bare skin. I felt a flicker of sensation at the inside of my right thigh when she licked it.

"Sensitive spot number two!" Sal crowed. As she lingered over the spot, I pinched my nipples and gasped.

Sal kept going. The backs of my knees, a spot on my right ankle, the bottom of my left foot—at each of those points, I felt something and the discovery hit me like a tidal wave. Overwhelmed, I cried out Sal's name. She made her way back to my hips and paused.

"Please," I whimpered. "Don't stop..."

She slipped my legs over her broad shoulders and bent down to kiss my mound. Her lips grazed my pussy and another flutter, like the memory of a memory, rose up inside me. I couldn't feel what she was doing, but I could see it. I could see the smile grow on Sal's face as she ran the tip of her tongue along my crevice then buried her face in my dark curls. I could see her mouth rub against my pussy and then come up again to glisten wetly in the moonlight. Without warning, I grabbed Sal by her short spiky hair and pressed her hard against me.

"Do it!" I growled.

Sal went down on me with a vengeance. She grabbed one of my hands and set it over my cunt. I felt her hot tongue swirl between my fingers and over the slick folds of flesh. Her hands went back to stroking the sensitive spot at my hip. Somewhere between my hip and my fingers, between the sight of Sal going down on me and the distant sensation of her touch, a pent-up storm of need surged inside me. It faded in at the gray area at my waist and roared up to fill my entire torso. Suddenly, I was floating on the ocean again, riding the biggest wave I'd ever encountered. When it came crashing down, I let it pull me under. I drowned in my orgasm as I screamed Sal's name.

"You see," she told me when she finally came up for air. "You're not broken, after all. You're beautiful."

*　　　*　　　*

I'm pleased to say, I gave as good as I got that night. After Sal had her way with me, I flipped her over and took my time exploring that fine piece of tail. Her pussy tasted like fresh scampi, and I was happy to eat until she came in my mouth. After that, we continued taking turns making love to each other. By the time the sky lightened to grey in the east, I was exhausted, but content.

The sun was sneaking up over the horizon when we finally returned to Ray's Raw Bar. Sal brought me back to the slip where we first met and gave me a lingering kiss.

"That was a pretty good first date," she said as she lifted me back onto the pier.

"So what do we do for a second date?" I asked.

"More swimming lessons. Maybe by the end of the month, we can scare up some scuba gear for you and go on an adventure. There's an old shipwreck I know—a Spanish galleon. We could go diving for sunken treasure."

"And in the meantime, we keep diving for pearls?"

"Count on it, doll face."

I heard the door to Ray's swing open. We turned and watched George shuffle out, pushing my wheelchair. He parked it on the slip next to me and grimaced.

"What's the matter, George?" Sal asked. "You look like you got your trouser trout caught in your fly."

"Been waiting up all damned night for you, that's what's the matter." He glanced at me. "You left your chair on the dock. Figured you might want it when you got back."

I shrugged. "I suppose I can use it when I'm not in the water."

"Now Marnie, let's show George a little more appreciation than that!" Sal cooed. "After all, he wouldn't have waited up if he didn't really love us. Ain't that right, sweet cheeks?"

Before George could answer, Sal leapt up and planted a sloppy kiss on his shocked face. Choking and sputtering, he swatted her away, but not before she gave his butt a good pinch.

"See you tonight at six!" she called to me as she hit the water and swam off.

George shuddered. "Tell me you're not meeting her here tonight!"

When I nodded, he groaned and rubbed his behind. "Damn mermaid!"

"Mermaids," I corrected as I watched Sal head off into the sunrise. "There's two of us now."

Skin

"Do you love me?"

I cower naked before my goddess, fearing her answer. She stands before me, sleek and aloof. Shiny black leather encases her from head to toe, hugging every curve. Thigh-high boots, opera-length gloves, a cat suit, and a scalp-hugging hood—this is her raiment, her carapace, her skin. Only her eyes and mouth show from beneath that impervious exterior. Those holes and the long silver zipper that run down her back are the only chinks in her armor. Otherwise, my goddess is untouchable, unattainable, dark and terrifying. She is black Kali, destroyer of men. She is the smell and creak of burnished leather, the crack of the whip on soft, naked flesh. She is perfect.

"Do you love me?" I beg to know.

She laughs, twirling a flogger in her hands. "At $200 an hour? Why not? My heart is yours. Now assume the position, Danny boy."

I drop to my hands and knees in shivering supplication. Her whip and flail are also leather, as is the collar she buckles around my neck. The thick strap chafes as she pulls on the leash.

She pushes my face to the toe of her boot. "Worship me, dog!"

My goddess is cruel. There is no pleasure without pain, no excitement without humiliation. I hump her leg, grinding my hard cock against her booted calf. My arms are pulled behind my back, forearms laced together with a leather thong. My shoulders ache and I cannot feel my hands, but I can't stop humping her leg. I am so close, so close!

"You like this, don't you, Danny boy? Maybe you like it a little too much." She steps away before I can come. I fall over, sobbing then screaming as she unbinds my arms. Feeling shoots through my hands like fire and ice, an infinite number of searing pinpricks dancing along my fingers.

"You're supposed to use the safe word, dumbass." She sneers as I writhe on the floor. "Now I have to punish you for being so stupid."

"Please!" I beg. I don't know which hurts worse, my hands or my cock.

"Please nothing. Jerk yourself off. I'm too pissed to touch you."

I try my best, but my hands won't cooperate. It's divine retribution. I should have used the safe word, but if I had, she would have stopped and rebuked me for being weak. Now my goddess is angry and my hands are so clumsy I can't even hold my cock. Tears of frustration stream down my face.

"You're pathetic," she says before wrapping her fist around my erection. For an extra $50, my goddess decides to be merciful. In her gloved hand, I come hard and quick.

My goddess is supreme. I have worshipped her once a week for the last three years and I have never been disappointed. She is demanding and imperious and very expensive, but worth every penny. Leather is not cheap, she tells me, so I must pay extra for her attentions. I don't mind. She is everything I want, heaven and hell wrapped in a supple black hide, the slap of the paddle and the taste of polished boots. I adore her and fear her in equal measures.

Until the day I discover she's a fraud.

I spy her one afternoon in a shopping mall. I have never seen her unmasked before, so I do not recognize the face. I only know her by the sound of her voice and the tilt of her head. At first my cock gives an involuntary jerk. Then it withers and dies as I take in the faded t-shirt and ripped jeans, the curling red hair and the pale freckled flesh. Without her leather shell, she is as appealing as a flayed carcass. She turns and sees me, gives a knife blade smile. Horrified, I watch her strut toward me.

"You know who I am, Danny boy?"

I don't want to answer. It's not her. It can't be her! Where is my black leather goddess? Where is the dark temptress, the sacred Amazon, the destroyer of men?

She studies my face and snorts. "Yeah, you know all right. Don't worry, I won't tell anyone about your little secret, so long as you behave."

That's not what frightens me, though. When she reaches to touch my face with her bare hand, I turn away, sickened, and run.

My goddess is weak and imperfect. She is nothing without her carapace. She is a rotting sack of meat that only pretends to be divine, but I know how to fix that. When next I come to worship her, I bring a gift—a bottle of red wine.

"Do you love me?" I whisper, watching her drink.

"I already told you, idiot. My heart belongs to you. If you've forgotten, maybe I should dig out a knife and carve the answer into your ... into your ... skin..."

The drink slips from her fingers. The false goddess staggers on her stiletto heels and falls to the floor. The skin around her eyes and mouth grows pale and waxy. Her staring eyes turn to glass.

"I haven't forgotten," I say, digging out *my* knife from the pile of clothing I left at her door. I set the point above her chest. "Your heart is all I need."

At home, I stitch together a new goddess—thigh-high boots, opera-length gloves, the cat suit and the hood. I sew the mouth and eye holes shut. My goddess doesn't need them anymore. Same goes for the zipper. She will never shed her skin again. Her limbs I stuff with cotton batting, dead leaves, dryer lint, whatever I can find. It doesn't matter because, except for her heart, it's not what's inside that counts. It's what's outside. It's her skin, her perfect black-leather skin.

I kneel before the slumped figure and place the leash in her hand. "Do you love me?" I beg. "Please?"

The collar tightens. My goddess lives.

The Water Babies

I don't recall wanting to drown. I only remember swimming out to sea, where the waves were strong enough to carry me away. Away from the shore, away from Hal, away from the life I'd grown to hate. I was floating free for the first time in years, and when the current pulled me under, I was content to go with it. I was a mermaid, had been ever since the day my mother taught me to swim, and what did a mermaid have to fear from the sea? Not a damn thing. So down I went into the clear blue depths, where silver light played over darting fish that spiraled around me in a spectral dance.

Down, down, ever down. The water filled my mouth, my nose, my ears, and then all the empty places inside me until I was part of the sea and it was part of me. That's when the water babies came to me with their lithe bodies and long streaming hair. I called them babies because the wonder of innocence filled their eyes, but they had the bodies of young men, rippling muscles clearly visible beneath their pale, delicate skin. They wore no clothing, no decoration but a shining jewel hanging at each throat. When I reached out to touch one, he placed my hand on his chest and then guided it down to his slender hips. The other drifted behind me and undid the bindings of my nightgown, letting the white silk disappear into the deep. No, these two were no babies. They were as old as the sea, as seductive as the waves, and their touch set a tide of lust coursing through me.

I floated between them, naked and wanting. At first, they swam around me in lazy circles, but then they began exploring with their hands and mouths. They fed on me like hungry little fish, nibbling at my body with sharp kisses. One latched onto my breast like a lamprey while the other dove lower to suckle my cunt. With greedy hands I clutched them to me, catching them in the net of my desire.

Then the water above us churned and the roar of an engine shattered the sea. Above the noise, I heard shouts of rage. The water in my lungs turned to ice and suddenly I was struggling, the mermaid was struggling, fighting against the sea. The water babies saw my distress and pulled me up to the surface, gasping and screaming for air. Then a hand, Hal's, grabbed me by the hair and ripped me from the sea, landing me on the bottom of the boat like a fish on a hook. I retched and heaved until there was more water inside the hull than out. All the while, Hal kept screaming.

"You stupid girl! What the hell were you doing?"

I couldn't answer. All I could do was weep as the water babies swam away.

*　　　*　　　*

I don't recall wanting to drown, and for a long time, I couldn't recall the water babies either. Shock and depression erased my memories of that day. That was the doctor's diagnosis. I said they were buried beneath a mountain of drugs, but no one listened to me. I was mentally unstable. Hal said the pills were all that kept me in the real world, and he forced me to take them.

So I forgot about the water babies until the night of Hal's party. My husband was a lawyer striving to make senior partner. The party was meant to impress members of his firm. The only impression I knew how to make was a bad one, so while Hal made the rounds, meeting and greeting his guests, I escaped to the back deck of the beach house to bask in the sound of the ocean waves. Hidden beneath their endless rush and crash, I heard the susurration of idle gossip.

"Poor thing, they say she almost drowned."

"I heard she was under so long she suffered brain damage."

"How can they tell? She's never been quite right."

"Neither was her mother. You know *she* drowned."

"I can't imagine how Hal copes..."

Senseless prattle, all of it. I pushed the voices aside and focused on the sea. That's when I saw them.

Like ghosts they emerged from the shining waves and glided toward the shore. At first, I thought they were just a couple of college boys out skinny-dipping, blithely ignoring all the "Private Beach" signs Hal posted along the property lines. But something about them seemed familiar, something that tickled at the edges of my mind. As I watched, they drifted through the surf and washed up on the beach below. The waves, dyed red by the setting sun, lapped at their naked bodies as they stretched out on the sand.

"Mariel?"

I ignored the call and kept watching the two figures loll in the breaking waves. When they began touching each other, I gasped and leaned over the rail of the deck, the muddled memory tugging at me like the tide. One water-slicked head bent over another in a lingering kiss. A hand trailed up the inside of a glistening thigh to fondle a rising cock. I leaned even farther, goaded on by the sudden heat between my legs.

"Mariel!"

Hal's voice yanked me back. "Come away from the railing. There's nothing to see."

I wrinkled my nose at the stench of his cigar, but turned anyway, blocking his view of the lovers below. "I'm watching the sunset."

"You're watching the damn waves. All that light and motion, it'll lull your feeble little brain. Before you know it, you'll fall over the railing and hit the rocks below."

I rolled my eyes. "Please, if I hit those rocks it'll be because I jumped, not because I fell."

Hal sucked in a breath so sharp it should have slit his throat. He grabbed my arm. "Don't you dare say things like that, don't you dare ruin tonight for me!" he hissed.

He propelled me inside to the living room where strangers milled around, blathering and sipping their drinks. They all turned and gawked when I entered. Hal smiled and nodded at his guests, then slipped an arm around me in mock affection. He pulled me over to an older couple, a fat man with goggling eyes and a spindly woman whose smile was as fake as the pearls around her neck.

"Mariel, you've met the Sommes."

It was a command, not a reminder.

"Alice and Peter, yes. How nice to see you again."

The woman nodded, her fake smile threatening to split her narrow face. I offered a similar smile of my own. The man trapped my hand between his blubbery palms and refused to let go.

"Such a lovely girl," he wheezed. "You're a lucky man, Hal."

Hal beamed. "She's my pride and joy, aren't you, love? We've been married thirteen years."

"How lovely," the woman said to me. "Most marriages don't survive that long. Of course, I heard you almost didn't survive last summer."

"That was just an accident," Hal jumped in. "Mariel went sailing one morning and fell out of the boat. Fortunately, I was nearby to save her."

"How romantic! Your husband is your hero, then."

Hal squeezed me so tight I could barely breathe. "Yes," I lied. "Hal is my hero."

*   *   *

"I thought I told you to stay away from the deck."

I scanned the shoreline, searching for two lovers under the moonlight. They were nowhere in sight.

"You afraid I'll jump?" I asked.

Hal came onto the deck and frowned. "Don't get smart. Pete Sommes told me there's a couple of queers hanging around the area, trespassing on people's private beaches. So come inside, now."

"Before the queers get me? Honestly Hal, the beach is down there and I'm all the way up here in the house. Can't I get a little fresh air?"

"Open your bedroom window if you want air."

"I can't. You put a safety lock on it."

He caught my arm. "I'll put a damned lock on the door to your room if you don't come inside right now."

"Fine. Whatever."

I let him lead me back in. He wasn't kidding about the lock. So far I'd been able to convince him to leave the doors alone, but there wasn't a window in the house I could open.

"Did you take your pills?" he demanded as he maneuvered me down the hallway.

"Not yet."

"Take them now."

He pushed me into the bathroom and handed me a cup of water. From the pill minder in the cabinet, he retrieved three brightly colored tablets. I popped them into my mouth and then drained the cup.

"You can leave now," I said. "Or do you need to watch me pee?"

Hal glowered but backed off. "Get ready for bed," he ordered as he stalked out.

I took my time, brushing my hair and washing my face. I even read a magazine article while I sat on the john. When I flushed, I spit out the

57

meds I had hidden beneath my tongue. I waved bye-bye as the water carried them away.

"Gone in a flush," I joked and reached for the nightgown hanging on the bathroom door.

As my hand slid over the white silk, an image flitted across my mind of another gown lost beneath the waves. I felt two sets of hands caress my bare breasts, tasted two different mouths covering my own.

"Mariel!"

Hal banged on the door and I jumped. The lingering touch of strangers vanished, but the wetness between my legs remained. Flustered, I threw on the gown. Before Hal could rattle the doorframe again, I turned the knob and stepped out.

"What the hell are you doing in there?" he demanded.

I did my best impression of a glassy-eyed zombie. "Reading an article ... about flower arranging..." I waved my hand at the magazine sitting by the toilet. "Can we get some flowers tomorrow?"

Hall shook his head. "All right, you're done for the night. Let's get you to bed."

I let him carry me back to my room and pretended to nod off as he piled me into bed and turned out the light. But the moment the door shut my eyelids flew open. I listened to the darkened house, straining my ears until I heard the rumble of Hal's snores in the room next to mine. Then I rolled out of bed and crept to the front door.

Moments later, I was outside, running past the rock garden beside the house and headed down the path to the beach. My feet barely touched the ground. My nightgown fluttered like a shroud. Only my pounding heart let me know I wasn't a ghost. When I arrived at the beach, I stumbled to a halt and searched the receding waves. What was I looking for?

I wandered the shoreline, sharply aware that I looked as crazy as Hal made me out to be. I was chasing figments of my imagination, and if Hal caught me out at this hour of the night he'd lock me up for sure. I was about to give up when I saw them lying on the moonlit sand. Two boys twined together, legs tangled as they rocked in time to the somnolent waves. I crept closer and closer, my heart pounding in my chest. They started to roll in the sand, as though wrestling. I was near enough now to see they were two distinct creatures—one tall and dark-haired, the other smaller with fair locks gilded silver by the moonlight. The dark-haired boy came up on top and pinned his companion beneath him. He eased his lover's legs apart and made ready to spear him on a thick ivory cock. My whole body shuddered as the two came together and a flood spilled from between my legs, soaking my gown. I groaned and dropped to my knees, overwhelmed by my orgasm.

They both looked up then and I froze. One wrong move and I knew they would disappear back into the sea. The wind blew, sweeping beneath my nightgown to transform my nipples into diamond points. Finally, the boy on top extended his hand. I crawled over to join them.

We never said a word. When I touched fingertips with the dark-haired one, he pulled me closer for a kiss. His companion slid an arm around my waist and slowly unbuttoned the top of my gown, baring my breasts to the night. As he rolled the hardened tip of a nipple between his forefinger and thumb, the other pulled up my hem. He traced lazy fingers between my damp thighs and pulled on my tight curls of hair. I spread my legs wider, hoping to lure his teasing fingers inside me. Instead, his hands moved to my hips and I was pulled around to straddle the fair-haired boy lying in the sand.

Fair-hair stroked my clit with his thumb while Dark-hair cupped my breasts from behind. A shivering current ran from my breasts to my cunt and back again. I braced myself against Fair-hair, setting my hands on his shoulders as he continued to torment me. That's when I noticed the glowing jewel on his chest. I felt an overwhelming urge to snatch it from him, as though doing so would make that beautiful boy mine forever. Just as I slipped my fingers beneath the chain, I heard a shout from the beach house above.

"Mariel!"

Shit! Hal had woken up and found me gone. I felt the boys tense and suddenly we were all scrambling—them to get back in the water, me to get back to the house. I flew up the path, trying to fix my gown. Behind me, I heard two splashes. Ahead of me, the house lit up one room after another as Hal searched. I'd never make it inside. I stopped at the rock garden and dropped to my knees at its granite border. Only then did I see the shining jewel clenched in my fist. Hal shouted again and I dropped the treasure into the gravel bed, piling a handful of stones to hide it. Just as my husband came stampeding out the back door, I rammed a finger down my throat and vomited.

"Mariel! What the hell are you doing out here?"

I started to cry.

"I c-c-couldn't find the bathroom... I f-f-feel so sick..."

59

"Oh Jesus Christ."

Hal carried me back into the house. I sobbed, but inside I felt a curious glow, like that of the buried jewel. The memory that had tormented me all evening finally surfaced. I remembered those boys.

*   *   *

"Open your mouth."

There was no use in arguing. I obeyed, and Hal fed me a pill.

"Now swallow it."

Again, I obeyed and let the poisonous tablet slide down my throat.

"Show me."

I opened my mouth again to let Hal inspect. Satisfied that the pill was gone, he grunted.

"Anita, do not let Mrs. Locke leave the house today. She stays inside, got it?"

"Yes, Mr. Locke."

I slouched on the sofa, stuffed to the gills with cereal, fruit— whatever I could find in the kitchen. The stuffing was deliberate. I knew Hal would dope me before he left. The extra food was supposed to slow down the pill's effects. Still, my eyelids were already drooping. I prayed Hal would leave before I was completely snowed under.

"You behave today," Hal said as he pulled on his blazer. "I can't afford anymore gossip, understand me, Mariel? Mariel?"

My only answer was a soft snore. I slumped on the sofa with my head thrown back, a little drool hanging from my lower lip for added effect. Hal came over and poked me a few times. I gave a brief snort and promptly went back to "sleep".

"About damn time," he muttered.

While I pretended to snooze, Hal grabbed his briefcase and left. I waited until I heard the car pull out of the drive. Then I jumped off the sofa and ran to the bathroom. Anita, my nurse, ran after me. For the second time in twenty-four hours, I stuck my finger down my throat and puked. All of breakfast came back up, along with the pill. It wasn't pretty, but gorging and purging were the only defenses I had against swallowing that poison.

"Mrs. Locke, that's not good for you!"

Anita stood there and wrung her hands while I wiped my mouth. I liked Anita. We had an agreement, she and I. I let her raid the liquor cabinet and she didn't rat me out when I misbehaved.

"I'm going out," I said as I headed for the door. "I'll be back before Hal gets home."

"Mrs. Locke, please! I could get fired."

I pulled the keys to the liquor cabinet out of my pocket and handed them to her. "Enjoy your day."

A moment later I was out the door; still drowsy but coming alive in the salty breeze. I stopped at the rock garden and found the jewel I'd hidden the night before. Then I skipped down to the beach. When I hit the sand, I kept going around the curve of the bluff. On the far side was a tiny cove that used to be home to two boats—a small sunfish for me and a black and yellow runabout for Hal. Hal got rid of the boats after my so-called accident. Now the cove was empty save for the wooden pier. I picked my way over the creaking boards until I reached the end, then slipped off my deck shoes and dangled my toes in the water.

As I sat there, I pulled the jewel out of my pocket and fastened its chain around my neck. It was a dazzling thing that changed colors as I watched, from ultramarine to emerald to amethyst and back again. The brilliant hues chased the last bit of fog from my brain and left me with a sense of peace no pill could ever give. Too bad I couldn't keep it, but I knew its owner was coming to claim it.

I didn't have long to wait. Two shimmering shapes appeared beneath the water, gliding toward the pier with preternatural speed. Dark-hair surfaced first, followed by Fair-hair. They floated over to me, eyeing the jewel at my throat.

"Hello," I said. "I'm glad you came back."

They said nothing, but their eyes drifted from the jewel to my face.

I offered a smile. "We haven't been properly introduced. I'm—"

"Mariel," Dark-hair said. "Which means 'sea bright.'"

That surprised me. "You know my name."

"We know you."

"Tell me your names," I said.

"I'm Dylan," Dark-hair said. "He's Bryce."

Bryce smiled slightly, his hair burnished gold in the daylight. He lifted a hand out of the water to stroke my bare calf. "You have something of mine."

"Yes, I do." I touched the jewel. "You know, if someone steals a mermaid's comb, she has to grant three wishes to get it back."

"We're not mermaids," Dylan said. "And that's not a comb."

"But I bet it's worth three wishes."

Dylan glanced at Bryce, who gazed up at me. Their eyes changed colors just like the jewel. "Three wishes," Bryce said. "That sounds fair. So what do you wish for, Mariel Sea-Bright?"

I laughed. "I'm a lonely woman, and you're two pretty young men. I wish... I wish you would stay with me. For a while at least."

Dylan's gaze flicked up toward the house. "What about the man?"

"Don't worry. He's gone for the day."

Bryce nodded. "So we stay. And do what?"

"What were you doing last night?"

Dylan and Bryce smiled as I settled back and grinned. Without further prompting, they turned to each other and started kissing, long deep-throated kisses that sent shivers up my spine. I glanced down and saw their cocks bobbing in the water, getting harder by the second. Bryce started rubbing up against Dylan, nibbling his lover's neck then dropping lower to flick his tongue over Dylan's coral-tinged nipples. All the while, he kept his hand on my calf, stroking my leg as he teased Dylan's nubs into hard little knots. When Bryce clamped down on one and began sucking hard, Dylan and I both gasped.

Bryce came back up for a kiss and Dylan boosted him onto the pier between my legs. He leaned back against me, dropped his golden head on my shoulder and sighed. Mesmerized, I watched Dylan come up out of the water to mouth the smooth stomach before him, leaving a trail of kisses that went all the way down to the silky curls between Bryce's legs. He came closer and closer to his lover's swollen cock until, at last, his mouth closed over its purpling head.

Bryce buried his face in my neck and moaned. I nearly came on the spot. His legs came up over Dylan's shoulders and he thrust his hips forward. Dylan opened his mouth and swallowed the entire length of Bryce's cock. For the next several minutes, he sucked furiously while Bryce cried into my hair. When Bryce came, I smelled the salt of the sea in his scent.

Then he slid off the pier, pulling me with him. I came down into Dylan's waiting arms. While Dylan pulled my shirt over my head, Bryce tugged at my shorts. Soon I was naked as a babe and splashing in the water. Bryce murmured as he stroked my breasts.

62

"Come swim with us."

"Come play," Dylan whispered as his hand grazed my thigh.

Then they were off, diving beneath the water and headed out to the sea. I dove in after them, the mermaid returned home once more. We raced out of the cove and into open water, playing tag in the waves. When we washed up on the beach, Dylan and Bryce wrapped their arms around me and we kissed. Bryce caressed my breasts, tracing slow circles around my nipples with his fingers. Dylan stroked my thigh, teasing me until I rolled over and pushed him down on the sand. I straddled his hips, impaling myself on his ivory cock. Bryce came behind me and slipped his fingers between my lower lips until he found a little pearl of flesh. My hips rocked back and forth. Then Dylan thrust into me hard and I screamed as my orgasm crested and crashed inside of me.

We collapsed to the sand in a tangle of arms and legs and drifted off together, lulled by the sound of the surf pounding against the sand. It felt so peaceful, so safe. Then I heard another pounding; heavy footsteps racing across the beach. I woke up and screamed.

"You goddam whore!"

Hal grabbed me by the hair and struck me. I heard a shout and saw Bryce reach out to stop him. Hal spun around and kicked him in the face. Bryce fell back with a spray of blood flying from his mouth. When Dylan came at him, Hal just laughed and dropped me on the ground. My beautiful boys were no match for the monster who called himself my husband. Hal pummeled them with his fists, knocked them both to the ground, and started kicking them in the ribs. As their blood stained the sand, I let out a furious shriek.

"Stop it! Leave them alone!"

I leapt onto Hal's back and shredded his face with my nails. He roared and swatted at me, but I sunk my teeth into his ear and bit down until a piece tore off in my mouth. Hal bellowed and flung me to the ground. I threw a handful of sand into his eyes and ran as he blindly staggered.

"Get up!" I hauled Bryce and Dylan to their feet and pushed them toward the water. "You have to go!"

"We can't! You wished us to stay..."

They stared at me, blood trailing down their faces. I ripped the jewel from my neck and shoved it into Bryce's hands. "Now I wish you would go," I whispered.

Bryce wept and cradled the necklace in his hands. Dylan pulled him away and they stumbled into the water. A moment later, Hal knocked me aside and waded in after them, but he was too late.

They were already gone.

*   *   *

I didn't want to drown. Not like this.

"You say you were out here on the deck when you saw them?"

"Yes, they were down there on the beach."

I was in my own bed, floundering in a heavy fog. Voices drifted to me through the suffocating mist, but none of them made sense.

"How the hell did she get down there, Anita? I thought I paid you to watch her!"

"Mr. Locke, that's enough. Anita, can you describe the men who attacked Mrs. Locke?"

"What are you asking her for? I already gave you a damn description!"

Thunder crashed. A storm was brewing. I sank even further into the mist.

"Your wife asked to go to the hospital..."

"She's already seen a doctor."

"Is that why she's doped up?"

Not doped. Drowning. Couldn't they see that?

"It's a sedative. My wife's schizophrenic. This incident could cause her another breakdown."

"Then she should go to the hospital—"

"Mariel's not going anywhere!"

"Mr. Locke, I'd like to know your wife's wishes in this matter..."

My wishes. Those words stretched out to me like a lifeline. I'd only made two—one to keep Dylan and Bryce, and one to send them away. What did I wish for now?

"I wish I was free," I whispered.

The fog lifted, just enough for me to breathe. I rolled off the bed and groped my way to the living room. No one saw me. They just stood on the back deck and argued. I went out the front door, taking Hal's blazer with me. At the rock garden, I pulled on the jacket and tucked two heavy stones into the pockets. Then I ran, one last time, down to the beach. The shouting didn't reach my ears until the water was up to my knees. When the waves came up to my waist, I started to swim. I kicked and stroked with all my might while the coat grew heavier, and the frantic figures on the shore faded to a distant memory.

I swam until the current pulled me under, and then I sank beneath the waves. Goodbye, Hal. Goodbye, pills. Down, down, ever down I went. I opened my mouth and drank deep, letting the sea fill all the hollow places inside me. The heavy coat slipped off my shoulders, but I didn't need it anymore. Two figures reached toward me from the shadowy depths below. Their hands entwined with mine, pulling me into a loving embrace. I gave up my last breath with a smile. The mermaid had finally come home to the clear blue sea where silver light played over darting fish, and the water babies waited for me.

He Who Plants A Tree

"But this is *Shady* Banks! You can't cut down the trees!"

Mrs. Green wrung her hands while Garth scowled and started up his chainsaw. "Lady, it's my yard. I bought this place. I can do whatever I want."

All further protests from Garth's elderly neighbor were drowned out by the roar of the saw as it ripped through a towering maple. The tree crashed to the lawn; others soon followed. He dealt with the roses next, ripping them out by their roots, then the tulips, the herbs, the ivy, the lawn. All day, Garth sweated and swore. Damn the previous owner and his green thumb!

"I *knew* I should have stuck with my old apartment," grumbled Garth as he wrestled with the honeysuckle that clung to the picket fence.

That evening, he surveyed the yard. Broken branches and tattered leaves littered the muddy ground. The butchered segments of the maple tree rested on the curb. Everything green was gone. Satisfied, Garth headed to bed. He would buy concrete tomorrow and pave the whole thing over.

That night, though, a tiny sprig of green blossomed from the slaughtered tree. It grew into a vine that raced across the yard and coursed up the house to the bedroom window. Garth awoke to find verdant creepers twining around his limbs. As he writhed in their grip, the plants transformed and a creature bloomed before him.

"What the hell are you?" Garth gawked at the slim, supple body crowned by a leafy head. Long graceful arms sprang from its narrow torso and in the fork of its crotch grew a dark red flower.

"I'm a dryad," the creature replied. It pointed to the felled maple outside. "The previous owner planted that tree for me, and today you killed it. *Plant me a new one.*"

The vines tightened. A single tendril wrapped around Garth's cock, pressing needle-sharp thorns into his flesh.

"But winter starts tomorrow!" he lied. "It's too late to plant—"

66

"Is that so?" Willow branches sprouted from the dryad's fingertips. The vines flipped Garth over and laid bare his buttocks and thighs. He yelped as he felt the first punishing lash. "Then I must stay here with you until spring," the dryad said. "Pray the season comes early."

The next morning, Garth limped to the bathroom, the dryad in his arms. He attempted to confine it to a cactus he kept there, but that only made it prickly.

"You call this a home?!" it demanded, jabbing Garth in the buttocks as he tried to use the toilet. "I need sunlight! More water too!"

So Garth transplanted the dryad to the living room and placed it before the north-facing picture window.

"Ah, much better," it sighed as it basked in a golden pane of light. The dryad wriggled and undulated in its terra cotta pot, lithesome hands stroking the ruby-colored flower between its twiggy legs until the blossom grew twice its size. Garth shifted from foot to foot in the corner, suddenly aware of a startling growth in his own pants.

"What are you?" he asked again in a choked voice.

The dryad arched its back, running its hands over silver-green skin. "I told you. I'm a dryad."

"But... I mean, are you male? Female?"

"Ha! Why don't you tell me?"

The blossom between its legs opened, unfurling to reveal a cluster of stamen and pistols sprouting from within the deep well of scarlet petals. Entranced, Garth reached forward to touch the bobbing bulbous head of one of the stamen. It shuddered and sprayed golden pollen all over Garth, who convulsed and released his own seed in return.

"Oh my god," he groaned, crawling away to hide the dark wet stain on his pants.

The dryad giggled as he escaped the room. "My, you are an animal, aren't you?"

That night, Garth locked his bedroom door. Even so, the vines crept around the edges and through the keyhole. Once again, he awoke to find himself bound by verdant growth, the dryad straddling his hips.

"Fertilize me," it demanded, stroking its whip-like fingers across Garth's stomach. The scarlet flower opened once more to swallow Garth's burgeoning cock and suck it dry.

Day after day, night after night, the pattern repeated itself. Garth tried to avoid the dryad, tried to keep it locked in the living room, but it quickly overgrew the entire house. Runners tripped his feet, sharp thorns tore at his clothing. And always, the willow whips chastised him wherever he went. Then at night, it came to him, bound him, and rode him—sometimes taking Garth inside its flowering sex, sometimes thrusting a stamen or two deep inside his ass or mouth. The pollen was everywhere.

"I think you missed a spot," the dryad crooned as Garth scrubbed in the shower.

He felt leafy fingers brush against his backside and looked. Sure enough, yellow-gold dust glittered along the long red welts that cut across his ass.

In the dead of winter, Garth stood outside in his blighted yard.

"I bet you miss those trees now, don't you?" said Mrs. Green as she peered over the fence. "Trees keep a house warm in the winter, you know."

Garth shook his head before returning inside. The old lady had no idea.

Around February, the dryad grew swollen and slow. Garth ran his hands over its bulging belly and felt the fruits of his labor growing inside.

"Spring is coming," the dryad whispered, stroking Garth's hair. "Plant me a tree."

"What kind?"

"The right kind," the dryad teased. "The kind that shows how much you love me."

The next day, Garth went to the nursery and picked out a red birch. It was fine, strong, and healthy, and he felt a sense of pride as he planted it in the front yard. He carried the dryad outside and lifted it up into the branches.

"Home at last!" it cried. The flower between its legs burst open and a flood of green spilled forth across the bare dirt yard. Lush grass swept across the ground, chasing away the last of the snow. Crocuses sprang up at Garth's feet. Herbs and roses, honeysuckle and shrubs—all that he had destroyed months before came flourishing back.

Next door, Mrs. Green rushed out of her house, staring at the once-dead yard.

"My goodness! This place was a ruin! Where did all these plants come from?"

Garth smiled up at the dryad, who smiled back.

"I guess Spring came early this year," he said.

To Birdman With Love

"At last I shall have victory!"

I stood before a shiny metal control panel overloaded with lights, buttons, and gauges and roared with glee. For months I, the Silver Panther, had plotted to destroy Super City with its own nuclear power plant. Now that the moment had finally come, I could barely contain my feline delight. I arched my back and stroked my whiskers, striking an ominous yet seductive pose. The spandex-clad young man I had shackled to the light fixture overhead merely rolled his eyes.

"Whatever, old man."

"No, no, no!" I hopped up and down in frustration. "Reddy, that's not what you're supposed to say. I am an evil villain about to destroy all of Super City. You don't just say 'Whatever.' Now let's try this again."

I struck another menacing pose before the control panel and roared again, this time wiggling my hips to make the tail on my costume swish back and forth. The overhead lights gleamed against my silver cat suit, highlighting my aging but still-ferocious feline physique. "At last I shall have victory!"

"Yeah, yeah. You'll never get away with this, Panther," Reddy droned.

I threw back the hood of my costume, snarling. "Would it be too much to ask for a little enthusiasm, hmmm? You're so pathetic. My god, what does the Atomic Eagle see in you anyway?"

The Atomic Eagle was, of course, Super City's all-time favorite superhero. His origins were the stuff of legend. While on a field trip with the local Audubon Society, mild-mannered ornithologist Alvin Erkwyler stumbled across a gang of poachers from the planet Apteryx attempting to steal a rare harpy eagle. Heroic even then, Alvin grabbed the bird and fled, only to be zapped by a ray gun as he escaped. The radioactive burst of energy enveloped Alvin and the harpy eagle and fused the two creatures into one, creating a magnificent human-avian hybrid. With a wingspan of over fourteen feet and a keen eye for justice, the Atomic Eagle quickly soared to the top ranks of heroism and became the patron savior of Super City.

Reddy, on the other hand, wasn't so interesting. The Eagle's freckle-faced sidekick was barely five-foot-four and far from imposing. Unlike his mentor, Reddy didn't have a wingspan of fourteen feet. Hell, he didn't even have wings. His only claim to super status was his ability to scream—or crow, as he called it—at super-human volume, something he usually did at the first sign of danger. Oh, and he had his so-called tail feathers, a clump of stubby orange-red feathers that sprouted from his behind in a fashion vaguely reminiscent of a rooster's tail. They were more fluff than feather, really—nothing at all compared to the glossy silver-black pinions of the Eagle. Like all sidekicks, Reddy was just another wannabe superhero, annoying and pathetic, and really only useful as bait for my trap.

"Hey Panther," he called out. "How long do you plan on leaving me hanging here? My arms are going numb."

I ignored him and double-checked the controls of the power plant. Any minute now, the reactor core would go into meltdown and Super City, the home of the world's most super superheroes, would cease to exist. Of course, so would I if *somebody* didn't hurry up and save the day.

"Where is he?" I fumed, checking my watch. "I spent months planning this gig. Why is the Eagle late?"

"Maybe he's out chasing the Violet Vixen," Reddy suggested.

"Don't you dare mention that tinted tart's name!" I hissed. "That purple hussy is so low in the hierarchy of villainy she might as well collect canned goods for the local food pantry. I mean, really, has the Vixen committed any truly significant crimes as of late? I think not."

Reddy shrugged as best he could with his arms tied overhead. "She did have over $2000 in overdue library fines last month."

"Oh please. That's not a crime."

"The Eagle thought it was. When he caught the Vixen, he gave her a spanking like you wouldn't believe."

"A spanking?" I gasped. "I don't recall seeing *that* on the Eagle Cam!"

"Yeah, well some of the Eagle's more arousing adventures don't always show up on the Cam." Reddy favored me with an obnoxious grin. "So what do you want with the Eagle, anyway, Panther? What's the deal?"

"It's ... personal," I said, returning my attention to control panel.

"Oh, I get it," he mused. "You got the hots for the Eagle. It's the feathers, isn't it?"

"What! How did you...? I never told anyone—"

"Relax, Panther. Everyone loves the feathers, even me. You know, I even tried to duplicate the effect. I deliberately bungled an experiment in my old high school zoology class, hoping I could recreate the accident that turned Alvin into the Eagle. It, uh, didn't quite work as I had hoped." He glanced at his rear-end. "Maybe if I had used a hawk instead of a frozen chicken..."

"So that's how you ended up with those puny tail feathers," I muttered, taking a long hard look at Reddy's bottom.

When I chained Reddy up, I deliberately posed him to expose that ludicrous feathered rump, figuring it might be fun to spank him while I waited for the Eagle to show up. Paltry feathers aside, though, Reddy had a rather nice rear view, very firm and well-muscled. In fact, his whole figure rippled with lean muscle mass beneath his spandex tights. His costume included a hole cut at the base of his spine to let out his rooster tail. I grinned as I realized whoever tailored his costume cut the hole a little too large, giving me a peek of his tight little derriere.

"Reddy, you're not wearing any underwear, are you?"

"Okay, pops, do not stare at my butt like that." He tried to twist around to hide his behind, but to no avail. "You're creeping me out."

"Really?" I purred, sidling up to him. "You don't *feel* creeped out."

I slipped one hand over his crotch and the other down the hole in the back of his costume. Definitely not wearing underwear. Reddy groaned as I pulled on his tail feathers. "Let's see if I can make this rooster crow," I murmured.

Extending a claw, I tore the hole around his tail feathers until it ran all the way to the front of his groin. Reddy's cock, freed from its spandex restraints, sprang up proudly from a nest of auburn curls. I had to admit I was impressed. Reddy might have been a lowly sidekick, but he definitely packed some super-sized equipment. I gave his dick a squeeze.

"Feel good?" I whispered.

"You dirty old alley cat," he muttered as he thrust eagerly into my silky paw. "You'll never get away with this..."

"Say that again?" I urged. My hand slipped under his tail and between his buttocks.

"You'll never get away with ... this ... oh god, don't stop ... please ... yeah, just like tha—"

"Unhand my sidekick, you fiendish feline fiend!"

Like a thunderclap, the Atomic Eagle crashed through the ceiling of the control room and swooped down upon us. As he landed, he struck a manly pose and scowled.

"Wherever there is evil, the eagle eye of the Atomic Eagle will seek it out—oh, uh, sorry. Are you guys busy?"

"Yes!" Reddy shouted, still thrusting into my hand. He came up onto his toes as I slipped a finger between his ass cheeks. "We most certainly are!"

"Um, should I turn off the camera, then?" The Eagle pointed to his Eagle Cam, the free-floating high definition camera that followed him everywhere. It was a pretty neat device. While the Eagle fought the bad guys, the camera captured it all in real time and beamed the footage directly to his website. I tell you, who needed cable when you could watch a hunky avian stud muffin get all hot and sweaty 24/7?

"You're recording this?" Reddy shrieked. His face went from crimson to white and back to crimson again. His dick jerked violently in my hand.

"Of course," the Eagle replied. "I record everything. My adoring public wants to know what I'm doing at all time—"

"Turn it off! Turn that fucking camera off! And you! Quit pawing at my dick like it's a cat toy!"

I continued stroking Reddy while the Eagle chased after the suddenly very elusive Eagle Cam. "But sweetheart," I purred, "we only just started. If we keep going, I'm certain we could produce the most amazing money shot."

"Does that mean you guys want the camera to stay on?" the birdman asked.

"No!" Reddy squawked, his hips still pumping furiously. "God, I fucking hate you people!"

"Yes, leave it on!" I demanded. I released Reddy's cock and stalked toward the Eagle. "I want all of Super City to see what I'm about to do next."

"And what is that?" the Eagle demanded.

I pushed up against him, grinding my hips against his leg.

"I'm going to choke your chicken!"

"I already told you. Leave Reddy alone, you vile villain!"

"He's not talking about me, you pecker-head!" Reddy screeched and ranted behind us, trying to hide his not-so-private parts from the Eagle

Cam by crossing his legs. "And somebody get this damned camera away from my crotch!"

"Atomic Eagle, Super City's nuclear power plant is on the verge of meltdown. You will submit to my desires or I will destroy this city and everyone in it!"

I extended my claws and slashed at the Eagle's costume, hoping to tear away the entire front so I could finally, *finally* get an answer to the most important question in the world—did the Eagle sport feathers between his legs or not? Okay, so the question was only important to me, but I had to know. The super-sexual fantasy of a lifetime depended on it!

My claws sliced through the air and snagged the Eagle's chest. Down, down, down they tore through his form-fitting uniform until, at last, they reached...

His metal utility belt. Damn.

"Unhand me, Silver Panther," the Eagle commanded, grabbing me by the scruff of the neck.

"Ah! I can't. Dammit, my claws are stuck on your stupid belt!"

"Then get down there and un-stick them."

He forced me—well, not exactly—down onto my knees in front of him so my head was level with his bulging crotch. Oh glorious day, what a position to be in! I felt like the early bird about to feast on a really big worm. Just as I was about to give his groin a lengthy and invigorating cat bath, the door to the control room swung open.

"Oh! Hi guys. I didn't know anyone was in here."

A woman in a pink cardigan and pleated pants waltzed into the room. "Oh my god! Atomic Eagle! It's actually you! I'm Sylvia Holstein, remember me? You rescued my parakeet Binky from the Rabid Rodent last Christmas."

"Ah, yes, Sylvia. How is Binky?"

"He's not bad. It's molting season so he's a little cranky right now."

"Do you mind?" I growled. "We have important business going on here!"

"Oh!" Sylvia took a step back. "I'm sorry. Am I interrupting ... something?"

She glanced at me and then at Reddy who had taking to kicking at the Eagle Cam to keep it away from his naked crotch. When he noticed her staring at him, he squealed and went back to crossing his legs.

"It's all right, Sylvia," the Eagle replied. "Reddy and I were just apprehending the Silver Panther. Apparently he's trying to blow up Super City again."

"Oh, is that why the reactor is on the fritz?" Sylvia walked over to the controls and flipped a few switches. The reactor gauges, which had been in the red, slowly dropped back to green. "Well, that takes care of that. Do you want me to call the cops?"

"If you wouldn't mind," the Eagle said.

"No! No cops! I don't need any more people to see me in this humiliating position!" Reddy ranted, but Sylvia was already dialing the phone.

An hour later, as the police prepared to haul me away, I smirked at Reddy. The Eagle had released him from the shackles in the control room and borrowed Sylvia's cardigan to tie around Reddy's waist. Naturally, it was too small to properly conceal his ... embarrassment.

"Can't you find me a pair of pants?" he whined to the Eagle. "This sweater's only gonna cover my front or my back, not both!"

"Now, now, little chum. I couldn't possibly ask Sylvia to give you her pants *and* her sweater. It wouldn't be polite. Besides, we can't waste anymore time fixing the battle damage to your uniform. Dastardly Dick just robbed the sausage factory downtown, and we must leave immediately."

"But I can't fight dressed like this!"

I laughed. "Who said you were going to fight, Chicken Little? You're a sidekick. The moment you reach that factory, Dastardly Dick will capture you and string you up just like I did. You better watch out. He may try to stick a sausage in your buns, and I hear that man packs a lot of meat."

Both the police and the Atomic Eagle burst out laughing at my little joke. Sylvia tittered to one side. Reddy rounded on me, his face boiling over with rage.

"I ... will ... get ... you..." he threatened. He turned to point at the Eagle. "You too, you pecker-head! You guys are going to regret the day you laughed at Reddy Rooster!"

He stalked out of the control room, clutching the sweater to his groin. Still chuckling, the Atomic Eagle followed, his Eagle Cam swooping after Reddy's naked buttocks and stumpy little tail.

"Okay boys," I told the cops. "Take me away. The sooner you lock me up, the sooner I can sit in the prison lounge and watch today's Eagle Cam. I don't want to miss a moment of it."

"Same here," they agreed.

*   *   *

For weeks after, Reddy's performance on the Eagle Cam was the talk of the town. Naturally, the Atomic Eagle removed the incriminating footage from his website as soon as he got home that night, but by then it was too late. Every super-villain in Super City had downloaded it, copied it to disk, and then e-mailed it to twenty of their best-est evil friends. Some enterprising fiend was even selling DVDs of it on the street corners, calling it *The Slutty Sidekick*—or something like that.

I became an instant star in the Super-Villains' Social Club thanks to my part in helping expose Reddy to the public, and I eagerly hoped for the chance to repeat my performance once I broke out of jail. Reddy wasn't the Atomic Eagle, but he did have feathers, and I could see myself getting off on playing with his plumage. Unfortunately, the Eagle Cam footage turned out to be the last time anyone saw Reddy. He disappeared after that. According to Super-Villain Weekly, he was just too humiliated to show his face in public.

Imagine my surprise, then, when Reddy came to visit me in jail three months later.

"Well, well, well," I purred, draping myself on the bars of my cell door. "If it isn't my favorite cock."

"That's rooster!" he hissed. Instead of his usual costume, he wore a large fedora pulled down over his face and a non-descript raincoat that didn't quite hide the bulge of his stumpy tail.

"Of course. So why are you here, Reddy? And what's with the getup? You look like the Poultry Pervert. Are you going to flash me? You don't need to, you know. I ordered a copy of *The Slutty Sidekick* last week. Once it arrives, I'll be able to look at your goodies anytime I want."

Reddy turned bright crimson, but otherwise kept his cool. "Actually, I came here to thank you," he said.

"Thank me? For what? That unfinished hand job? You must not see a lot of action, hero."

"No, I wanted to thank you for helping me figure something out. I've come to realize over the past few months that I no longer want to be a sidekick."

"You mean you're quitting?" I arched an eyebrow at him. "But sidekicks don't quit. They work for their heroes until they die! Or wait, perhaps you've already died. Of shame."

Reddy gritted his teeth. "Look, I just wanted to say thanks for helping me find a new ... direction in life. And to prove that there are no hard feelings, I wanted to give you this."

An impish smile crossed the former sidekick's face as he reached into his overcoat and pulled out a long, silvery-black feather.

"Is that—? But no, it couldn't be!" I reached for it, not daring to believe what he was handing me.

"It is. It's a tail feather from the Atomic Eagle." He placed the feather in my trembling hands. "And there's plenty more where that came from."

"What do you mean?"

Reddy shrugged. "I know you got a thing for the big bird, so I was thinking maybe I could set you up on a blind date. After all, you are his favorite super-villain."

"Am I really?" My heart thudded in my ears.

"Oh yeah. The Eagle's always going on about how cunning you are, and how sleek and distinguished you always look in your silver cat suit."

"Ah, that's the advantage of maturity," I confided. "Being older does give me a certain grace."

"Yeah. Anyway, I think the Eagle could really go for you. It's just..."

I gripped the bars of my cell. "Just what? Tell me!"

"He's got this thing. You might call it a fetish, really."

"A fetish? You mean like something kinky?" Oh my heavens, it was my most favorite sexual fantasy come to life. The Atomic Eagle was secretly a pervert!

"Yeah," Reddy went on. "There's something he's got to have to get off. It's not a big deal, but it does make him happy, if you know what I mean."

"What is it? Tell me!"

Reddy glanced from side to side, as if to make sure no one was listening. Then he leaned in close to whisper.

"Spaghetti!"

"Spaghetti?" I straightened up, confused. "What the hell do you mean spaghetti?"

"Shhh! Don't broadcast it to the entire city! Do you want everyone to know his superhero weakness?"

"Sorry!" I moved closer and whispered. "What do you mean *spaghetti?*"

"He's part bird, right? Well, to him, spaghetti looks like worms," Reddy explained. "And you know how excited birds get over worms."

"Yes..." I frowned. "But then why spaghetti and not actual worms?"

"Because he's also part human, dummy! A plate of real worms would gross him out. A plate of spaghetti though..."

"Would turn him on!" I finished. "Yes, I see it now!"

Reddy beamed. "Good. So here's the deal. You break out of here day after tomorrow, Valentine's Day, and head to the old warehouse by the city docks. Be there at six, and make sure you bring spaghetti. Oh, and don't wear anything but a bathrobe and a smile. Once the Eagle sees that pasta, you won't have much time to get undressed."

"Got it!" I whispered back. "But wait! What about the sauce?"

"Sauce?" Reddy asked.

"For the spaghetti! What do you think? Marinara or Alfredo?"

"Of, definitely marinara. It'll look good smeared all over the Eagle's naked body."

"Yes!" I clapped my hands with joy. "Thank you, Reddy. You have no idea how much this means to me. If there is ever anything I can do for you, you just let me know." I clasped his hand to pull him close. "Perhaps we could even get together again, just you and I, for a little one-on-one action?" I whispered. "I do so love feathers."

Even with the bars of my cell between us, Reddy couldn't help but feel my growing erection. He just shook my hand, grinning. "Maybe some other time, Panther. For now, you just make sure you're at that warehouse day after tomorrow. The big bird will be waiting for you. I promise."

*   *   *

Two nights later, I hid in the shadowy recesses of the old warehouse, waiting for the Atomic Eagle to appear. As Reddy had instructed, I wore nothing but my best silk bathrobe and an ear-to-ear Cheshire grin. On a cargo box behind me sat a large bowl of steaming

77

spaghetti, dripping with spicy red marinara. My whiskers trembled with anticipation. I felt like the cat about to eat the proverbial canary.

I chuckled to myself. "Ah, but there are no canaries on the menu tonight. Tonight, I feast on Eagle!"

The sound of a heroic whoosh reached my ears and I instinctively crouched lower. Moments later, the warehouse doors burst open and in flew the avian Adonis himself. The Eagle landed gracefully in the shattered doorway, taking a moment to preen for the ever-present Eagle Cam before boldly striding inside.

"I know you're in here, Panther. Give yourself up now, or there will be consequences."

Oh, the luscious sound of that commanding voice! I ached to obey, but I was not ready to repeat Reddy's recorded misadventure.

"Turn off the Eagle Cam first!" I demanded. My voice echoed in the cavernous space of the warehouse.

He huffed with impatience. "Must I? I have an adoring public to consider."

"Some things are better handled in private. Turn off the camera and I promise to play nice."

"Very well." He snatched the Eagle Cam out of the air and jabbed at the power button. The camera fell dead from his hands to roll across the floor. "It's off. Now give yourself u—"

Before he could finish, I pounced. Springing from my hiding place, I landed before him, the bowl of spaghetti in hand. A quick tug on the belt of my robe revealed my naked ambitions.

"Hello, my fine feathered friend. See anything you like?"

"Uh..." the Eagle replied. He stared at me blankly.

"Now, now." I waggled a finger at him. "Don't play shy. A little birdie told me all about your pasta perversion, and I'm here to say I don't mind at all. If noodles turn you on, then I'm more than willing to cook up a little excitement for us both."

"Well, Panther, that's, uh, very nice of you to make me dinner, but I'm on a low-carb diet..." The Eagle backed away from me, holding up his hands. I paced after him like a tiger on the prowl. "Wow, this really is all so ... sudden. Perhaps I should go—"

"Not so fast, Eagle. You and I have a date to keep!"

A voluptuous vulpine figure bounded toward us from the back of the warehouse. I caught a flash of violet hair and groaned.

"Oh look, it's the Purple Cow."

"That's Violet Vixen!" the femme fatale snarled as she reached us. She was dressed only in purple garters and stockings, with a tiny lavender thong to cover her "fox hole".

"You look more like Super Whore to me," I replied. "What are you doing here, Vixen? This is a private party."

"Yeah, and you're the clown they hired for entertainment. Nice costume, by the way. It's definitely bound to get some laughs." She cast a glance at my open robe. While I sputtered in rage, the Vixen strutted toward the Eagle, a foxy smile playing across her face.

"Anyway, I'm here for a date with my favorite feathered foe," she announced, producing a large, copper-bottomed pot from behind her back. "And I even brought dinner."

She pulled off the lid and presented a mound of spaghetti to the astonished Eagle.

"I hope you're hungry, because once you're done eating that, there's pie for dessert."

Vixen pointed to the thong and wiggled her hips. I nearly hawked up a hairball in disgust. The nerve of her!

I stepped in front of the Vixen and gave her a not-so-friendly shove. "Back off, bitch! I was here first."

The Vixen pushed back. "So what? Forget this poser, Birdman. I know he's not the pussy you want to play with."

"Why you hyacinth hussy!" I leapt at her, claws out, and snagged her thong before she could dart away.

"Aha!" I shouted, pointing at the brown curls of her exposed crotch. "I always knew you dyed your hair!"

She shrieked. "You flea-bitten feline freak! I don't care how many lives you have, I'm gonna kill you for that!"

I squared off against the Vixen, hissing and arching my back. Out of the corner of my eye, I saw the Eagle raise his wrist-radio to his mouth.

"Back up! I need back up! Somebody, anybody, this is the Atomic Eagle. I need back up right now!"

"Ooh, I got your back up right here, big bird."

The Eagle squawked as a pair of brawny arms snaked around him. Gape-mouthed, Vixen and I turned to stare at this latest intruder.

"The Red Lantern?!" we gasped simultaneously. After the Atomic Eagle, the Red Lantern was the most popular hero in Super City.

"Red Lantern, thank goodness you're here," the Eagle cried. "These villains have gone crazy!"

"Crazy in love, I'm sure." The Red Lantern held fast to the Eagle and started rubbing his hips suggestively against the other man's tail feathers. I noticed then that most of the Red Lantern's costume was absent from his muscular frame. In fact, the only thing he wore was the ruby-studded ring from which he derived his super powers and a suspiciously overstuffed G-string.

"Uh, Red?" The Eagle squirmed in his grasp. "Are you feeling okay?"

"I feel just fine, lovebird. But how do you feel? Hungry, perhaps?" He spun the Eagle around and whipped away his G-string. Spools of slippery spaghetti poured from his crotch to land at the Eagle's feet.

"Good lord, not you too! What's *wrong* with you people?" The Eagle broke away from the Lantern and rounded on us. "You're super people. Sure, some of you are evil and some of you are good, but if there's one thing you should all have in common it's your propensity to wear spandex. Right now, not a one of you is wearing a damned thing! And why the hell are you all trying to feed me spaghetti? I hate spaghetti! I'm a bird of prey, for god's sake. I eat rabbits and voles and furry pests—"

"Then you should have no problem going down on us."

As one, we turned to see the Rabid Rodent, flanked by the Wicked Weasel and the Gassy Gopher. None of them wore their costumes, but all three held out plates of spaghetti.

"And what are *you* doing here?" I demanded.

"Oh, I came to play 'Hamlin Town' with the Eagle," the Rodent rasped, foam dripping from his lips.

"Hamlin Town?" the Eagle replied warily.

"Yeah, you blow my pipe and I'll follow anywhere you go."

"That's it!" I shouted. I grabbed the Eagle by the arm and pulled him toward me. "I came here to spend some quality time with *my* arch-nemesis, and you losers are *not* invited to join us. So why don't you all leave and go back to whatever rocks you crawled out from under—"

"Leave?" a voice boomed out. "But we just got here!"

Oh damn. I spun around. From every corner of the warehouse came a swarm of superheroes and mega-fiends, either naked or clad in the scantiest of lingerie, every one of them bearing bowls or pots or plates of spaghetti. They came with marinara, they came with Alfredo, they even came with pesto. I wanted to scream in frustration. How the hell had they all discovered the Atomic Eagle's secret?

The answer occurred to me immediately. Reddy had told them, of course, but why? I had no time to figure out that conundrum. The swelling mob congregated around the Eagle, blocking off every exit. Closer and closer they advanced, everyone intent on taking the Eagle for themselves. The Vixen, Red Lantern, and I took up defensive positions around our bewildered hero, but there was no way the three of us could fight them all off. We had to move fast.

"All right, you two," I growled. "Here's the deal. Red Lantern, you blast a path through this mob so I can take the Eagle out the back. Then you and Vixen cover our retreat. Once we're all safely out, we'll regroup at my hideout in the Kit-Kat Club. Then we can all have a turn with the birdman." The others nodded eagerly until I added, "I get him first, of course."

"Hold up. Why do you get a crack at him first?" the Vixen demanded.

"Yeah, why are you calling the shots?" the Lantern jumped in. "You're not exactly a neutral party here."

"No, more like a *neutered* party," the Vixen sneered. "Why don't you go home and play with some nice balls of yarn, Panther, 'cause those are the only balls you've got!"

Oh, that was the last straw. I tore off my robe, flexed my feline physique, and yowled, "You want to see balls, you purple prostitute? I'll show you balls. Cat fiiiiight!"

The moment I leapt upon the Vixen, all hell broke loose. The Eagle spread his wings to fly off, only to be tackled by the Red Lantern, who was in turn tackled by the Rabid Rodent and the Wicked Weasel. The Gassy Gopher cut loose with an eye-watering blast that knocked several others down, causing them to spill their spaghetti. I don't know who threw the first handful of noodles, but soon the pasta was flying everywhere. The Vixen and I rolled through piles of the stuff until we were knotted together in sticky strands.

"Get off of me!" she shrieked.

"Gladly!" I yelled back, but the more we rolled, the more tangled we became.

As we fought, more naked super-characters continued to arrive, each of them beating the others bloody in an attempt to steal the Eagle. Even Doberman Daisy, the dog-faced dyke, showed up, demanding a piece of tail feather. But the worst came when the Myopic Cyclopic showed up, ripping off the roof of the warehouse to spray us all down with his giant one-eyed monster. Oh, the super-humanity!

In the midst of the fray, my superior feline senses detected a high-pitched mechanical hum. The sound nagged at my brain. I had heard it before, but where? As I struggled to free my head from the stranglehold of the Vixen's thighs, the answer literally hit me in the chest.

"What the hell?" A small, round object with a glass lens dropped onto the floor next to me and rolled a few feet before launching itself back into the air.

"Eagle Cam?" I whispered with dawning horror. Then I screamed, "Eagle Cam?!"

"What? Where?" The Vixen released me and sat up, scanning the air. "Oh my god, there's another one! And look, there's two more!"

"Eagle!" I shouted. "I told you to turn off those bloody cameras!"

"I did!" he shouted back, struggling to fend off the bovine affections of Buffalo Bullocks. "Those aren't mine!"

Bullocks grabbed a double handful of the Eagles costume and pulled. A wide swath of spandex tore away to reveal a tantalizing glimpse of pectoral pinions. One of the cameras zipped by for a close-up of the Eagle's feathered nipples. I yelped as another of the whizzing balls shot between my legs to buzz my testicles.

"But if they're not yours, then whose—"

"They're mine!"

Everyone looked up. High up in the rafters I spied a familiar, redheaded figure. Reddy Rooster looked down at us and waved.

"Hey Eagle. Hey guys."

"Reddy!" the Eagle shouted. "What are you doing up there?"

"I'm launching my new career!"

"What career is that?" I asked, fearing I already knew the answer.

Reddy smirked. "Why, the career you and the Eagle introduced me to a few months ago—pornography. With the help of my Cock Cams, I'm ready to expose everyone here as the perverts they really are!"

The Eagle ducked as two more cameras careened toward him. "But Reddy, you're my sidekick, one of the good guys! You're supposed to help people! You're supposed to help me!"

"You mean the way you helped me back at the power plant?" He leered down at us. "I put up with an awful lot of shit as your sidekick, pal. Wearing that stupid chicken costume, being captured and tied up while you got to fly in and save the day. Sure, the job sucked, but at least I was getting paid. But then you had to go and air that stupid video to the whole city!"

"Reddy, I told you already, that was a computer glitch. I never meant for that video footage to go on-air."

"Oh really?" Reddy turned to look at me. "Hey Panther, remember when I told you the Eagle's most arousing adventures never made it on the Eagle Cam. I lied. Take a look at this!"

Reddy hit a button on his utility belt and all the Cock Cams pointed to the center of the warehouse. As one, they projected a flickering holographic image of a sexy, feline figure on its knees before a spandex-clad crotch.

"Oh yeah, Panther, lick my dick with your raspy tongue..." a deep voice rumbled off screen. "Do it, you big pussy..."

Mortified, I watched myself lean forward to nuzzle the unidentified bulging groin, my recorded self's hand caught in the utility belt above it. In the background, I saw sleek metal control panels covered in lighted buttons and wavering gauges—the control room of the Super City nuclear power plant.

"Oh you bastard," I hissed. Just as my tongue stretched out to bathe the Atomic Eagle's dick in a loving caress, the image cut to a close-up shot of a naked bottom decorated with a fuzzy purple foxtail.

"Oh yes, spank me, big boy! I've been such a bad girl! Spank me hard!"

"That's right, Vixen, beg for it..." came the off-screen voice again. "Beg for it, you foxy slut..."

A utility belt whipped across the screen, catching the Vixen sharply across both ass-cheeks. From the corner of my eye, I saw the villainess beside me blanch. "That lousy fuck! He told me the camera was off!"

The shot switched again, this time to a full-length shot of a naked bronzed torso slick with soapsuds. A hand wearing a ruby-studded ring slid down rippling abs to stroke the rigid cock that sprouted from a shaved pubis.

"You like this, lover? I did it just for you..."

"You want me, bitch," said the off-screen voice. "You know you do..."

At this point, the camera shot zoomed back to reveal the frame of a high definition TV. As pornographic images of heroes and villains alike continued to play across the screen, the camera focused on a large feathered figure seated before the TV, frantically flogging his cock.

"Do it, Lantern. Bend over and show me that ass!"

As if on cue, the Lantern on the TV complied. A gloved hand reached toward his upturned buttocks and slipped a finger inside.

"I'll kill him," the Lantern growled. The veins in his neck stood out visibly. "I'm gonna squeeze that turkey's neck and choke him dead!"

More shots followed. The Rabid Rodent felating the Wicked Weasel; Doberman Daisy on all fours, pussy splayed as she begged someone off-screen to do it to her doggy-style; a naked slap fest between the Femi-Nazi and the Gay Gladiator. Apparently no one had escaped the eagle eye of the Eagle Cam. Through it all, the Eagle narrated and masturbated until, at last, he sprayed long ropes of hot sticky semen across the TV screen. When the holograph finally flickered off, we all turned to stare at him.

He laughed nervously, hands up. "Um, look, those movies were supposed to be private—"

"Yeah, so private I was able to buy a copy on the street corner last week," Reddy announced. "In case anyone's interested, the movie the Eagle was watching in that little home video is called *Super Sluts*. It's produced by the same folks who brought you *The Slutty Sidekick*; in other words, the Eagle."

"You're selling this?" the Rodent howled, frothing at the mouth.

"Well, you know, the Aerie needed remodeling and then I had to buy a new engine for the Bird of Prey, plus the cost of costumes more than doubled recently. Hey, being a superhero is expensive. I had to make money somehow!"

"Speaking of money," Reddy called out, "I'm prepared to pay one million dollars to the first person who makes the Eagle blow his load on camera, two million to whoever gets him to beg for a spanking, and three million to anyone who can get him to cry for Daddy while being fisted. If it helps, his real weakness isn't spaghetti, it's his tail feathers. Pull on those babies and that slut will do anything. Trust me, I know."

The cameras flickered on again, projecting another hologram in the air above us. This time it showed the Eagle in a sixty-nine position with Reddy, the former sidekick tugging on the superhero's tail feathers for all he was worth while riding the Eagle's face.

"Um, okay, that movie was also supposed to be private..."

"Oh, I'll bet," I hissed. "Let's get him!"

The Atomic Eagle let loose a high-pitched scream as we all lunged toward him, snatching at his rear end. I'm not sure who made him come

84

first—it was either me or the Vixen, we always were so competitive. I do know it was the Rodent who made him beg for a spanking, followed by the Femi-Nazi, Buffalo Bullocks, and several others. But the real vengeance came when the Red Lantern slipped his fist between the big bird's feathered ass-cheeks.

"Who's your Daddy, you feathered freak?" he roared.

"You are!" the Eagle cried, bucking hard on the massive fist buried inside him. "Oh yeah, Daddy, please! Please! Give it to your little boy!"

Through it all, we pulled at his feathers—tail feathers, wing feathers, the crest on his head, even the chick fluff that covered his balls. Pretty soon, the Eagle's pinions were coming loose in our hands, but we didn't care. We were out of control by then.

Overwhelmed by lust, we turned our attentions to each other. The Femi-Nazi chewed on Doberman Daisy's box while the Gay Gladiator thrust his battering ram into her iron-clad behind. The Violet Vixen somersaulted across the warehouse to land on the Wicked Weasel. As he writhed beneath her, she lowered herself onto his erect dick, singing, "Pop goes the Weasel's cherry!"

As for me, I wound up in familiar territory, on my knees before a spandex-clad pelvis, fingers entwined in the bushel of feathers that sprouted behind it.

"Eat all you want, Panther," Reddy drawled as I tore at the crotch of his costume to get at his cock. "It tastes like chicken."

Indeed it did.

Several hours later, the police showed up to put an end to our orgy. Reddy and his Cock Cams had long since disappeared, along with the dignity of every hero and villain in Super City. As the police led me away, I glimpsed a pathetic naked figure attempting to conceal his pink, dimpled flesh with salvaged scraps of spandex. It was the Atomic Eagle. We had plucked him bald.

That was the end of my career as a super-villain. I spent three days in jail on charges of obscenity and public lewdness. It would have been longer, but Super City simply didn't have the space to hold every villain and hero who had been involved in the warehouse fiasco. Reddy contacted me as soon as I was out.

"I hear you're looking for work," he crowed. "Why don't you stop by my roost? I think I might have a position for you."

That evening, I watched Reddy's first movie, *Mission Im-pasta-ble*, while hanging upside down over the edge of his bed.

"Sales have been huge," he told me as he spread some lube between my cheeks. "I'm thinking of doing a sequel. Maybe something like *Feline Felatio* or *Pussy In Peril*. What do you think?"

"Depends," I grunted as he pushed his cock deep inside me. "Would I have to wear spandex?"

"Nah, I'm thinking leather or maybe rubber. Not like it matters, really. Nobody watches these movies for the costumes."

"True..."

The audition process was rigorous, but I got the part in the end. While it's not nearly as glamorous as being a super-villain, it is a job and the hours aren't bad. Some days, I never even leave the bed—a real bonus for someone with my feline disposition. And I get to play with the boss's tail every once in a while. So I'm content.

Too bad the pay is chicken feed.

GRAVITY

"Let me tell you something, girl. Gravity sucks."

The fat woman spoke in a heavy voice that nearly rolled me flat with its declaration. The sound of it was a perfect match for her body. She was massive, no taller than 1.7 meters, yet she weighed over 200 kilos. At least, she did on Earth, the woman confided. Here on the moon, she felt light as a feather.

"I had to leave," she rumbled as we rolled out of the spaceport "Take off *might* have killed me, but gravity definitely *would*. Couldn't move down there." She waved a bloated hand toward the glowing Earth. "Couldn't even get out of the damned bed. They had to hoist me into the rocket by crane."

As we headed into the station, I marveled at how she moved. She bounced along the metal hallways with a slow, heavy grace, each ponderous step sending ripples through her distended form. Adipose overwhelmed her face, and she had more rings around her center than Saturn. She was a wonder to me, an icon of abundance and overindulgence from another world.

"What's your name?" she asked as I helped her check in.

"Luna."

She chuckled. "Luna, the moon girl. You're thin."

"Born on the moon," I explained. "Never been planet-side. Everyone here is tall and thin."

She nodded. "Gravity doesn't weigh you down. Well, it won't weigh *me* down either, anymore."

We made love that night. My interest surprised her, I think, but I had never seen anyone like her before. The moon was a harsh place, full of dry dust and dead rock. Here, everything was rationed—the food, the water, the air. The people were as sparse and tenuous as the recycled oxygen, and we were all just a breath away from death. Not her, though. I dug my fingers into the folds of her flesh, wallowing in the furrows and crevices of her landscape. I scaled her mountainous breasts and tumbled down the rolling hills of her belly.

"Eat as much as you want," she said with a laugh as I burrowed between her legs. "I got plenty to spare."

After that first night, I was bound to her, unable to escape her sphere, though she wouldn't even tell me her name.

"Left it behind with the gravity," she joked. "Too heavy to carry around."

So I called her Gaea. She had as much money as she did fat—how else could she have afforded the trip?—and she hired me to be her guide.

"I want to go *everywhere*," she told me. "Now that I can, I want to *move*."

We bounced through the station—her leading the way, me trailing behind. We didn't go far, at first; she was unused to the exercise and the recycled air. Over the weeks, though, Gaea's orbit expanded until she ran laps around the station. I was excited for her. She seemed so happy with her newfound freedom. But I soon noticed the laws of physics were wearing away my love. Without the full force of Earth's gravity to hold her in check, she had become an object in constant motion. As her velocity increased, her mass decreased. Like the Earth hanging in the endless night above, my beautiful Gaea began to wane.

In bed, I stumbled over the skeletal ridges of her once ample hips. Where were Gaea's mountains and hills? Where was the abundance of flesh? Gone. She had grown as flat and sparse as the lunar plains.

"You should eat more," I said, struggling to gain a handhold on her dwindling form. "You're rich. You don't have to starve."

Gaea scoffed. "One can never be too rich or too thin."

I tried feeding her more, anyway, sneaking half of my rations into her meals. The sacrifice left me dizzy with hunger, but Gaea grew round and full once more. Overjoyed, I feasted on her bounty. Then the extra kilos began to weigh on her mind.

"I still feel it," she said one night as I suckled at her breast. "Even here, on the moon, gravity still has a hold of me. I'm heavy again."

"It's nothing. You've just acclimated to the moon. Don't worry—"

She jumped up, propelling me off the bed and into the nearest wall. As I struggled to right myself, she catapulted toward the observation port.

"I have to escape." She pointed to a blinking red light in the glittering sky. "The orbital supply station... Can you take me there?"

I shook my head. "It's dangerous. Besides, there's nothing up there; it's just an abandoned hulk of metal."

"Exactly. There's nothing, not even gravity. I'd be completely free. Make the arrangements tonight."

I did as she asked, but reluctantly. The orbital station had been closed for years. When we got there, we glided through its hollow corridors then went outside to walk along the cratered hull. A rocket lifted off from the moon below us and Gaea whooped with joy.

"Look at me!" she shouted over the com on her EVA suit. "I can fly!"

She leapt into the starry night, sailing to the limit of her tether. The sight of her tumbling free-fall chilled me to the bone.

"Gaea, come back! We should return to the shuttle."

"No." Her voice crackled in my ear. "I'm staying here."

"What? But—"

"I made arrangements. I'm staying." She drifted above me, cold and distant. "I know about the food, Luna. I know what you've been trying to do. You've become a stone around my neck. I need to cut you loose. Besides," she said, spinning away from me, "I'm not attracted to you anymore."

I felt as though someone had cut off the oxygen to my helmet. While I struggled to breathe, Gaea moved farther away. Without thinking, I reached for her tether and unhooked it from the anchor point. Gaea didn't notice until it was too late.

"Luna? Luna!" She jabbed at the controls on her jetpack, only to set herself further adrift.

"You were right," I said as she flailed around in the void. "Gravity does suck. It holds us down and crushes us in its grip. But it also holds us together and keeps us safely in our place. Too bad you never appreciated that."

Gaea fired her pack once more and hurtled away into space. I watched her go, and then I returned to the moon, alone.

THE HONEY BEE

The long, yellow spadix of the giant anthurium jutted aggressively from the bowl of its single scarlet leaf. Deacon stripped off his glove and ran a forefinger lightly over the bumpy surface of the flower's phallic protuberance, watching it shiver at his touch. Another had shivered that way once when Deacon touched him. Thanks to Deacon's wife, Meredith, that other was now gone.

Deacon adjusted his trousers and crouched until his face came level with the plant. He continued stroking the spadix, heedless of the pollen attaching itself to his fingers. He was alone, hidden in a greenhouse at the southernmost edge of the Huffington estate, and as far away from his wife as he could get that afternoon. Two weeks after discovering his infidelity, Meredith had decided it would be best if they sought the company and advice of an older married couple. Her distant cousins, the elderly Lord and Lady Huffington, had proved more than willing to oblige.

"We can be happy together," Meredith told Deacon as they jounced about in a coach headed toward the estate in Kensington. "You'll see. Lady Huffington and her husband have been married for more than thirty years. We shall learn from their example."

Deacon did not bother to point out to his wife that a long marriage did not necessarily mean a happy one.

His opinion did not matter to her anyway. They were here now whether he liked it or not. After two days of forced companionship with their hosts and two nights of forced romance with his wife—a scenario that always ended in tears—Deacon decided to escape.

On the afternoon of the third day, he donned his sack coat and planter's hat and slipped away from the manse. Outside, he let himself wander, following the gravel paths of the garden until he came to a disused topiary maze near the edge of the estate. The lawn there grew wild and unkempt, and was choked with straggling weeds. The verdant sculptures were in such desperate need of trimming that Deacon could barely discern what they were supposed to be. Was that bay laurel meant to look like a lion or a dog? And that one over there, it might have been a man once, but lack of care had devolved it into a hunched-back monkey.

Deacon started to turn away—in his current mood, he had no heart for abandoned places—but then he caught the scent of flowers, strangely sweet and spicy. The heady fragrance lured him into the maze.

The moment he stepped within the labyrinth's bounds, walls of overgrown shrubbery rose up to shut him off from the rest of the world. As Deacon ambled along the neglected path, his mood lifted. The maze eventually led him to a wide clearing at its southern end where the greenhouse that he now occupied stood. Though the building showed signs of decay and neglect, he had approached without hesitation. The floral scent that had guided him seemed to come from within. He followed his nose through the grime-coated glass door and entered into a verdant paradise.

Palms, ferns, and other exotic plants crowded against the walls of the greenhouse. Chipped clay pots overflowing with orchids and camellias lined the stone benches. At the center of the cracked tile floor stood the raised wall of a pond, in which pristine lotuses floated in surprisingly clear water.

Deacon's eyes darted in every direction at once as various species clamored for his attention. Then he spotted the bright scarlet anthurium and could not look away.

He had approached the red flower to admire it, losing himself in the memory of better times. It was easy to do in this place. Deacon had always been happiest when surrounded by green, growing things. He had spent much of his youth studying plants, observing and sketching their characteristics after the fashion of Darwin and Hooker. He had once dreamed of becoming a naturalist and, over the years, he'd filled several notebooks, but now he had only one—a slim leather-bound treasure filled with his best work. It survived only because he had kept it hidden from Meredith. She had burned the rest right after she sacked Gareth.

Gareth. Back in the present, Deacon straightened up from the anthurium and adjusted his coat, smearing the pollen from his fingers along his collar. How many years had he suffered alone and in silence before Gareth walked into his life? And how many years would he continue to suffer, shackled to a woman he could never love? Meredith was a fine lady, beautiful and wealthy, but she could never compare to his Gareth. It had never mattered to Deacon that Gareth was a commoner with dirt under his nails and grass stains on his trousers. In fact, Deacon had been rather fond of those grass stains; he'd been the cause of them on several occasions, though he never told Meredith that.

"He's so coarse," she had complained one afternoon as they watched Gareth toil in the garden. "And vulgar too."

Yes, coarse and vulgar, but also firm and gentle, with a soothing voice and deep brown eyes that had beguiled Deacon from the moment they first met. Deacon had not so much agreed to marry Meredith as he had chosen to be with her family's gardener, the man whose touch could revive an ailing plant or rouse his lover's penis to rigid anticipation.

The scarlet anthurium bobbed before Deacon, the spadix looking for all the world like an erect cock. At least, that was how Gareth had always described it to him. He had planted scores of them in the greenhouse, and then brought the fresh-cut flowers into the main house to let Meredith fuss over them, unaware of what they meant. It had been Gareth's way of making a joke and seducing his lover all at once. Even now, Deacon couldn't look at one of the plants without growing aroused.

He touched the plant again and shivered. It was a lovely specimen. Deacon hadn't drawn anything in weeks; he should sketch it. He pulled out his notebook from a coat pocket and turned to a blank page, but his inspiration died before he could make the first mark. All he could see on the page was Gareth's face, Gareth's body.

With a grimace, he flipped the notebook shut and turned away from the anthurium. How many times would he have to remind himself? Gareth was gone. Meredith had caught the two of them together in the garden one night and, screaming, had thrown the gardener half-naked into the street. Afterwards, she had destroyed all the anthuriums she could find, tearing them out of their pots by the roots and trampling them underfoot.

"I will not have these disgusting things in my house!" she had shrieked at Deacon. "They're unnatural, and so are you!"

"Unnatural," Deacon murmured, echoing the memory of his wife's hysterics. "What would Mr. Darwin make of men like me?"

He pondered his question, watching the amber light of late afternoon stream through the glass panes of the ceiling. It was getting late. Meredith would be looking for him soon. He stepped toward the greenhouse door. As he reached out for the handle, a voice called to him.

"Leaving already? You've barely set foot in here."

Deacon spun on his heel. A man appeared from behind a screen of palms. He was tall and slender built, with black hair and a long straight nose. The tilt of his dark eyes hinted at an exotic eastern ancestry. His clothing was elegant, but worn and several years out of date. The frayed cuffs of his frock coat didn't quite reach his wrists. His pants flapped about his ankles. He should have looked like a clown dressed like that, yet the man carried himself with such assurance and contentment that Deacon felt a green stab of envy.

"Do you like it?" The stranger nodded to the scarlet flower. "*Anthurium andraeanum*, also called the boy flower, for obvious reasons. It came all the way from the West Indies."

"It's ... lovely," Deacon managed to say. Was his mind playing tricks on him or had the floral scent that he had followed to this place suddenly intensified? Deacon shook his head. It must be something nearby in the greenhouse. Men did not exude such an amazing fragrance.

The man smiled. "I'm Florien," he said, holding out his hand.

Deacon shook it, surprised by the warmth of the touch. "Are you...?" No, he couldn't be the gardener, not dressed like that. "Are you a friend of the Huffingtons', come to visit? Lady Huffington didn't mention you."

Florien shrugged. "I live here. I take care of the plants. And you?"

Deacon fumbled with his notebook, aware that the stranger was staring at it. He shoved it back into his coat pocket before answering. "I'm just a guest."

"A guest with a name?"

A flush of embarrassment crept up the back of Deacon's neck. "Deacon. I apologize. I'm in a hurry. I need to get back—"

"To whom? Your wife?" Florien cocked his head and gazed pointedly at the gold band on the ring finger of Deacon's left hand.

Deacon flushed again. "My wife...," he began.

"Do you love her?"

Deacon started. What sort of question was that? Before he could form an indignant reply, the stranger gripped his hand.

"Stay, if only for a little while. I so rarely have guests. I'll give you a tour of the greenhouse."

Florien offered another smile. Deacon wanted to pull his hand away and refuse his offer. Or did he? He knew he should leave. It was late. Back at the house, the servants were already setting the dining room table for supper. The Huffingtons had invited other guests, important people, friends of his wife. Meredith would be furious with him if he were late. If he ran now, he could be back at the mansion and cleaned up with a few minutes to spare. Then he could spend the evening dining and chattering with people he barely knew and a wife he had come to loathe.

Oh.

The scent of flowers hung thick in the air, tickling Deacon's nose. Florien squeezed his hand ever so slightly. When he let go, his fingertips stroked Deacon's palm the way Deacon had stroked the anthurium. The boy flower, Florien had called it. Deacon glanced at the scarlet bloom with its provocative appendage and licked his lips.

"Very well," he said at last. "A tour. Lead the way."

The greenhouse was larger than it had appeared on the outside. The ramshackle structure boasted a collection of exotic flowers and plants that would have made the Queen's gardeners green with envy. Florien strolled along the narrow aisles, pointing out the various specimens. Here were exuberant sprays of pampas grass; over there was the brilliant red-orange burst of Kaffir lilies. Carmine hibiscus towered in their pots, while the drooping heads of pink vireyas nodded on their branches.

For over an hour, Deacon followed Florien through the greenhouse. His delight at the variety and abundance of tropical plants was slowly surpassed by a growing fascination for his quixotic host. The man never spoke of Lord and Lady Huffington, nor did he explain his relationship to them. Was he a relative of theirs, or a servant—the gardener, perhaps? But what gardener would dress in outdated finery? Florien's frock coat, long and black and trimmed in velvet, was better suited to a ballroom twenty years ago than an ageing greenhouse.

But he had dirt under his nails, Deacon noticed, and calluses on his hands, just like Gareth had. And the way he handled the plants, gently but firmly bending nature to his will—that was also like Gareth. The further they went into the greenhouse, the more the similarities began playing havoc with Deacon's emotions. Florien and Gareth were two very different men, at least physically. Gareth was shorter and broader across the shoulders. Years spent laboring under the sun had bleached his hair to the color of wheat and tanned his skin to rosy brown. Florien, on the other hand, was tall, dark-haired, and fair of complexion. Deacon could never mistake the stranger for his lover. But little things about Florien's attitude—the tilt of his head, the intensity of his gaze as he spoke about his botanical charges—these things roused bittersweet memories in Deacon's heart. Here was Gareth's kin in spirit if not in body.

Near the back of the greenhouse, Florien guided Deacon to a strange plant that sprouted large cup-like appendages at the end of its leaves. Above each cup was a lid in the shape of a heart.

"Is that some sort of carnivorous plant?" Deacon asked, peering at the bizarre specimen.

"Yes, a pitcher plant. *Nepenthes raja* to be exact," Florien replied. "Found in Borneo and brought back here."

A honey bee buzzed about, hovering over the tiny brownish flowers that clustered along the apex of the main stem, high above the lidded traps. The flowers gave off an intense sugary smell.

"Such a sweet scent," Deacon said, inhaling. "How many insects have been lured to their death by it, I wonder?"

"Quite a few." Florien pointed to one of the mottled magenta cups. It nearly overflowed with the corpses of flies and other insects that had slipped inside and starved to death.

Deacon shuddered. "It devours so many creatures. But how does it know not to eat the bee that pollinates it?"

"It doesn't. The bees are interested in the flowers, not the pitcher. They don't usually get near enough to the traps to get caught. But should one make the mistake of getting too close..."

Florien shrugged. Deacon looked at the gruesome contents of the pitcher plant again. This time, he spied a yellow and black striped corpse.

"It kills indiscriminately. That's horrible."

"No. Its traps are passive. It only eats what's presented to it."

Florien leaned over the pitcher plant to trim away a dying leaf. A lock of dark hair fell into his eyes. Visions of Gareth, in the same pose, rose up in Deacon's mind. Without thinking, he reached for the stray lock and brushed it back from the other man's face. His fingers caressed Florien's cheek, just for an instant. Florien looked up at the touch, a question in his eyes. Deacon drew back, horrified. What had he just done?

"I'm... I must go!"

He turned and bolted, racing through the greenhouse, desperate to escape. He heard Florien call out to him and he ran faster, twisting through the narrow aisles. He came out at the end of a row of camellias, only to find himself at the back of the greenhouse again instead of the front. He turned and ran back. This time, he came out on the east side, near the calla lilies. The door was nowhere in sight. Damnation, the place was worse than the topiary maze outside!

"Deacon, wait!"

The sound of footsteps approaching set him racing down another aisle. This one was the right one, finally. He could see the glass door at the end, but as he hurried toward it, his notebook slipped from his coat pocket and skidded across floor. Florien stepped out of the nearest aisle and snatched it up.

"What's this?"

Deacon lunged for the notebook and missed as Florien sidestepped him. He flipped it open to the first page and smiled at the image of a blossom with petals spattered in crimson and cream.

"*Stanhopea tigrina?*" Florien asked. "I grow these here in the garden. Come, you must see!"

Florien dashed off with Deacon's notebook clasped in his hand and a devilish smile on his face. Deacon chased after him, sweating. He must retrieve his notebook before the other man delved any further into its pages. There were secrets in there. Gareth was in there.

Florien turned a corner and disappeared behind some cinnamon ferns. Deacon scrambled to catch up. He rushed past the ferns and nearly ran headlong into his quarry. Florien turned triumphant and held up the notebook.

"*Stanhopea tigrina,*" he said and pointed to a simple clay pot on a gardener's bench.

Deacon looked at where he indicated. An intricate blossom sprouted from the vessel, its brilliant crimson and cream spotted petals stretched open like the arms of a lover.

"Beautiful..." he muttered. He felt a trickle of sweat run down his back. "Now if I may have my journal back, please. I really must be going."

"But there's still more to see."

Florien folded his arms around the journal and nodded pointedly at the bench. Deacon took a deep breath and glanced at the other flowers there. He clasped his trembling hands together tightly and fought the urge to snatch the notebook from Florien's grasp.

"*Dendrobium heterocarpum, Papilionanthe teres, Zygopetalum maxillare...* yes, you have an impressive collection of specimens here."

"As do you." Deacon looked back to see Florien flipping through the pages of the book. His heart leapt into his mouth as the book fell open to one particular page.

"Who is he?" Florien asked. He held open the notebook to a sketch of Gareth, shirtless and reclining with a wicked grin on his face. The sight of that grin made Deacon's cock twitch even as his blood ran cold at the knowledge that a stranger had stumbled upon the evidence of his darkest secret.

"He is no one. A former servant who worked in our garden."

"Hardly 'no one', I should think." Florien continued to turn the pages. More images of Gareth passed under his gaze, intimate moments caught forever on paper. "These drawings are quite detailed. You must have studied him at great length," he said as he came upon a sketch of Gareth, naked and fully aroused, one hand stroking his erect penis, the other holding a freshly cut anthurium to his face. "The boy flower. You must have known him very well."

Deacon's mouth filled with dust. He was ruined. Meredith had chosen to keep his secret rather than risk her own public humiliation, but this man had no such considerations. What would happen if he exposed Deacon? How would the world judge him, a degenerate who lusted after other men?

"You must have loved this man." The words came to Deacon from very far away. "It must have broken your heart to lose him." Florien handed him the journal. "I'm sorry for your loss."

Deacon stared at the journal. Was that it? No denouncement, no contempt? No threats or ridicule? He stared at Florien, uncomprehending. The man smiled back and raised his hand to caress Deacon's cheek.

"It's hard to be different. I know," he said.

A flood of anguished relief cleared the dust from Deacon's mouth and he found his voice again, though the words came halting and painfully.

"My wife ... says our relationship was unnatural."

"What is unnatural about desire?"

Deacon gave a bitter laugh. "You mean, what is unnatural about a man who will not touch a woman? How will such a man progenerate? How may he contribute to the survival of his species if he produces no offspring? My wife wants children, but I am useless to her. I am useless to the human race, an evolutionary failure. There is no need for a sodomite among mankind."

"I need you."

Florien grabbed Deacon by the wrists, causing him to drop the journal. His grip was like steel, inescapable. When Deacon tried to pull away, Florien dragged him closer.

"I need you," he repeated. "I desire you. You are essential to *my* survival."

He planted his mouth on Deacon's, forcing his tongue between the man's teeth. Deacon felt Florien's arms wrap around him, ensnaring him even further. Their bodies rubbed together in a fashion Deacon found painfully sweet. Only one other had ever held him like this. Only one other had ever truly known him.

And look what had resulted from that.

Deacon shoved a hand in Florien's face, struggling to get away. "Someone will see us!"

"No." He held Deacon tight and tried to kiss him again. "No one comes to this place unless I invite them."

"*I* came here."

"You were invited."

Florien grabbed Deacon by the collar and drew the man's face into his neck. The now-familiar scent of flowers flooded Deacon's senses.

"This is my invitation," Florien whispered. "I have issued it for more years than you can imagine. You sensed it. You are the only one in all that time who has ever sensed it and followed it here to me."

Deacon breathed deep, drowning in the mellifluous waves of Florien's perfume. Florien released his shirt collar to hold him close again. His hands slid down Deacon's torso in a long, firm caress until they slipped under the sack coat to pull at the waist of Deacon's trousers. Florien's voice droned on.

"We are alone. No one will come. I could strip you naked and press you up against the glass windows to have my way with you and no one would ever know. Would you like that?" One questing hand undid the fly of Deacon's pants and slid inside to squeeze his growing erection. Florien murmured into Deacon's hair, "Yes, I think you would like that very much."

Deacon shuddered. He buried his face once more in Florien's neck. "I am a fly trapped in your web."

"If you wish. Shall I bind you with silken thread and feast upon your body?"

Deacon gave a trembling laugh. "I thought you were a gardener, not an entomologist."

"I am many things, including your lover."

Florien released his grip on Deacon and, as promised, began stripping him naked. The planter's hat and sack coat fell in heap on the floor, quickly followed by Deacon's waistcoat, shirt, and trousers. Florien

98

reserved the cravat, waiting until he had stripped away Deacon's undergarments to bind the narrow silk tie around his wrists.

He took Deacon to the south-facing wall of the greenhouse and made him stand there, naked and shivering, while he rearranged several pots to clear a space before the begrimed windows. He raised Deacon's arms over his head and pushed him against the glass, facing him toward the outside world. Should anyone come by, in spite of Florien's insistence that they would not, Deacon would be fully exposed to them. He shut his eyes and pressed his cheek against the glass. Another push of Florien's hand against his backside forced his naked cock to rub against the smooth, sun-warmed surface.

Deacon heard a whisper of cloth from behind him—Florien, disrobing. This was followed by the faintest touch of fingers against his buttocks.

"Tell me what you did with that other man," Florien whispered in his ear. "The one you claim is no one."

"He's gone now," Deacon protested.

"Yet he remains with you, here..." A finger tapped against Deacon's temple. "And here." Florien pulled Deacon away from the glass just enough to touch his swollen cock. "Where else is he hiding, hmm? Here?" A kiss blossomed like fire on Deacon's neck. "Or perhaps here?" Another kiss on his shoulder. "Or even here."

Deacon gasped as he felt Florien's fingers slide down the crevice of his buttocks. The other man chuckled and pressed the digits into the crack, spreading his cheeks apart.

"Yes, I think your previous lover most definitely left traces of himself here. Did he plow your furrow with his cock? Did he plant his seed deep within you? I surely intend to plant mine."

A solitary fingertip brushed over Deacon's anus, causing him to yelp. Florien shoved him against the glass again. With one hand he grabbed Deacon by the hair and held him fast. "Don't fight, you are mine! I will take you and use you and you shall enjoy every minute of it!"

The fingertip pressed hard against Deacon's clenched opening. He grunted as it wormed its way inside him. He felt something else, longer and harder, rub up against his buttocks and panicked. "Wait! Please! I'll tear!"

"No, it's just a finger, nothing more. A way to tease you, torment you, a means to heighten your desire for me..." The fingertip began moving back and forth. It barely breached Deacon's sphincter, but it was enough to send a thrill of panic through him. "I need you," Florien went on. "I need you to want me, to be mine!"

"Yes!" Deacon rocked his hips in time with the minute thrusts from Florien's finger. His cock rubbed against the windowpane until the tip leaked. It left a smeared trail on the glass. Florien pressed harder, until Deacon felt the whole of his finger inside him. The hand in his hair slipped down to his chest and trapped one of Deacon's nipples. Florien squeezed it until Deacon thought it might burst like a ripe berry.

Waves of sultry pleasure washed over Deacon. His aching heart and tormented body remembered and welcomed the sensations. He was on the verge of climax. A few more moments, a few more strokes of his cock against the greenhouse window, and he would spill his seed all over the glass, one more stain added to the grime. Just a few thrusts more...

Florien pulled him back abruptly. Deacon cried out, "No! Let me finish!"

But Florien only spun him around. Deacon stumbled and landed on his knees to come face to face with Florien's groin. Deacon gasped. The organ that sprouted from between Florien's legs resembled the spadix of the anthurium more than a man's cock. It was long, slender, and rigid, like a spike, with hundreds of tiny bumps covering its surface from the fleshy pink base to the brilliant scarlet tip. On an anthurium, those bumps were actually tiny flowers, male and female. What were they doing on a man?

"What are you?" Deacon whispered.

Florien didn't answer. Instead, he twined his fingers in Deacon's hair again and brought the man's head toward the strange, erect organ. He shifted his hips and brushed the tip against Deacon's cheek. A swirling cloud of golden dust rose from the rigid shaft, accompanied by Florien's bewitching scent. The dust clung to Deacon's skin and he moaned.

"I am the gardener and the flower," Florien said, rubbing his cock all over Deacon's slack face. "And what are you but the honey bee, come to feed on my essence?"

He tugged on Deacon's hair, tilting his head back. Deacon opened his mouth wide to engulf Florien's cock. The rough surface sloughed against his tongue, coating his lips and mouth with more of the glimmering powder. Deacon sucked hard and tasted nectar so sweet it set his brain buzzing. Yes! This was natural and good, the honey bee and the flower. He feasted on Florien's cock, slavering on the scarlet head until Florien began to moan.

"More ... more, little bee..."

He shuddered and drove his cock into Deacon's mouth, fucking it with desperate need. Deacon clung to his thighs. Florien shuddered and pulled back on his head, withdrawing his cock from Deacon's greedy mouth. The tip erupted with a spray of shimmering particles, more gold dust that gilded Deacon's face and chest.

That was the first orgasm. Florien dropped to his knees and pushed a dazed and euphoric Deacon onto his back, spreading his legs wide apart. He grabbed Deacon's cock and began pumping it. Deacon writhed on the broken tiles, animalistic sounds pouring from his lips. Florien's cock rubbed against his, erupting with another burst of dust, and then another, until a heavy film coated Deacon from head to hips. He rolled about in the granular mess, smearing it all over himself, tasting it in his mouth, inhaling it through his nostrils. He was drugged, enraptured, frantic, screaming. Florien worked at his cock, drawing him deeper into the wells of ecstasy than he had ever been before. Just when Deacon thought he would lose his mind from sheer sensual delight, Florien squeezed one last time. Deacon's entire being quaked and streamed out through his cock to spatter across his belly.

*   *   *

Nightfall peered in through the panes of the greenhouse when Deacon awoke. He lay on the floor, curled up on his side behind Florien, an arm wrapped around the other man's waist. A fine luster of gold sparkled along his wrist—the dust. Deacon rolled onto his back. God, he was painted with the stuff, especially around the groin.

"Are you alright?"

Deacon looked up. Florien rolled onto his back to study him.

"I'm fine," Deacon replied. "A bit of a mess, but not unhappy about it."

A grin fluttered across Florien's lips. "Good."

"Florien, what are you? Where did you come from?"

The other man turned his gaze toward the glass ceiling overhead. "What am I? I can't say, really. I don't think you'll find me in any of your taxonomies. Once, I lived in a beautiful forest very far from here. But one of your kind found me and brought me here. He built this greenhouse to keep me..."

"Alive?"

"No, just to keep me. He was a collector, and I was a rare specimen, the prize of his collection."

"What happened to the man who brought you here?"

"He died years ago, and I have been trapped here ever since."

Deacon moved closer to Florien and placed a kiss on his shoulder. "Not anymore. Let me take you from this place. I'll build you a new greenhouse, a garden all your own. Or else we'll travel the world. If we search, perhaps we can find the place you came from and bring you home."

Florien shook his head. "No. I've been here too long. I've put down roots and become bound to this place. I can never leave."

The words hung in the air between them. Deacon sat up, suddenly feeling cold. "Well, maybe you can't leave, but I must. It must be past midnight now. My beloved wife will be furious with me."

He brushed at his body, trying to wipe away the dust. Florien grabbed his hand.

"Leave it," he demanded.

"I have to clean up. It's late and I must return—"

"Return to your wife?" Florien rolled over and locked gazes with Deacon. His eyes, so vibrant and compelling before, had become dark hollows in a face oddly pale. "Yes, go back to her, but don't clean up."

"And why not?" Deacon snapped.

"Because your wife isn't the only one who wants children."

Deacon froze, his hand hovering above his gold-dusted thigh. "What do you mean?"

"This is my seed. I've given it to you, and now I need you to spread it among your kind."

"What? How?"

Florien dropped his head back against the floor. "How do you think? By seeking out healthy mates. Begin with your wife..."

"No!" Deacon shouted. "How dare you ask me to touch her after what we've done here?"

"Because you must. I am the last of my species, and I am dying."

"Dying?" Deacon stared at Florien. The man's breathing was labored. A waxy sheen had replaced the vital blush of his skin. "What have you done?"

"I told you. I gave you my seed, my essence. All that I am I poured into you. Now you must find a mate and pass it on to her, or everything that I am will vanish from the Earth. I will become extinct."

A sob, sharp and painful as shattered glass, escaped from Deacon's throat. He grabbed Florien by the shoulders and shook him. "Are you mad, to kill yourself so that I might sire your offspring? Why did you do this?!"

A wan smile crossed Florien's grey lips. "I am the flower, you are the bee. That is simply the way things are. You can do this. You must. For me."

With a wail, Deacon turned away from Florien. He wrapped his arms around himself and wept. Tears mingled with the dust on his skin. No, not dust, he thought to himself. Pollen. The sudden realization caused him to suck in a sharp breath. Florien's scent, fading but still sweet, invaded his senses. He gasped as it went to work on his brain, suppressing his grief and infusing him with a compulsive need to do as Florien willed. He fought against it, but half-heartedly, and lost.

"All right," he said at last. He turned his tear-streaked face to Florien. "I will do this. For you."

*   *   *

A short while later, Deacon rushed out of the greenhouse. He had gathered his clothes and dressed in haste. The moon floated high overhead, a cold eye to watch his desperate flight. How much time did Florien have left? Deacon didn't know. He ran through the topiaries, finding his way effortlessly in the dark, guided now by the acute need to fulfill his purpose. Once through the shadowy labyrinth, he sprinted through the gardens back to the mansion. He reached the back door and pounded on it until an anxious maid arrived to let him in.

"Sir, we've been looking everywhere for you!"

Deacon pushed past her. "Where is my wife?"

"In your room, sir! She's most distressed—"

Deacon ran off, leaving the bewildered servant behind. He took the steps to the second floor two and three at a time and within moments burst through the door of their room. Meredith sat on the bed, her face pale and taut with anger.

"Where have you been?" she hissed. She rose to her feet, hands curled into claws. "You missed supper! I had to face all our friends alone and say you were ill, but then someone remembered seeing you head out into the gardens. I have never been so humiliated—"

"Meredith, shut up."

Deacon shoved her backwards onto the bed. She landed with a shriek.

"What are you doing?!"

He tore open her robe and yanked the hem of her nightgown above her waist. "My duty as your husband. You say I have been remiss? That is about to change."

Deacon dropped on top of his wife, pinning her to the bed. With one hand, he undid the fly of his trousers; with the other, he trapped Meredith's wrists. When she screamed, he covered her mouth with his. Florien's scent did its work and Meredith went limp, a bemused look spreading across her face.

"What is that lovely scent?" she murmured. She pawed at Deacon's shirt, trying to undo the buttons. He pushed her hands away. He had only one reason to be there, and he wanted to get it over with quickly. He fumbled his cock into his wife's waiting sex. He was erect, but only because Florien's scent caused him to be so. Deacon had never slept with a woman before, had never wanted to, and the only thing that kept him going now was the thought of his lover dying in the greenhouse. He thrust into his wife once, twice, a third time. The pollen spread from his body to hers, the process blessedly quick. Meredith cried out on the fourth thrust and passed into unconsciousness.

Deacon rolled off of her. He pulled his wedding ring off and dropped it onto the bed beside her.

"Madam, I am done with you. I pray I never look upon your miserable countenance again."

He dropped to his knees on the floor. He wanted to wretch, but he wasn't done yet. Florien had said to start with his wife. That meant he must find others, and quickly. Without bothering to do up his fly, Deacon got up and stumbled out of the room. He ran back downstairs and searched the house until he found the maid who had let him in.

"Come with me," he said, grabbing the plain-faced woman by the hand.

"But sir! Where are we going?"

"Outside."

He dragged her to the kitchen garden and pressed her up against an ivy-covered wall. Like his wife, once she inhaled Florien's scent, she offered no resistance. When he was done with her, he sent her to fetch someone else. She came back, giddy and giggling, with a gap-toothed

104

scullery maid. He rutted briefly with the girl while the maid watched and then sent them both to bring others.

Three more women came to him that night. One was another maid, sister to the first. The other two were well-bred ladies, guests of Lord and Lady Huffington. They had come to the garden, leaving their sleeping husbands unaware.

Deacon performed his duties mechanically, depositing Florien's seed into each woman. When he finished with the last one, he got up and staggered away. Florien's scent was fading. Most of the shimmering pollen was gone from his skin. In the east, a faint light tinged the sky. Dawn. Deacon ran back to the greenhouse as fast as he could.

*　　　*　　　*

Florien still lay on the floor where Deacon had left him. His condition had grown worse. His skin had the ashy pallor of a corpse. His breath came in sharp, shallow gasps.

"It's done," Deacon said. He knelt on the cracked tiles beside Florien. "Six women in all, and I hope to God I never touch another of those creatures again."

Florien gave a pained laugh. "What a busy little bee you've been! Six women? At least one is bound to produce offspring. What a shame I will never see the results..."

Tears filled Deacon's eyes. "Please, you can't die."

"I am spent," Florien wheezed. "I poured my vital essence into my seed. I have almost nothing left."

"No! I lost one lover. I can't lose you too. There must be something I can do to prevent this!" He cast his gaze about the greenhouse. "What do plants need to survive? Soil, water, sunlight..."

"Deacon, don't... It won't work..."

"Why not?!" he shouted.

"Because I am not wholly a plant. I have some of the characteristics of one, but I'm also a man. I don't live off sunlight alone, and you cannot simply plant me in the ground and expect me to survive."

"I cannot let you die!" Deacon wept. "I would rather die myself than lose you."

"Really?" Florien's eyes gleamed with a feverish intensity. "You would do that to save me?"

105

Deacon gathered Florien in his arms and pressed his face in the other man's hair. "I love you. Without you, my spirit will turn to dust and my body with it. I am alone in this world. I have nothing else to live for."

"Then I will not let you die in vain." Florien pulled Deacon to him and gave him one last kiss. Then he moved his mouth to Deacon's neck. His arms twined like vines around Deacon's limbs, holding him fast. His teeth, sharp as thorns, pierced the skin, the muscles, the veins. Deacon cried out, but only a little. After all, what other purpose would his life ever serve?

*   *   *

Edward crouched before the brilliant red anthurium and contemplated the honey bee that rested on the spadix. The insect's hind legs were coated with the sticky yellow pollen produced by the miniscule flowers crowding the surface of the fleshy spike. Exactly how many flowers there were there on a single anthurium, Edward didn't know. Perhaps he should count them. All of them. But then that might take hours and Edward would miss his own wedding. Wouldn't that be a shame?

With a sigh, Edward stood up and adjusted his morning coat. The dove grey garment felt awkward on his lanky frame. He wanted to strip it off and roll up his shirt sleeves, maybe get down on his knees and spend some time tending to the treasure trove of plants he'd just discovered. He would get dirty, of course—soil trapped under his nails, stains on his trousers. That wouldn't do for the wedding. No, it wouldn't do at all.

Edward grimaced. It was time to face the truth. He was getting married in an hour, whether he wanted to or not. If he didn't show up on time, his father would hunt him down and drag him to the altar. His fiancée, Melissa, was a lovely girl, sweet-tempered and patient. He wondered how patient she would be, though, once she learned he had no interest in her at all.

Would he bed her tonight? Could he? Edward wanted to laugh and cry at the same time. He had never been intimate with anyone, never touched another person beyond shaking hands. But in his dreams at night, Edward wrestled with a lover who touched him in places he didn't dare think about during his waking hours.

And that lover was always another man.

He stared at the anthurium, entranced by the swooping curve of its reproductive organ. The thing was obscene, really. So much like a penis, only a penis covered with flowers. Edward bent to stroke it with his finger. The tip bounced beneath his touch much the same way his erect cock bounced on those rare occasions when he indulged in his own lingering caress.

"Do you like it?"

Edward whirled to find a man with dark hair and eyes standing behind him. The stranger wore an old-fashioned sack coat that had to be at least thirty years out of fashion. A battered planter's hat rested on his head.

"Like what?"

"The flower," the man said, nodding at the anthurium. "*Anthurium andraeanum*, sometimes called the boy flower, for obvious reasons. It came all the way from the West Indies. By the way," the man said, holding out his hand, "I'm Florien."

Alienated

"I wonder if it's male or female."

Joe Rose studied the alien sitting at the end of the bar, trying to decide on an answer to his question. There were maybe a hundred different species that came through the Staten Island transshipping station where he worked, and Joe knew almost nothing about any of them. Sure, he could tell a Latian from a Grizzt, and he knew enough to never shake hands with a Raelian—if you did, you got a palm full of green goop—but he didn't know shit about the intimate details of their biology. All he knew was that he couldn't tell the guys from the girls just by looking at them, and this particular creature sitting at the bar was no exception. It had a lithe, fur-covered body that curved in all the right places and luminous grey eyes with long lashes set above high cheekbones. Joe could almost swear it was female, but there was something about the set of its shoulders and the way it cradled its beer that just screamed *male*.

"Man, I really wonder," he muttered again.

"So why don't you go ask it, Rosie boy?"

His drinking buddy, Hank Lawson, punched him on the shoulder and grinned. A few of the other guys around them laughed.

Joe growled and hid behind his beer. "No fucking way."

"Why not?" Hank urged. His rough face split into a leering grin. "If you're lucky and it's a girl, maybe she'll show you how they do it up there in outer space!"

Joe glanced back at the alien. He had to admit that would be pretty damned lucky. The thought of cuddling up to all that fur made his cock twitch, and he couldn't stop staring at the way her uniform hugged her body. Or was that his body? Christ, he wished he could figure it out.

"Forget it, Hank, I'm not drunk enough to go ask."

"Come on, Rosie boy! You aren't scared of a little bitty alien, are you?" Hank jeered. "Go ask it what it is, and then ask it for a fuck. I dare you!"

With a meaty hand he pushed Joe off the barstool. The rest of the guys cheered him on. Joe wanted to say no, but then Hank had said those three little words—*I dare you*—and that was that. No way was he going to back down on a dare from Hank Lawson, especially not when the rest of the gang was watching. No fucking way.

So Joe picked his way through the mob at the bar and headed for the alien at the other end. Before he could reach her (him?), she turned and looked straight at him. The intensity of her gaze stripped away all his bravado and took his clothing with it. For an instant, Joe stood naked in the crowded bar, and the shock and embarrassment made him so hard he thought he'd come on the spot.

"Holy shit!" he muttered, unable to even move. Then the alien looked away. Freed from her paralyzing stare, Joe dropped his hands to cover himself only to discover he still wore his faded jeans and work shirt. He looked back at Hank, flustered. The big dockhand just grinned and flashed him a thumbs-up. The rest of the guys hooted and clapped as Joe squared his shoulders and went through with the dare.

"Hi," he said as he sidled up to the alien. "Care for some company?" She nodded and Joe slid onto the empty barstool next to her.

"Thanks," he said.

"You are welcome," she replied.

She had a nice voice, rich and melodic, one that sent shivers down his spine. It was a little too low for female, a little too high for male, and the ambiguity had Joe squirming in his seat. Fuck, what if this thing was a guy, after all, and he pissed it off by asking about its sex?

Come on, Rosie boy! You aren't scared of a little bitty alien, are you?

Scared? Him? Never. He stole a glance at the creature sitting next to him. She (he? it?) looked back expectantly, wide grey eyes mesmerizing him.

"Shall I pay for you?" she asked.

"Huh?"

She—Joe decided it had to be a she, because his cock sat up straight every time he looked at her—gestured to the empty mug gripped in his hand. "What do you wish to drink?"

"Oh!" He flushed as he tried to decide. "Beer, I guess. Lager."

The alien called to the bartender and tapped Joe's empty mug with a long finger that ended in a neat, tapered claw. Like a cat's claw, Joe thought as his drink was refilled. She looked just like a great big house cat in need of some serious heavy petting. Here pussy, pussy, pussy. Then he

109

swallowed as he noticed how long the claw was and decided she reminded him more of a tiger.

The bartender wandered off and Joe peeked at the alien again. The neon lights of the bar poured over her cascade of shoulder-length braids and polished the short nap of auburn fur on her face and hands to a velvety sheen. The rest of her was covered by her uniform—a fitted blue jacket cropped at the waist, a skintight white shirt, and gray leggings tucked into black boots with a heavy tread. Geometric shapes decorated the shoulders of her jacket—a sign of her rank, he supposed—and a long line of swooping gold characters decorated her left lapel.

"Um, is that your name?" Joe asked, pointing to the script. His fingertip hovered over the spot where the characters curved over her rounded breast. That part of her definitely looked female. He wondered if it was covered with fur too.

"Kazen, Nashaetra clan, from Daesha. Navigator for the Torlance."

"Huh?"

"Kazen," she repeated slowly. "Nashaetra clan, from Daesha. Senior navigator for the Torlance."

"Oh, Kazen." Joe pressed his lips together and nodded. "From the Torlance? Nice ship. My crew just finished loading your cargo today. I'm Joe Rose, by the way."

His gaze flashed back to Hank and the guys sitting on the other side of the bar. The big dockhand laughed at him and waved. Then Kazen shifted in her seat, pulling a twenty-credit note from her jacket pocket. Joe decided he'd better act fast if he was going to go through with this.

"Say, I was wondering..."

She stared at him again with those eyes and his earlier feeling of nakedness returned. Joe felt a thrill of embarrassment mingled with a little fear and excitement as he imagined her stripping off all his clothing right there in the bar, just so she could take a good long look at what he kept hidden underneath. Man, he'd undressed some women with his eyes before, but he could actually feel her hand slip between his legs to cradle his balls.

"What are you?" Joe blurted out. Then he winced. Christ, that wasn't exactly the smoothest pick-up line.

"Kazen," she answered. "Nashaetra clan, from Daesha—"

"No, no, I got your name. I meant, are you, you know, female?"

She stared, unblinking. His heart sunk a bit and his cock deflated.

"Okay, are you male, then?"

No answer but that startling gray gaze. Joe bit his lip.

"I just need to know, because there's something I wanted to—"

"Yes."

"Huh?"

He frowned. What the hell did *yes* mean? Yes, she was female? Or yes, she was male? Before he could ask, she stood up, dropped the twenty on the bar, and then walked out.

"Go get her, Rosie boy!" he heard Hank shout.

Joe grimaced, but his cock was straining against his fly again and Joe decided to follow where it pointed—out of the bar after Kazen.

He had to run to catch up. If she was female, she was pretty damned tall—taller than him, even—and her long booted legs quickly carried her down the block to a nearby hotel. Joe saw her disappear inside the building and he sprinted the last several yards, barely making it through the door in time to see her step onto the elevator.

"Hold it!"

He darted across the lobby, ignoring complaints from the desk clerk as he ran past. Just before the elevator doors slid shut, the alien reached out to hold them open.

"Thanks," he said, panting as he stepped into the car. The doors closed and Kazen pressed a button. The elevator began its slow, rumbling ascent.

"So, Kazen." Joe leaned back against the wall to catch his breath. "I didn't get your answer back there in the bar. Are you a guy or a girl?"

"Yes."

He clapped both hands to his head. "Okay, I don't understand that. Let's try this. Can you have sex with humans?"

"We are compatible."

Joe's cock jumped at that bit of news. "That's good! Would you, and I mean you personally, prefer to have sex with men or women?"

"Yes."

Did that mean she liked both? Joe shook his head, trying to figure it out.

Buttons lit up as the elevator continued upward. When it reached the fifteenth floor, the elevator rumbled to a halt and the doors slid open. Kazen stepped out and Joe quickly followed. "Perhaps I'm not making myself clear. Biologically speaking, are you male or female?"

111

The alien stopped in front of a door, room key in hand. "Daeshaen physiology is different from human physiology. This cycle, I produce eggs as a human female would, but I would need to transfer them into a potential mate for insemination and gestation. Does that answer your question?"

"Not really." Joe scratched his head. "I think you said you make the eggs and put them inside someone else to have a baby."

She nodded. "Yes."

"But you said *this cycle*. What's a cycle? And what did you do last cycle if you didn't make eggs?"

"A cycle is a breeding period. It lasts approximately forty-two Earth months. During my previous cycle, I could receive eggs from a mate, fertilize them, and carry them to full term to produce a child."

"Uh, with humans, it's the males that usually do the fertilizing and the women who carry the kids."

"So I have been instructed."

"But you're saying Daeshaen males carry the babies and the females do the fertilizing?"

"Not exactly. As I said, our physiology is different. We are not male and female as you would understand it."

Joe tried three times to open his mouth and utter an intelligent reply to that statement. In the end, the best he could come up with was, "Look, do you have a vagina or not?"

Kazen nodded. "I have genitalia similar to a vagina. You're interested in examining it?"

Joe blushed and laughed at the same time. "Well, yeah, I guess so. In fact, I want to do more than just look, you know?" He leaned closer to her and traced the lapel of her jacket with a finger. "I'd like to..."

Ask her for a fuck! Hank's voice echoed inside his skull, making Joe flinch. Hell, that was crude. He had his foot in the door. He didn't want to screw things up now by being vulgar. He took a deep breath and opted for a more subtle approach.

"Kazen, I'd like us to be intimate. You know what that means?"

For the first time, she smiled, and Joe's heart started to pound. "Yes, I understand intimacy. The question is, do you?"

"If I don't," he whispered, leaning closer, "I'd be happy to have you explain it to me."

He had to rise up on tiptoe to kiss her. Kazen parted her lips and let him explore her mouth with his tongue for a few moments. She tasted like cinnamon and fresh oranges, he thought.

Then she pulled back and said, "I'll show you mine if you show me yours."

She sounded like a coy schoolgirl, but her face was dead serious. Joe wondered what she'd look like wearing that expression and nothing else and his cock started to throb.

"A little show and tell? That sounds good to me."

Kazen slipped the key into the lock and pushed the door open. Joe followed her in, blinking in the dim light of the room. It was a standard suite with a king-sized bed and two night tables, nothing out of the ordinary here. It seemed odd to him that he was about to have sex with an alien in a place so normal, but then Kazen seemed so strange that perhaps a mundane setting was best.

"Which of us is going first?" Joe asked as he followed her to the bed.

Kazen pushed him down onto the mattress and climbed on to straddle his hips. Her clawed fingers worked carefully, unbuttoning his shirt and stripping it away.

"Okay, I guess I'm first." His voice grew hoarse as he watched her reach for his belt. His fly was next, and it came open so fast Joe could have sworn it had undone itself. From beneath it swelled the bulge of his cock, imprisoned within the striped fabric of his boxers. A small wet spot already stained the elastic waistband. Kazen touched the wetness and sighed.

"You like that?" Joe breathed. He slipped his hands beneath her jacket, feeling for her breasts. "You like that I'm turned on?"

"Yes. The human sexual response is very intense, very pleasurable to share."

"Oh yeah? How many human sexual responses have you shared?" he asked, laughing.

Without waiting for an answer, Joe slid the jacket off her shoulders and began tugging at the skintight shirt she wore underneath. He peeled the garment away from her body and discovered the fur on Kazen's hands and face extended to the rest of her, as well. Grinning, he skimmed his fingertips up her stomach and around her breasts, enjoying the soft fuzzy feel as he drew smaller and smaller circles around her almost human nipples.

"You feel so good," he said, looking up into her huge gray eyes.

113

"You feel so good..."

The words had echoed back to him in a woman's voice and, all of a sudden, Joe was on top, looking down at a brown-skinned girl with curly black hair. His hands reached down to cup her full breasts, gently squeezing the soft, buttery flesh.

His hands.

His hands were covered with auburn fur.

"What the hell!"

Joe sat up with a start, his heart racing. He looked at Kazen and she gazed back expectantly.

"What just happened? I saw a woman, and I think... I think I was you!" Joe blinked several times. "You made love to that woman."

Kazen nodded.

"And somehow you showed that to me? Christ, was that telepathy?"

"We call it intimacy," she answered. "A sharing of memory and experience."

She slipped a finger inside the waistband of his boxers and stroked the head of his cock. "You asked to be intimate. There are many, many experiences I could share, but I thought I should start with something familiar to you."

She found the slit of his cock head and pressed her fingertip against it, rubbing back and forth. Joe groaned and lay back on the bed.

"In the bar," he gasped, "when you looked at me, I felt naked."

"That was ... a challenge. To show you how exposed you would feel if you chose to be intimate with me."

"You knew what I wanted even before I walked up to you?"

"I felt your curiosity, very strong. I was glad when you answered the challenge. Curious lovers share the best experiences."

Joe shivered, suddenly understanding. "You show me yours, and I show you mine?"

"Exactly." She pulled down the waistband of his shorts to free his cock, and began rubbing the sweet spot just below the glans.

"You do this with everyone you fuck?"

Kazen nodded.

"Why?"

She paused. "Why does it matter to you if I am male or female? Humans call it sexual preference, but we call it alienation. You cut yourself off from potential lovers for the most superficial reasons—gender, race,

114

religion, age. Then you isolate yourselves even further by failing to connect with each other when you do celebrate intercourse. In fact, you do not celebrate it at all. You let your bodies perform the mechanics, but your minds never touch."

Joe shook his head. "Humans can't do what you just did. I can't put my thoughts into someone else's head. We just don't communicate like that."

"How do you know? Have you ever tried?"

He bit his lip. "I wouldn't even know how to begin."

Kazen leaned forward and kissed his neck. "You said if you did not understand intimacy, you would be happy to let me explain it to you."

Joe groaned. Her tongue flicked over his earlobe and her fingers went back to teasing his cock. "I did say that," he whispered. "But this ... this sharing thing, I don't know."

"Do you want to leave, then?"

"Yes. No. I don't know." He squirmed beneath her, trying to decide. "Can I see it first? I mean, I know this is gonna sound really superficial after everything you've just said, but can I see what you look like down there before we go any further?"

Kazen sat up and nodded gravely. "Of course."

She rolled off him and settled back on the bed. Joe reached over, released the straps on her boots, and pulled them off. Hands trembling, he reached for her pants. They slid down her hips and legs like silk. Underneath, she wore nothing but fur. The auburn down of her belly faded to pale gold between her legs. At first, Joe saw nothing but an uninterrupted surface of skin. Then, like an orchid at sunrise, everything blossomed. Four dark-veined petals unfurled from the smooth exterior of Kazen's groin to reveal a crenellated bloom of moist flesh, tinted pale pink to dusky maroon. Its frilled edges pulsed and swelled, drawing his eyes down to its center where he spotted a small hard bud set above a narrow opening. Beneath that slit appeared a short fleshy stem that he could only describe as the stamen of a rare flower.

"You can touch it if you like," she said, spreading her legs a little wider.

Joe reached out a tentative hand and brushed the damp outer petals. They fluttered at his touch. Kazen moaned and Joe grinned like a kid on Christmas morning.

"It's sensitive?"

She nodded. "Just like the genitals of a human female."

"What about this?" His fingers grazed the bud. Kazen arched her back and gasped.

"That's very sensitive. As is this."

The stamen twitched and grew longer as he stared at it. Joe shook his head. "That's a lot more complex than what I've got. What do you do with it all?"

"Let me show you, if you really want to know."

Joe swallowed. If she showed him something, then he'd have to show her something. Did he really want to open up to an alien like that? He looked back down at the strange sensual flower burgeoning between her legs and reached out again to stroke it. Just before he touched it, the outer petals wrapped around his fingers, pulling them all the way in. Shivering, Joe imagined what it would feel like to bury his cock inside those petals. What had Kazen said? Curious lovers shared the best experiences? He was certainly curious now.

"Okay. Show me."

Just like that, he was Kazen again, this time kneeling between the legs of another Daeshaen, one named Seera with silvery blue fur that shimmered beneath the glow of two moons. Seera, so sweet and gentle, wanted to spend one last night making love before they shipped out on different vessels. Joe watched Kazen's hands reach out and stroke the skin between Seera's legs until the outer petals of her sex opened up.

Beneath the vision, he saw his own hands following along, the memory of the blue Daeshaen superimposed over the real one lying on the bed before him. He continued caressing her undulating outer lips until both the remembered alien and the real one began to rock their hips and moan. Then Joe moved further inward, his fingers spiraling around the small bud of flesh he thought must be an alien clit. When he touched it, the bud released a pungent scent like ripe melon. Mouth watering, he leaned down to taste.

At the first lick, Kazen cried out and arched her back. Just like a human female would, Joe thought, and that sparked one of his memories. The blue Daeshaen faded and was replaced by Cheryl, his ex-girlfriend. Twenty-seven and still a virgin, she'd arched her back the same exact way the first time he went down on her. Then she grabbed him by the ears and pressed his face to her pussy, demanding more. Joe loved the way she tasted, like rosemary and olive oil. Just like his mom's Italian cooking, he joked with her later—sharp, fragrant, and delicious.

But right now, he tasted ripe fruit and he knew it was Kazen he was licking, not Cheryl. Cheryl left him two years ago because he wouldn't open up to her, she said. He shut her out, *alienated* her, because he wasn't good at expressing his feelings. Even though he loved her so much it scared the shit out of him, he was still young enough to play the field—and here she was asking him about marriage, and kids, and the future, and why didn't he want to settle down and spend the rest of his life with her? It was the same damn argument over and over and over again until finally he told Cheryl she was suffocating him. So she said goodbye and faded away as a thick blue gelatinous mass took her place on the hotel room bed.

He became Kazen again—a Kazen that shook with fear as the gel overwhelmed him, smothered him, and covered every inch of his body as it wended its way inside him. It filled every orifice he had—his mouth, his nose, even his genitals—sending him into a panic attack.

I can't breathe! he thought, but in the back of his mind he knew he could.

Oxygen passed through the viscous being that held him, allowing him to respire without hindrance. His fear eased as he realized the gel wasn't suffocating him. It had simply submerged him inside itself to love him more completely. Within its fluid embrace, Joe felt endless ripples of electric current running over his body. His cock stiffened with each pulse and the gel, sensing his excitement, wrapped more tightly around him, massaging and stimulating him until Joe thought he would pass out from sheer ecstasy. It was as if someone had taken his entire body inside their mouth to give him the ultimate blowjob.

Then he realized Kazen did have him in her mouth. Through the mirage of the gel, he felt her lips glide over his cock. Gasping, Joe reached down to stroke her face. God he loved touching that velvet skin. It felt so smooth and soft, it reminded him of Hank Lawson's crew cut. Hank, the guy he played high school football with, the guy he went to college with, the guy who stumbled into his dorm room late one night while Joe was jerking off and said, "Here, Rosie boy, let me show you how it's really done," and then got down on his knees and started licking the head of Joe's leaking cock. He'd never felt anything so damned good as Hank's tongue running up and down the length of his dick, and when the big guy took the whole thing in his mouth, Joe thought he'd damn near explode.

And he did, right inside Hank's mouth, but Hank just laughed as he swallowed and told Joe it was his turn. Joe said okay and got down on the floor with Hank and went to work. Hank had a nice cock, longer than

Kazen's stamen, but that was changing because that little beauty just kept growing with every lick Joe gave it until it was just as long, though not as thick, as Hank's cock. Then he was giving head to both Hank and Kazen, and the sound of the two of them crying out his name as he sucked on them was like music to his ears.

He and Hank had made that music all night long, he recalled, but come morning they were both sober and the song was over. Neither one of them could admit what they'd done. The two best friends couldn't even talk to each other anymore, so they went their separate ways. Joe eventually dropped out of college his senior year, and he didn't see Hank again until ten years later when he went to work at the Staten Island transshipping port. By then, they were okay. They could joke and drink, but damn, they could never look each other in the eye. They were *alienated*, cut off from each other by their stupid macho pride.

Pride, pride, stupid pride. It was stupid pride that got Kazen into trouble, claiming she could steer the Torlance even though she'd never set foot on a ship that big before. Well, she'd steered it, all right, steered it so close to Raelia's second sun that she'd scorched the hull and the captain now sat white-knuckled at his command post, too shaken to even swear at her. The senior navigator, Orxtl, scowled at her so hard Kazen knew she was going to lose her license.

But a little while later, old Orxtl pulled her into his quarters and teased her out of her uniform, laughing all the while because he'd done the same damn thing on his first flight out, many cycles ago, except his captain actually shit his pants from fear. Kazen laughed too, and then she sighed as Orxtl coaxed open her sex and played his long white fingers over her stamen cock until she was squealing with frustration. Then the old man opened himself up and slipped her right inside his flowering pussy, and rode her hard and fast until she came screaming inside him. Afterward, as she licked him clean, he told her not to worry about what happened that morning, because everybody made mistakes the first time around.

And there's always a first time for everything, but you never know how it's going to work out. The first time Mrs. Minnever invited him into the house, Joe hadn't expected anything more than a glass of lemonade. She was a proper lady, a fine lady, Mr. Minnever told him, and she didn't care for rude behavior, which meant if Joe was going to cut their lawn this summer, he'd best mind his manners. So Joe watched his language and said please and thank you to Mrs. Minnever. Every Saturday, he mowed and edged three acres of Kentucky bluegrass all for the bargain price of fifty bucks a week. It wasn't much, but when you were flat broke and heading off to college, every little bit helped.

Then one day, Mrs. Minnever invited Joe into the house and told him she would pay a hundred bucks if he'd just take off his clothes and let her touch him. Mr. Minnever was out of town, he was always out of town, and Mrs. Minnever was so lonely. Joe was a good boy, she knew that—a virgin, she was willing to bet. When Joe blushed, she laughed.

"Be a good boy for mama and take off your clothes," she said, and he did. Then Mrs. Minnever told him to undress her too, only he couldn't use his hands; he had to do everything with his mouth. Bit by bit, he pulled off her clothes with his teeth to reveal that beautiful curvy body covered in auburn fur. Then Mrs. Minnever was pushing him back into a kitchen chair and placing his hands on her velvety breasts as she straddled his eager cock. Forty years old and still tight as a drum, she bragged, and when the outer petals of her pussy reached down and grasped his cock and balls, he had to agree she was damn tight. She pulled him deep into the flowery folds of her sex and rubbed her stamen against his prostate.

"I'm gonna come, I'm gonna come," he chanted over and over again, and Mrs. Minnever said, "There, there, baby, come to mama, it's all right."

When he was done, she bent him over the kitchen table, pressed his face onto its green formica surface, saying, "Tit for tat, what's good for the goose is good for the gander."

He would have protested, but the first dollop of lube had already hit him right between the ass cheeks and next thing he knew, Mrs. Minnever—call her Barbara, please—had two fingers inside him. It felt strange as hell, but good, too. Then she put something else in there, something long and hard that kept Joe rocking and moaning for all he was worth.

And that, ladies and gentlemen, was how he lost two virginities in one day and made a hundred bucks in the bargain. In fact, he made a lot of money that summer, and never regretted how he earned it until the rumors started. Barbara said he shouldn't care about what people said. She was leaving Mr. Minnever, anyway, and twenty-two years age difference wasn't that big a deal—not when two people really loved each other the way she and Joe did. But it mattered to Joe; it mattered a hell of a lot what folks said and, even though he loved her, he lied and said he only did it for the money. Then Barbara screamed at him and slapped him. She said she hated him and they were *alienated* from each other because he was too fucking scared of what other people would think.

And on and on it went, from Joe to Kazen and back again, an endless stream of memories flowing back and forth, each one triggering another as they hurtled along. They were connected, with Joe on top, plunging his cock into Kazen's beautiful alien pussy and her beneath with her long velvet legs around his waist and her stamen, her cock, sliding into his ass. Joe felt it stroking inside him and he laughed.

What the hell did it matter if Kazen was male or female? She was in him and he was in her, and he couldn't tell anymore where one ended and the other began. Their desire had fused them together into a complete circuit of trust, intimacy, and love. And Joe did love her—he really, really did.

Then they both shuddered and the petals of Kazen's flowered sex convulsed around Joe's cock while her stamen thrust into him one last time. Joe cried out and shot his seed deep inside her as he flew through the last of their shared memories to land safely in her arms.

*   *   *

He walked Kazen to the docks the next morning and kissed her gently before she boarded the Torlance. Joe was back to being Joe and Kazen was Kazen again. They were two separate beings just like before, but connected now in a way he'd never known was possible.

"I'll be back in three weeks," she told Joe.

"I know. I'll be waiting." He pulled her close again for another kiss. "Thanks for last night. It was amazing."

She ruffled his hair and smiled. "You are welcome. Now share it with someone else?"

"Okay."

He watched her board the giant freighter and then turned to walk away. Hank Lawson waited for him at the end of the dock, a look of astonishment plastered on his broad face.

"Hey, Rosie boy, what the fuck happened last night? You never came back to the bar."

Joe nodded. "I spent the night with Kazen."

"Kazen, huh?" Hank scratched his close-cropped scalp and chuckled. "Well, well, well. I guess you got an answer to your question, then. So what was it?"

"Hmmm?"

For the first time in years, Joe looked Hank in the eye. He gazed at his friend and called up the memory of a night they'd once shared a long time ago. The big dockhand blushed as though he knew what Joe was thinking, but he didn't look away.

"Hey, Earth to Joe? I said, what was it? Spit it out. Was it male or female?"

"Yes," Joe answered finally, and he walked away grinning, knowing that Hank would follow.

Girls Gone Wild

"Dude! Harry and Dave sent another movie!"

Joe rushed into the house, clutching a package. Mick jumped up and down on the couch, whooping.

"Open it, man! Open it!" Mick chanted.

Joe tore apart the cardboard box and dug out a cheap plastic jewel case, labeled in black marker. "Oh sweet! This one's called 'Campground Adventures with Harry and Dave!'" He held up the DVD in one hand and slapped palms with his roommate in a testosterone-charged high-five.

"It's movie time!" Mick shouted as he snatched the disc from Joe. He flipped open the case and a scrap of paper fluttered out and floated to the floor.

"Dude, what's this?" Joe picked up the paper. "They sent us a note?"

"Forget that. We got beer and homemade porn. Grab a spot on the couch and get ready for some nasty girl-on-girl action!"

"All right!"

Mick slid the disc into the DVD player and grabbed the remote. He settled next to Joe on a threadbare couch that smelled like potato chips and farts. As the television hummed to life, Joe cackled.

"I so cannot believe these guys. Remember the last movie they sent?"

Mick groaned. "Oh yeah, three naked babes going down on each other in a tub full of Jell-O. Man, if only we could have gone on this road trip with them. Being broke sucks."

"Hey, at least we can enjoy their adventures vicariously. Besides, Harry and Dave promised to send home a souvenir. Some of these chicks might show up on our doorstep one day."

"Not the fat ones, I hope."

"But dude, the fat ones will do *anything!*"

Mick punched Joe in the arm. "Shut up! Movie's starting."

They turned to watch the screen, eyes glazing over as it filled with the grinning visage of a wiry young man in ratty t-shirt and jeans. His grungy urban clothes looked sorely out of place against the backdrop of wild spruce and pines.

"'Sup, dudes? It's me, Harry! Dave and I are in Alaska this week, visiting the Klondike Campground in search of some local wildlife. And we do mean wild! Rumor has it that the Klondike is a favorite spot for women campers, especially sorority chicks. So we decided to check it out for ourselves. Dave, you ready to hunt for some women in the au naturel?"

The camera bobbed up and down. "Ready, dude!"

"Then let's get going!"

With a smirk, Harry turned and hiked down a path. The camera followed, focusing on his backside as he strode along.

"So like, this is supposedly a girls-only campground," Harry said over his shoulder to the camera. "I mean, guys can come here, but for some reason they usually don't. Which means a couple of alpha males like me and Dave should have no problems tracking down some frisky femmes ... oh, and here they are now..."

Harry turned off the trail and headed into a campsite. Mick and Joe drooled as they watched their friend approach two women, one blonde and one brunette, setting up a tent.

"Oh my gawd," the blonde exclaimed. "Are there, like, actually men here? I thought this place was for girls only!"

"It's okay, ladies." Harry smiled and stroked his goatee. "I'm Harry and this is my good buddy Dave. We're here on special assignment. We're, um, like in film school? And we're doing a documentary on Alaska wildlife for our summer project. Right, Dave?"

The camera bobbed up and down again. "Riiiiight..."

"I don't suppose either of you girls has seen any interesting wildlife in the area?" Harry winked at the girls, both of whom giggled and smiled back. Mick sat on the couch, growing warmer as the camera zoomed in on the brunette's breasts. She wore a t-shirt, but no bra. Her nipples stood up beneath the thin cotton fabric, making tiny tents of their own.

"Un-fucking-believable," Joe said five minutes later as the camera showed the two girls, now topless, writhing against each other, their tent still only half set up. Harry narrated from off screen, in a loud whisper.

"Dudes, what you see here is the mating ritual of Tittius-Sororitus, better known as the big-breasted sorority chick. They'll hump each other like this for hours, French kissing and rubbing their nipples together. If we're very patient, they may even ... oh, there they go now..."

The brunette leaned down to suck on one of her partner's swollen nipples. She bit down and tugged gently, causing the other girl to moan, then unzipped the blonde's shorts to expose a cleanly shaved pussy. Mick sucked in a sharp breath as the brunette kneeled and lapped at her friend's cunt.

"Holy shit." Joe groaned on the couch next to him, sliding his hand between his legs. Mick shifted in his seat, trying not to be quite as obvious as he slipped a hand into his sweatpants.

"How the hell does he do it?" Joe asked, his fist pumping in slow rhythm inside his shorts. Mick didn't answer, but focused instead on the action on the television screen.

A few minutes later, the scene changed and Harry introduced Inga, Helga, and Gertrude, a trio of Swedish exchange students who spoke very little English.

"Dude!" Joe exclaimed as Helga pulled off her top and presented her double-D sized breasts to the camera. "How does he break the frikkin' language barrier?!"

Mick stroked his cock faster. "I don't know, but when it comes to girls, Harry's a fucking genius."

They continued jerking off as Inga stood behind Helga, her hands reaching around to pinch the other woman's nipples while Gertrude stripped to one side. A few minutes later, all three women lay in a circle on the grass, each one with her head between another girl's thighs. Tongues flicked over slick pussies, fingers slipped in and out of cunts. Harry chuckled off screen.

"And there you have it, dudes. A trio of rare Swedish birds, the golden clit-suckers. Bet you won't see that in National Geographic!"

More scenarios followed as Harry and Dave travelled from one campsite to the next. Everywhere they went, they found girls in pairs or trios, giggling and smiling, all willing to take off their clothes and perform for the camera. Occasionally, Harry suggested to the women what he wanted. More often, the women acted of their own accord.

"It's like they want us to watch them," Joe breathed as a freckle-faced redhead pulled an enormous dildo out of her backpack and used it to fuck her best friend.

Mick snorted. "You mean, they want Harry and Dave to watch them. They don't even know we exist."

"But they know he's recording it!" Joe replied. On the screen, the redhead pulled a second dildo from her pack and inserted it deep into her wet cunt. "They've got to know someone else is going to see this."

Mick shrugged. "They don't care, man. Once Harry turns on that million mega-watt grin, chicks will do anything for him. You know, he even got a couple of lesbians to suck him off once? They were fighting over him, too."

"Dude, I wish we had video footage of that!"

"Yeah, that would have been sweet..."

On the television, the scene changed once more. This time, Harry stood in front of a sign that read *Private Campground* in bold red letters. Below that, in smaller print was *Trespassers Beware!*

Harry flashed his trademark grin. "You know, we've seen some pretty wild things today—"

Joe choked on his beer. "They filmed all of that in *one day?*"

"—but to see something really wild," Harry continued, "we have to head off the beaten path. According to legend, the campground behind me is the ancestral territory of a band of real live Amazons, gorgeous women over six feet tall with enormous tits and voracious sexual appetites. Men who set foot in this place risk unspeakable torture at the hands of these beautiful but vicious femme fatales."

"Probably just a bunch of hairy-legged box-munchers," Dave muttered from behind the camera.

"Dude!" Harry doubled over, snorting. "Whichever it is, Dave and I are going in to see for ourselves. Are these women really ferocious man-eaters or just adorable pussies in need of some serious lovin'? Let's find out!"

For the next few minutes, the camera followed Harry as he hiked through the woods. The trees grew taller and closer together. The path narrowed then disappeared. As the woods grew dark around them, Harry stumbled over a root.

"Shit! It's getting pretty wild out here."

The camera jerked and wobbled as Dave trailed after him. "Yeah, about that, dude. We've been walking for a while now. I don't think there's a campground out here. Maybe we should turn back—"

"Shhh!" Harry held up a hand, motioning for silence. He turned slowly, ears pricked, the tip of his tongue between his teeth. "You hear that? That's women laughing! Come on, this way!"

He took off through the trees. Dave shouted after him.

125

"Harry, wait! Fucking idiot..."

The picture went dark. Moments later, it came back up. Harry stood to one side, peering through some bushes. "Through here," he whispered. The camera panned and zoomed in on a pond. Several shadowy figures, backlit by the setting sun, laughed and splashed in the water.

"Oh man, look at 'em," Harry breathed. "They're all naked and wet! This must be some sorta sorority bash. Look at the size of their ti—"

A loud growl, like the call of a mountain lion, cut Harry off. The camera image jerked up and shut off abruptly. Just before it went dark, it recorded a glimpse of a stern female face, dark brows knitted together in anger.

In the living room, Joe and Mick squirmed in their seats.

"Shit," Joe muttered. "What do you think happened?"

Mick chewed his lower lip. His erection had deflated the moment the camera went dark. "Dunno. DVD's still running though. Hold on..."

The camera came back up but at an odd angle, looking up at the scene as though Dave held it tucked under one arm. Harry stood in the midst of a gang of women. Most of them were naked, their wet bodies rippling with long lines of muscle. All of them towered over Harry by several inches, their faces cut off by the camera angle.

"Ladies!" Harry rocked on his toes, smiling as always. "We are so sorry to intrude. My buddy Dave and I were out hiking and we got lost. I guess we were paying too much attention on our work and not enough on where we were going. See, we're doing this documentary for our film class, and we were wondering if any of you beautiful babes have seen any interesting wildlife lately?"

Nobody answered. The same low growl they had heard earlier went up around the circle. Even though it came through the television's speakers, the sound still made the hairs on the back of Mick's neck stand up. On camera, Harry looked around at the women, still grinning, but now nervously fingering his goatee.

"Um, so are you all enjoying your camping trip? Looks like you've got quite a party going on here. Kind of a clothing optional thing, I guess. Which is cool, you know, because you gals are way too beautiful to be all covered up. Right, Dave?"

From off screen, Dave muttered over and over again. "Oh shit, oh shit, oh shit, oh shit..." The camera shook in his hands.

Harry's grin faltered. "Okay ... um, like I said, we didn't mean to intrude, so maybe we should just go back the way we came..." He took a step backwards and stumbled into one of the women. The camera came up suddenly and steadied, zooming in on Harry and the stern-faced woman they had glimpsed earlier. She wore nothing but a scowl and a pair of cut-off jeans that barely covered the curves of her ass. Her full, bare breasts hung at eye-level with Harry's face.

"Wow. You're really tall." Harry swallowed hard, tearing his eyes away from the woman's breasts. "So what's, uh ... what's your name?"

"Tia." A razor sharp smile cut across her angular face. "I think you should stay."

"Well, if that's what you want, that's cool..." Harry shuffled from one foot to the other as a wall of women formed around him, blocking his escape. "We've got this video camera, you know. If you'd like, maybe we could tape your party... You know, make a movie of you girls having fun..."

"Is that all you ever do? Just watch while the women play?" Tia trailed a hand down Harry's chest and hooked a finger under the hem of his shirt. Harry closed his eyes.

"Not always," he whispered as she pulled up his shirt. "Sometimes we like to join in..."

Tia pulled Harry's shirt over his head and tossed it to the ground. The other women began stroking his bare torso. Naked breasts pressed against his back and shoulders. Hands, slender but strong, reached for his fly. Harry's jeans fell to his ankles.

"You're excited." Tia brushed her fingertips against the bulge in Harry's shorts. He nodded, eyes still closed. He swayed in the midst of the women, his cock rising until it poked through the fly of his boxers. Someone grabbed the tip and pinched it.

"Ow!" Harry jumped back, falling over as his feet tangled in his jeans. The women laughed. "What the hell was that for?" he demanded.

"Foreplay," Tia replied. She stalked toward him, hips swaying.

Harry scrambled back. "You're kidding, right? Okay, we should definitely go. Dave, help me out here. Dave? Dave?!"

The camera turned and pointed at a second band of women. Dave stood in their midst, arms held fast behind him. His clothing was nowhere to be seen. He writhed and bit his lip as a statuesque blonde squeezed his balls. The camera panned back to Harry, who knelt on the ground, mouth working but forming no coherent words. Tia grabbed him by the hair and pulled him back to his feet.

"If you really want to go, then go," she growled. "We won't stop you. But if you stay, you play our games, by our rules."

She pulled at the waistband of Harry's boxers, running her fingers along the inside. Harry shuddered, and back in the living room, Mick shuddered with him. When Tia pulled the waistband out, the head of Harry's cock sprang free.

"You know this is what you've been looking for." She dragged a fingernail over the leaking tip. "All those times you videotaped those other girls? You didn't really want them to perform for you, did you? No, you wanted to perform for them. Well now's your chance, little man. So what do you say?"

She continued teasing the head of his cock, scraping the tip with her nails. Harry swayed before her, groaning. He nodded, once, and with a ferocious smile, Tia yanked his shorts to the ground. Her hand slipped between his legs to fondle his balls. Harry gasped and spread his knees. The women clustered round him, catching him and supporting him as he surrendered to Tia's touch.

The camera went dark again. Mick and Joe sat on the couch, shivering. Mick's sweatpants were bunched around his hips. He gripped his throbbing cock with both hands. Joe did the same, his shorts pooled in a damp puddle around one ankle. When the camera came back on, they both flinched.

The image bounced up and down now, the sound of breath, fast and heated, in the background. Trees whipped past. Ahead, two naked figures stumbled through the woods—Harry and Dave.

"Fuck!" Harry cried. "Where are they?"

"Just run, dude. Run!"

A chorus of wild howls went up. Harry and Dave froze.

"Oh shit, man! Here they come!"

The woods around the two men erupted with wild whoops and cries. A hand reached out of the trees and grabbed Harry by the neck. Dave turned to bolt. He made it two steps before he was caught as well.

"Told you we'd catch you." Tia stepped out of the brush and pushed Harry to the ground. In one hand she carried a long, supple switch. She made a circling motion with the other. Whimpering, Harry turned around.

"Head down, ass up," she ordered, eyes blazing. Harry complied, letting out an anguished howl as the switch came down on his exposed behind.

Another cut. This time the scene jumped to a campsite. Harry and Dave scurried around a bonfire on their hands and knees. The women reached out as they passed, swatting at their naked backsides. Long red welts striped both men's thighs and buttocks.

"Add more weight!" a woman's voice called out. Harry and Dave were pulled to their feet, their legs forced apart. Mick gasped as the camera zoomed in on Harry's groin.

"What the fuck?"

A leather strap wrapped around the base of Harry's swollen cock. Below that, shiny metal rings encircled his scrotum, stretching his testicles and forcing them toward the ground. As Mick watched, a woman's hand grabbed Harry's balls and added another ring. The sound of Harry's weeping came clearly over the camera.

"What's wrong, Harry? Do you want to stop?"

"N-n-no ma'am!" he blubbered. The woman's hand stroked his rigid dick until a bead of liquid seeped out of the tip.

"What about you, Dave? Had enough?"

The camera panned to another erect cock, this one encased in a cage of metal bands and leather straps.

"Oh god, please..." Dave groaned. One of the women held out her hand, just beyond the reach of his cock, and he thrust his hips at it.

"Oh, this one's nowhere near done," the woman said.

"Neither is this one!"

The camera zoomed out to show Harry on his knees, humping another woman's leg.

"Maybe we should let these two play with each other," someone suggested. Howls of laughter, like the baying of wolves, went up around the campfire. The camera made another jump cut and suddenly Harry and David were kneeling on top of a picnic table. The women lounged around on benches, watching as the boys kissed and fondled each other.

"Looks like these two have played together before," Tia drawled. "Harry sure seems to know what Dave likes."

As she spoke, Harry pushed Dave back on the table. The cameraman complied, spreading his legs to allow Harry to slide between them. Mick felt a slow, electric buzz trail from the base of his cock all the way to the tip as he watched Harry lick and suck another man's dick.

"Good boy," Tia said, stroking Harry's head as it bobbed up and down. Moments later, Dave arched his back and exploded in Harry's mouth. Harry sat up, gasping.

129

"Now smile for the camera." Tia stood behind him and wrapped her arms around his waist. He groaned as she pulled on his cock. "Tell me," she murmured in his ear. "Just what were you going to do with this little movie of yours, anyway, hmm? Was this for your private collection, or were you planning to share this with some friends?"

Mick felt Joe stiffen on the couch beside him. "Don't do it, dude! Don't tell!"

"It's for my friends..." Harry gasped. He thrust eagerly into Tia's grasp. "For Mick ... and Joe..."

"And where, exactly, do Mick and Joe live?"

"Denver... Oh god!"

Harry thrust one last time and went rigid as a spray of white-hot semen erupted from his cock. He fell back against Tia, limp as a rag doll. As the camera faded to black one last time, the woman stared directly into the lens, her eyes piercing Mick to the bone.

"Mother of God." Joe stared at the darkened screen of the TV. His hands and cock were as sticky as Mick's.

"The note..." Mick dropped to the floor and fumbled for the slip of paper that had fallen out when he opened the DVD. In Harry's familiar scrawl, he read:

Sorry, dudes. They're coming for you next.

Mick looked up, heart pounding in his chest. "Joe, did you lock the doors earlier?"

"What? I don't know..."

Mick's eyes darted to windows where shadows gathered. He spun around as he heard the knob of the front door rattle.

"Who's there?" he called out.

A low growl swept through the room, like the call of a mountain lion. More growls came from the windows and the sliding-glass door. The knob on the front door turned and the door swung open. Even as Mick's knees turned to water, his cock grew hard again.

The Ice Cream Man Cometh

"Vanilla must be the new chocolate. Everybody's asking for it these days."

This is what the ice cream man says as I hand him my money. I don't answer. Honestly, I don't give a damn what's in vogue right now. The day is blistering hot and the cooling system on my shield suit is fucked up again. I'm sweating to death inside the only thing that keeps me alive beneath the naked sun.

The ice cream man sits in his truck and counts my money. "The weather AI says the burn index is in the seventies today."

That means a seventy-percent chance or worse of developing a nasty black burn on any exposed skin while I'm outside. I double-check the seals of my suit. I've been burned before, and I have the scars to prove it.

"Can we get going?" I ask, sweat trickling down my back.

"Yep. Just as soon as you pay the rest of your money."

"The menu says eighty-five!"

"There's a dairy shortage. Cows in Canada got some disease. Fifty herds put down this morning. Prices went up before I drove out."

"Bullshit!" I'm dying of heat prostration now. "You're just greedy."

"Maybe. Tell you what. You let me watch and we're good. Okay?"

"Whatever." He can watch all he wants, record it even. I don't care. I just need my damned ice cream.

The truck door opens. "Come on in!" he says with a bow.

I step into the embrace of the truck's refrigerated air. Once the door closes, I strip off my suit. I'm wearing nothing underneath except my burn scars and a pair of sweat-soaked panties. In a moment, the panties are gone too.

The ice cream man busies himself at the dispenser. "Vanilla, right? You want anything with that? Cherries? Sprinkles?"

"Just plain vanilla."

"Male or female?"

"Male. Make him short, about my height."

"One plain vanilla male, short, coming up."

He hits a button and the dispenser starts up. I watch cold milk and sugar blend with infinitesimal nanotech. Moments later, the machine squirts a thick layer of ice cream into a humanoid mold.

"Plain vanilla." The ice cream man sighs as he peels away the mold to reveal a short but muscular figure beneath. "Lady, you are boring."

"Still want to watch?"

"Why not? I got a camera here in the freezer section. I'll keep an eye up front and leave you two alone."

He lumbers through the hatch to the cab of the truck. I seek out the glassy eye of the camera above the door. So he'll record it, after all. Oh well. The frozen figure on the dispenser table stirs, its nanotech coming to life. Nanotech is an ephemeral thing. It only works at certain temperatures. So long as they stay cold, those tiny little bots will combine to form a skeletal structure and a simple brain to guide it. But only so long as they stay cold.

These days, nothing stays cold for long.

The vanilla man sits up, staring at me with blind white eyes. I put a hand on his chest. The touch of his frozen body sends more than shivers down my spine. An endless ache of nostalgia mingles with the thrill of desire inside me. When I pull my hand away, it's sticky with melted cream.

"I bet you taste good," I whisper into his frozen ear. I lick his neck. I'm not wrong.

When I was little, the ice cream truck came to my street every summer day. My mother always bought a single cone of vanilla to share. Nothing fancy, just a simple treat. "It's the best way to keep cool on a hot day," she told me, ice cream dribbling down her chin.

That was a long time ago, before the ozone layer evaporated and summer and winter bled together into an endless season of burn. Mother is gone now, dead of radiation poisoning, but the ice cream man is still here, and so is his frozen delight. I take a big bite out of the vanilla man's neck, then slide down his front, smearing ice cream all over my belly and breasts. I'm too hot. He's already melting. I try to slow things down, just taking small licks here and there. It will be weeks before I can afford this again, and it's not even real ice cream. All that crap about cows and milk—the cows died a long time ago too. Doesn't matter. It tastes like real vanilla, and if I close my eyes, it'll take me back to before, when ice cream was just a simple treat for a hot summer day.

My mouth finds an icy cock and I can't hold back any longer. I swirl my tongue around the head and lap at its base. Then greed gets the best of me and I take the whole damn thing in my mouth to suck hard as I can. My fingers sink into buttocks of half-frozen cream. The vanilla man shudders, not from pleasure, but from the loss of integrity. He's heating up and the nanotech can't hold it together much longer. He starts to melt in my mouth, and I taste the old summer days, feel the sunlight that doesn't kill. I swallow more and more of the vanilla man, working up past his balls and into his belly as he melts around me. When the nanotech finally gives up, he disintegrates and I'm bathed in a white, sticky mess.

The hatch to the cab slides open and the ice cream man comes in to hand me a towel.

"Did I bore you?" I ask, wiping away the mess.

"No, ma'am." His eyes fix on my sticky face. "I, uh, come by every month. I give a discount to my regulars."

I nod as I pull on my shield suit. The cost of the discount will be more recordings, but I don't care.

I have to have my ice cream.

Husbands and Wives

Davy sat alone at a scarred wooden table outside a small café. Twilight draped the sky above him in velvet shades of blue and purple. Stars studded the far horizon like crystalline splinters of ice. Their glinting light sent a chill down Davy's spine. This was his ninth evening in the city of Matrimony, and he still had yet to find his bride.

The door to the café banged open, startling the young man. A matron, heavy-set and gray-haired, pushed through carrying a pitcher. The hinges squealed in protest as the listing door swung shut behind her.

A week ago, the café had overflowed with patrons and the door had been brand new, painted in a checkerboard of bright red and green, the colors of marriage and fertility. The whole city had been new and bustling back then, built in the midst of the barrens to provide a meeting place for the throngs of prospective husbands and wives who came every season for the wedding festival. But the city, like the festival, was short-lived. Its temporary structures were little more than plywood shacks and canvas tents. None of it was meant to last. The paint on the café door, so bright and pretty eight days before, was now cracked and peeling. The awning above it sagged and all of Matrimony seemed to sag with it, tent stakes slowly pulling loose from the crumbling ground. There was nothing beyond the city's tarpaulin borders to support it—just miles and miles of sunburnt grass waiting for the place to fall. After tomorrow, it would, and Matrimony would become nothing but a memory to be packed up and put away for the next season.

The matron, a kindly woman named Magalia, wandered over to Davy, holding up the pitcher in her leathery hand. "Another drink, dear?" she asked.

"Yes, ma'am. Thank you."

He watched her refill his empty mug. "Don't you worry," Magalia told him. "It's not too late. There are still plenty of good women out there looking for a fine young man like yourself. You'll walk out of here with a bride tonight for sure."

Davy gave a weak smile in response and the matron shuffled off. The hinges squealed, the door swung shut, and he was alone again. His hands shook as he lifted the drink to his lips. He hoped the old woman was right. His mother and sisters were depending on him to make a good match, to marry a wealthy woman who would support her husband's kin. Of course, the richest brides had long since wed, having snatched up the most promising husbands on the first day of the festival.

Davy winced as he recalled that day, the day he had ruined his best chance. He had stepped off the dusty train that had carried him all the way from his home on the East Coast to Matrimony and was thrust into a maelstrom of shouting, frantic females.

"Are you healthy? Have you ever been ill?"

"How many children does your mother have?"

"Do you have sisters or brothers? Any children from them?"

"Are you a twin? A triplet, even? What about your mother or father? Are there any multiple births in your family?"

Prospective grooms filed off the train to become the immediate targets of intense scrutiny and speculation. The women turned them around, looking them up and down, all the while barking out their questions. The men could barely get a word in edgewise, but when they did, they parried with sharp queries of their own.

"Who is your family? What's their business?"

"How much money do you make?"

"What families are you allied with? What are their prospects?"

"Will you give my sisters a job?"

"Can you pay my mother's debts?"

The questions were as old as the wedding festival itself, and had become part of the ritual over the years. Men looked for wealthy wives to support their mothers and sisters. Women looked for husbands from healthy, fertile families to give them children. And Davy? He was looking for a place to hide.

A woman—thin, blonde, and sharp-featured—came up as he tried to make his way through the crowd and began to interrogate him. Scared, he backed away, only to run into a second woman who spun him around to check his teeth. A third woman came up from behind him and put her hand on his ass to give it a squeeze. With a wild howl, he twisted away and ran, shoving through the mob, desperate to escape the grasping feminine hands that reached out to stop him.

It had been too much, too terrifying. Before that day, the only women Davy had ever known were his mother, Joanna, and his sisters, Alicia and Grace. His entire world had consisted of them and the little bower where he lived in the back of their house, with its windowless walls and small enclosed garden. The only time he had ever been anywhere beyond the garden's high stone fence was on the day he had been born, and that was only because he'd come too soon, catching his mother unawares as she piloted her ship along the Elizabeth River.

After his birth, Davy's family met with one financial downfall after another. No matter how hard his mother and sisters worked, they could not dig themselves out of their growing debt. Though they never said so, Davy knew he only added to the burden, being an extra mouth to feed and an extra body to house and clothe. He couldn't work.

"Boy children are so precious," his mother often sighed. "If you left this house, strangers might steal you away!"

His only contribution to the family's finances lay in his potential as a future husband and father. Over the years, as the family business declined, more and more of his family's hopes became pinned on him until, at last, he was the only hope they had left.

"Marry well!" his mother had pleaded, wringing her hands as he boarded the train for Matrimony. "Our future depends on it, Davy. Make sure you marry for money, not love!"

Love. To his impoverished family, it was a luxury they couldn't afford. So was fear, but that hadn't stopped Davy from fleeing the swarm of voracious females buzzing around Matrimony's train station. He ran blindly through the city, feet pounding the dusty roads in time with his racing heart, until he collapsed at the red and green door of old Magalia's café. There, he curled up beneath one of the tables and sobbed. He wanted his mother and sisters, the only women he had ever known, ever needed. He didn't want those horrid creatures who pulled him this way and that like a dog on a leash. Why had his family sent him into this madness, he cried, wrapping his arms tight around his knees? Why?

Because of the baby, a small voice reminded him. Why else?

Three weeks before Davy left home, his sister Grace had given birth to a daughter. He remembered the infant, all pink and wrinkled, with eyes impossibly blue and wide with wonder. Grace had insisted on pressing the wriggling bundle into his arms, wanting him to appreciate the first good thing that had happened to their household in years. The vitality emanating from that tiny, perfect form had shocked him and he wept when he finally handed her back. He could still recall her sweet, fleshy scent and the tiny fingers that had gripped his own. As he hid beneath the table in Magalia's café, he wished he could see her again. He knew he never would.

It was his memories of the baby that finally brought Davy back to his senses. She needed food, clothing, a roof over her head that didn't leak, a warm bed at night, and so much more. No, she didn't just *need* these things. She *deserved* them. All his life, Davy had depended on his mother and sisters to care for him, and they had given him everything he needed until they were bankrupt. Now it was his turn to provide for them, to find a wife who could help his family get back on their feet and make sure the baby had whatever she needed, no matter what.

So Davy had crawled out of his hiding place, dusted off his clothes, and stumbled into the mob of anxious men and women, looking for his bride. The women came and went, asking their questions and answering his in return. There were several he would have wed, but his intentions went unrequited. He was a healthy, attractive male, but his family was so poor even the richest women refused to take on their debts.

He spent nine days and eight nights wandering through Matrimony, continuing his search. The matrons did their best to help, especially Magalia. Whenever she saw him hesitate, she coached him on what to do. But even with all that, he still had no luck. And with every passing day, his chances diminished. All around him men and women met, got married, and consummated their relationships. Then they disappeared, their business in Matrimony complete. Of the hundreds who had flocked to the transitory city, only a few dozen still wandered the streets, the last lonely candidates looking for a mate.

Davy set down his mug with a weary sigh. He should have braved it out at the train station and found himself a rich woman there. Instead, he had let his fear overwhelm him and that had cost him his best, maybe his only, chance for a good match. Tonight was his last night to find a wife, then came Beggar's Day, the last day of the wedding festival. If he was still unmarried by dawn tomorrow, the matrons would select a bride for him from among the only women left. Beggar's Day brides were notorious for their poverty. There would be little chance one could pay off even a tenth of his family's debts.

Not that there was much chance he could still find a rich woman tonight. It was so late. But the longer he waited, the poorer his wife would be. He needed to get out there and start looking. Maybe he'd get lucky. Maybe. Besides, wouldn't it be nice if he chose who he married, rather than have a wife assigned? In truth, it was the only choice he'd ever get in life. Better to take it while he still had it.

Davy pushed back from the table. Time to get moving. He'd walk the streets all night if he had to. He stood up, straightened his jacket, and looked out at the city.

And promptly sat back down.

A woman stood on the dusty path leading into the café. She was tall, with long dark hair and a flowing cotton dress. Swirling tattoos trailed down her bare arms in delicate henna spirals, depicting the traditional symbols of life and fertility. A smile played over her lips as she studied Davy.

"Hello," she said.

Davy stared at her. He had seen so many women in the past several days, more than he ever would have believed existed. No two had been exactly alike, but his reactions had always been the same. Alarm, dismay, frustration, apathy—he had run through a gamut of adverse emotions. But this woman was the first to elicit something different from him, something new and positive.

She did not stalk toward him, preparing to pounce on him and carry him off to the wedding chapel if he turned out to be good husband material. Rather, she approached him quietly, the way he'd once watched his mother approach a fallen baby bird before picking it up to put it back in the nest. A strange but pleasant prickle ran over Davy's skin as the woman walked toward him, and he felt as though he'd just woken up for the first time in his life.

"May I join you?" the woman asked.

His mouth gaped as he tried to form words. Why couldn't he speak? She stepped closer. Her dress swayed as she moved. The fabric was so delicate Davy could see the curves of her body outlined beneath, backlit by the fluttering lamps of the café.

"Are you all right?" she spoke again.

"Nice," he whispered, studying her curves. He felt the urge to reach out and wrap his arms around her ample figure. Then he shook himself. "No, I mean, fine! I'm fine."

The woman chuckled. "Hello, Fine. I'm Caroline."

Davy laughed with her, although he didn't understand the joke. His sister Alicia had warned him about dealing with women. "Laugh when they laugh, and listen when they talk. Whatever you do, don't just sit there with your mouth hanging open like an idiot!"

Which was exactly what he was doing now. Davy snapped his mouth shut and stood up quickly, knocking over his chair. He blushed, righted the chair, and then held out another seat for the woman who called herself Caroline.

"Would you... I mean, if you're not going anywhere..."

"Yes," she said. "I would love to sit. Thank you."

She gathered her skirts and settled on the sturdy wooden chair. Davy sank back into his seat, heart pounding. He thought his mother and sisters had told him everything he needed to know about Matrimony and the wedding festival, but somehow they had failed to mention this. His palms were sweaty, his face flushed. His privates felt rock hard beneath his jeans. What was happening to him?

With a start, he realized he'd let the silence stretch on too long. He was supposed to say something to the woman, but what?

"My name is, uh, Davy," he stammered. "I'm from the East Coast. Susannahtown on the Chesapeake. It's very nice to meet you."

The woman grinned. "As I mentioned, I'm Caroline. I'm from Bethany, in the Allegheny."

She held out her hand. Davy surreptitiously wiped his on his pants leg before clasping it. Her slim fingers felt warm in his grasp, with just a touch of calloused skin.

"Caroline, from Bethany. That's not too far from my family's home."

"No, it's close actually, especially if you travel by water."

They lapsed back into silence again. The woman, Caroline, settled back in her chair. The winsome smile he'd seen earlier returned to her lips. Davy's mind raced. This was very different from his other interviews. She wasn't pelting him with questions. What was he supposed to do? If he didn't talk, would she leave? Desperate to get the conversation going again, he said the first thing that came to mind.

"I, uh, I'm in good health. And I have all my teeth."

A look of surprise crossed the woman's face, followed by uproarious laughter. Davy cringed and covered his face with both hands.

"I didn't mean to say that." He could barely hear his own voice over her laughter. "I'm such an idiot!"

"No, no you aren't," the woman replied, wiping a mirthful tear from her eye. "You poor thing. Is that all anyone's asked you about? Your health and your teeth?"

He nodded, his face still buried in his hands. He heard her cluck her tongue.

"Oh now, don't hide. I didn't mean to laugh like that." She pulled his hands down and tucked a finger under his chin, tilting his face up to meet hers. "Come on, give me a smile and show me all those lovely teeth everyone wants to know about."

She was still chuckling, but the sound made Davy want to laugh with her in spite of his embarrassment. He felt a lopsided grin sprawl across his face.

"Oh, very nice. You've got a beautiful set of teeth, and a handsome face to go with them."

Her hand slipped from under his chin to stroke his cheek. Davy's heart skipped a beat. Her gentle touch was a far cry from the clutching and clawing of the harpies at the train station. He could happily marry a woman with a touch like that.

Marry for money, not love!

Inwardly, he groaned. The image of his mother beseeching him even as the train pulled away from the station rushed back into his mind. He didn't want to talk to this woman about money! But he had to. Stuttering again, he summoned up all the important questions his mother had drilled into him.

"Caroline, I was wondering... uh, what do you, uh, do? I mean, what's your family's business?"

The last words came out in a rush, and he felt like an even bigger idiot than he had when he'd told her about his teeth. But Caroline simply nodded and replied.

"My family owns a distillery. We make alcohol for spirits and medicines. The business does well. Very well, actually. We've even added a brewery for beer and we're thinking of buying some vineyards in a few years."

"Really?" He tried to keep an excited squeak out of his voice. "That sounds ... big."

"I suppose it is big. We ship our wares all over the region. By wagons and mule trains over land, and by boat down the river. We sell all up and down the James. Richmond's seen a boom in population the last few years, so we've been doing a lot of business in that area. Of course, we'd like to expand even further eastward, but—"

She stopped abruptly, shaking her head. "I'm sorry, Davy. I didn't mean to bore you with women's talk. Sometimes I just get carried away."

140

"What? No, please, I want to hear more. You were talking about doing business in the east? My sisters work at the docks in Susannahtown, for the warehouses there. They handle the incoming ships, unloading and sorting cargo. If you wanted to sell to the merchants there, you should talk to them. They know all the markets in the area, and they know who's buying what. And my mother knows everything about sailing on the river. She's a ship's captain. She's sailed up and down the James for years. She has charts too, old ones from before-times. They're the most accurate charts of the Chesapeake you can find!"

Caroline leaned forward and listened as he rattled on about his family. He needed to build them up until their years of experience and knowledge outweighed their misfortunes. If she understood how valuable they were, how hard they worked, she might marry him regardless of their debts. When he finally stumbled to a halt, the dark-haired woman let out a laugh.

"My god, you're very well educated," she said. "How did you learn all that, about ships and business? Did your mother and sisters teach you?"

He ducked his head. "Sort of. They talk a lot about business. I just listen. Sometimes, I even sneak downstairs at night to hear what they say when they think I'm asleep. I suppose I shouldn't eavesdrop on them like that. Not that I'll ever get the opportunity to do it again."

His last words hung in the air, a somber reminder of his fate. He would never go home again, never hear his sisters complain about their work or his mother worry about money. That was all in the past now. Marriage was his only course.

Strains of music drifted overhead, filling in the silence. Davy glanced up and saw Magalia hovering in the background behind Caroline. She smiled at him and jerked her head toward the street. A trio of matrons stood beneath the lamppost. The tallest played a soft melody on a teardrop violin. Her companions joined her on guitar and flute. Davy looked back at Magalia, who mimed a dancer with an invisible partner, then pointed at Caroline.

"Would you like to dance?" he said, breaking the stillness between them. "My sisters gave me a few lessons. I promise I won't step on your feet."

Caroline shook her head. "I'm not much of one for dancing, I'm afraid."

"Oh." Davy shrank back in his chair.

"Perhaps we could go for a walk instead?"

He jumped up, knocking over his chair again, but he didn't notice. Caroline took him by the hand and led him away from the café. Magalia waved them off, as teary-eyed as his mother had been on the day he left home. Davy's feet didn't seem to touch the ground. He floated by the musicians under the lamp, who smiled at the happy couple. He smiled back with a grin so wide he thought his face might split. He knew he must look like a fool beaming like that, but he didn't care so long as he was with Caroline.

She took him down the main avenue and then into one of the small parks that dotted the city. It wasn't much of a park—just a few benches, some potted trees, and a low stone wall surrounding a shallow pool of water. The pool had a roof over it with a crank and bucket, meant to look like a wishing well. Caroline sat on the side of the well and pulled Davy, still grinning, down next to her.

"Here." She fished into her skirt pocket and pulled out a coin. "Make a wish."

Closing his eyes, Davy clutched the coin in his fist before tossing it in.

"What did you wish for?" she asked.

"Toys. For the baby. One of my sisters had a little girl before I left. I want her to have nice things."

"That's very generous of you, to use your wish for someone else. You must love the baby very much."

He stared at the coin still visible in the well's shallow depths. The smile on his face diminished. "Grace named her Daphne, because it sounds like Davy."

"Then Grace must love you very much."

"She does. They all do. They've loved me all my life."

"And you love them."

"Yes."

"How much trouble are they in?" Caroline asked gently.

Davy looked up, fearful.

"It's all right." She squeezed his hand. "I just want to know."

He let out a shuddering sigh. "You'd find out eventually anyway. There's almost no money left. My mother lost her ship in a hurricane a long while back. She hasn't sailed in three years. No one will hire her, not even for crew. They say she's too old. My sisters work, but all their money goes to paying old debts, while new ones keep stacking up." He looked at Caroline's hand entwined with his. "My mother meant to keep me home

142

for at least another year, but with the baby in the house now, they need the money. So here I am. You're a rich woman, exactly what they hoped I'd find. You can support them for the rest of their lives. But they've got nothing to offer you except a mountain of bills."

"And you," Caroline added. "Isn't that something?"

He gave a bitter laugh. "What good is a husband? He serves one purpose, and that's it. A man from a rich family can do it just as well as a man from a poor one. And the rich man is a better deal. You won't have to support his family for the rest of their lives."

Caroline stood up. "You know, Davy, I think you spent one too many nights staying up late, listening to your womenfolk talk. You learned their business, but you also learned their despair and cynicism too."

"All I learned was the truth," he shot back.

"Did you?" She pulled him to his feet. "Then let me teach you a different truth."

"Where are we going?"

"To the chapel. We're getting married."

She dragged him along, ignoring his protests. How could she even think of marrying him after what he'd just told her? Yet her hand stayed clamped around his wrist in a gentle but firm grip and she pulled him, slowly, deliberately toward the center of the city.

The chapel was the heart of Matrimony, a sprawling tent of white canvas with a pair of interlocked red rings painted above the main opening. A matron, waiting out front, lifted the flap door and ushered them inside. Within, they found long rows of rickety tables, each stocked with papers, bottles of ink, and quill pens. In the midst of the tables, a series of heavy, scuffed cabinets squatted. A trio of matrons, dressed in the black robes of the Matriarchy, clustered before one of the cabinets, muttering amongst themselves as they sorted through one of the drawers. One of them looked up as Davy and Caroline approached.

"Ah, another happy couple. Come in, come in."

The oldest matron Davy had ever seen broke away from the trio and waved them over to a desk. A broad smile split her seamed face, but her eyes looked tired and sad.

"I'm Mother Janet, one of the officiators. This is Sister Rebecca and Sister Terry," the old woman said, gesturing to her companions. "They're acting as our witnesses tonight. So, you two all ready to get married?" Mother Janet didn't wait for an answer as she briskly sorted through a pile of folders on the desk. "Wedding contract ... wedding contract ... you'd think we'd have these out and ready to go, wouldn't you? But it's been so slow tonight... Ah! Here we go." With a flourish, she pulled out a sheet of paper from a folder and set it on the desk. "Bride's name and home town?"

"Caroline Gunston from Bethany in old Virginia."

"Good, good," the matron muttered as she inked a quill pen and scribbled across the page. "And the groom?"

Davy shot Caroline an anxious look. She squeezed his hand. "Go on," she said. "Unless there's someone else?"

He shook his head. "Davy. Davy Amherst from Susannahtown, also in Virginia."

"Oh, sweethearts from the same region. That's always nice." The matron added his name to the sheet. "Terry, do we have their registration letters?" Behind her, Sister Terry searched through the file cabinets until she found two papers and pulled them. She handed them to Mother Janet who laid them beside the wedding contract.

"Now I have a few questions for you two." She straightened up and took a deep breath. "Caroline Gunston of Bethany, this young man's mother offers her son to you as a husband. In return, do you offer support to her and her kin, to repay the loss of her child with sufficient dowry?"

"I do."

Mother Janet glanced at the registration letters on her desk. "Let's see. His mother asks for ... oh my." Her eyes, suddenly worried, flickered to Davy and back to Caroline.

"I'll pay it," Caroline said.

"Child, do you realize how much she's asking?"

"I'll pay it," Caroline repeated. "And you can add to it jobs for Davy's mother and his sisters, plus a trunk of toys for his sister's baby, Daphne."

Mother Janet's eyes widened with surprise.

"My goodness, that's a generous gift!"

Caroline smiled at Davy. "He's worth it."

Mother Janet beamed, the sadness in her face lifting for a moment. Then she turned to Davy.

"And you, young man. Do you understand the duty you are expected to fulfill? That the purpose of this marriage is to produce children?"

"I do."

"And your mother explained to you what would happen on your wedding night?"

"Yes, she did."

Mother Janet sighed. "Very well, then. Make your marks here."

She turned the contract to them, showing them where to sign. Caroline's flowing script seemed to overwhelm Davy's small block letters. The two sisters added their signatures below, then Mother Janet stamped a heavy seal on the contract and handed it along with their registration letters to Sister Terry to file.

"I now pronounce you husband and wife. May your union be fruitful and blessed with children. Sister Rebecca will show you to your tent."

Sister Rebecca led them through the chapel and out the back entrance. Outside were dozens of shelters, smaller versions of the chapel tent. Davy gripped Caroline's hand as they walked to the nearest one.

"You have until dawn to consummate the marriage," Sister Rebecca said, lighting a lantern posted in front of the tent. "Someone is always nearby, so if there's a problem, just call for us. Otherwise, we'll leave you alone until morning."

She walked off, looking like a grim shadow as she strode back to the chapel in her long black robes. Davy and Caroline stood outside the tent until she disappeared.

"Are you ready?" Caroline asked him.

"Yeah, I think so."

She grabbed the lantern and led him inside, ducking beneath the canvas flap. Davy followed on unsteady feet and nearly tripped over the piles of pillows and blankets spread out across the tent floor. He couldn't believe he was married. Caroline hadn't even flinched at the dowry his mother had asked for. And the toys for Daphne?

"Why are you doing this?" he asked suddenly. "You're rich. You were supposed to marry a man fresh off the train. Why did you wait to marry a pauper like me?"

Caroline set the lantern down. Its light cast long shadows across her face. "I've been here three times before, Davy. Three wedding festivals in the past eight years. And every time, I did exactly what my mother demanded. Marry a man from a well-off family. I've pulled husbands off the train depot, and married them within an hour of their arrival. I hated it every time. My mother died last winter, so I'm head of the family now. I

145

decide who marries and when. And one thing I've decided is that at least once in my life, I will marry for love, not money."

"You love me?"

"Yes, Davy. I love you."

She placed her hands on either side of his face and kissed him. His mouth went slack, giving his face the same idiot look he'd worn when he spotted her at Magalia's café. She kissed him again, slipping her tongue between his open lips.

"I love you," she whispered, "because you have nice teeth and a handsome face. And because you feel so warm."

Davy felt his jacket slide off his shoulders and land on the tent floor. His shirt followed. Caroline ran her hands over chest. The faint calluses of her fingertips brushed over his tingling nipples. His groin tightened in response.

"Caroline!" he gasped.

"It's all right." She snuggled against him. "Don't worry. I promise you, I will make this the best night of your life."

She kissed his neck and shoulders before kneeling on the blankets before him. When she nuzzled at his crotch, Davy groaned. His privates felt impossibly huge. Caroline tugged at the buttons of his fly, one by one, until his penis bounced free from its confines. With soft fingertips she stroked it, sending electric tremors up its length and along Davy's spine. When she slipped her mouth over the tip, his legs turned to jelly.

"Down," he gasped. "I have to lie down!"

He almost collapsed on top of her. He rolled onto his back, letting Caroline place a pillow beneath his head. She stripped off the rest of his clothes until he lay naked on the makeshift bed of the tent. The night air leaked through the seams of the tent, caressing his bare skin.

"What happens after tonight?" he asked, trembling. "Where will I go?"

She leaned over him, letting her dark hair tumble over his face. "You'll go home, with me. It's very beautiful. We live high up in the mountains, surrounded by woods. My sisters and I have a big house on a large tract of land. The place is full of children and laughter. There's a barn for the horses and cows, and we have a garden for vegetables. There are cherry trees too. They're in bloom right now. We've got pink and white blossoms everywhere." She paused. "There's a special house for the husbands. We built it on a hill overlooking the homestead. All the husbands are there, mine and my sisters'. It faces east, so it always catches the first light of day."

"Will we have a child?"

"Yes," she replied. "I'm certain of it."

They didn't say anything else after that. Caroline unbuttoned the top of her dress and put his hands on her full breasts, letting him feel their fleshy warmth. Her nipples tightened beneath his fingers. He kissed them both, hesitant at first, then with more confidence as his wife moaned. His wife! Seized by a sudden possessiveness, he pulled away the rest of her dress, touching her everywhere. He wanted to kiss every inch of her body, squeeze her round buttocks in his hands. His fingers glided over her rounded body, exploring every curve, every nook and cranny until they slipped through the tufted hair between her legs and found a secret wetness there. His penis stiffened at the discovery.

They went on like this forever, touching and kissing each other through the dark hours of the night. Davy never wanted it to end. But outside, the darkness began to fade.

"Dawn's coming," Caroline whispered. "Are you ready?"

His heart stopped. He felt her hand clutch his. He wanted to tell her no, the night had been too short. He needed more time. But then he looked in Caroline's eyes and saw the tears there. One night was all they'd been given.

"Show me how," he said.

She pulled him on top of her, fitting his hips between her legs. With one hand, she guided his erection inside her. The other she kept pressed to his face.

"Like this. Push in..."

He did, feeling her body close around his. The sensation struck up a fire in his groin. He'd never been so close to anyone else before. He pulled back and pushed in again, and then again. Each thrust was harder than the one before. Caroline lay beneath him, chanting his name. Her hand stayed on his face.

Another thrust and he felt something happen inside him. Something vital erupted from deep within and passed from husband to wife. Davy cried out and collapsed on top of Caroline.

The cold set in quickly, an icy tingle that started at his groin and spread to the rest of his body. "Caroline?" he whispered. He shivered.

"Davy, it's all right. I'm here, I'm right here."

Tears streamed down her face. She rolled him onto his back and stroked his cheek.

"I'm so cold..."

"Don't worry. It will be over soon... Oh Davy!"

He reached for her hand with numb fingers. "Do you love me?"

"Yes. I love you! I will always love you! And I will take you home with me and lay you to rest in the husbands' house on the hill. And our child will grow up happy and healthy, and I will take care of your family for as long as they live. I promise. I love you, Davy!"

"I love you too," he gasped. Then he closed his eyes and was gone.

Caroline sat for a while, holding her husband's cold hand. When the matrons came, they helped her dress and then wrapped Davy in a winding sheet. Mother Janet performed the final rites.

"This is the fate of all men," she intoned, her seamed face grave with sorrow. "To be born of woman, live out their days, and return to a woman's embrace at death. Let us hope Davy's sacrifice bears fruit. He will live on in his child."

Caroline kissed Davy's cold lips one last time and prayed. Please, God, let their child be a daughter.

A son would break her heart.

FUTURE PERFECT

"Sahir came... Sahir comes ... is coming, will have come..."

It sounded like a lesson in verb tenses, but it was actually the beginnings of a prescient vision, the kind Nadine only got when she was on the verge of a twenty mega-ton orgasm. The word *come* sounded promising, but my name was Aaron, not Sahir, and it kind of bothered me to hear Nadine call out another man's name when things were getting hot and heavy. Not that I thought she was involved with anyone named Sahir. It's just that after spending two years as her boy-toy, it would have been nice to hear my loving domme shout *Aaron, Aaron!* when she was about to blow.

"Sahir will come ... will come..."

Well, at least she was with me physically. Gray eyes glazed, vision turned inwards, Nadine cinched a piece of surgical tubing around my freshly shaved balls. All the while, she kept muttering about Sahir. I bit the penis-shaped gag stuffed in my mouth and groaned. I should have realized playtime wasn't her top priority when she brought me into the lab instead of the apartment upstairs. Most dominatrices have a dungeon. Not Nadine. She was a scientist, so she had a lab and a test subject, a very willing test subject.

From the start of our relationship, she'd measured all my responses, tested my physical and mental capacities, and analyzed my phobias and fetishes. Feminization ranked as my fifth-worst fear as well as my second favorite turn-on, which meant wearing frilly panties got me so hard it scared the hell out of me. So naturally, Nadine had transformed me into a little girl for this particular session. I stood before my latex-clad domme, hands secured behind my back, wearing a lacy pink baby-doll dress with matching socks and patent leather shoes. A pair of itchy ruffled panties hung around my ankles. I had cried when she made me put them on, then breathed a sigh of relief two hours later when she finally yanked them down to torment my cock.

"Sahir comes ... comes up to the register ... he counts the till..."

Damn, still talking about Sahir. Sahir was the guy who ran the convenience store a few blocks from Nadine's house. He got robbed once a month, but she'd never had a vision about it before now. Why the hell was he so important this evening?

"Sahir counts the till ... a boy is hiding ... hiding in the store..."

Beads of sweat formed around a series of flat metal disks pasted to Nadine's forehead. More disks lay hidden beneath the red latex suit that encased her from neck to ankle. The wireless electrodes, one of Nadine's early inventions from the days she worked for a biotech firm, stood out as stark white patches against her dusky brown skin. They transmitted her brainwave activity to a nearby computer where all Nadine's visions were recorded for later analysis.

"The boy pulls out a gun ... Sahir doesn't see ... he counts the till..."

As her vision grew more intense, I stole a peek at the computer's monitor. A series of wavy lines crawled across the screen. The third line from the bottom, the one Nadine said represented her theta waves, began to spike. Did that mean she was close to coming, or was that a symptom of the vision she was experiencing?

Wham! The stinging smack of a paddle on my ass drove any further questions from my mind. Even through the vision, Nadine had sensed my straying attention. To correct me, she picked up a small leather flogger and began slapping my cock with it. With every stroke, my tortured dick bounced up and down.

Nadine continued muttering about Sahir and the hidden boy. I writhed before her, caught in a hellish mix of agony and ecstasy. Beneath the surgical tubing, my balls swelled and ached. The throbbing head of my cock turned purple and started to leak. A buildup of pressure at the base of my dick told me I was almost home, but just as I was about to drop to my knees and explode, Nadine tossed the flogger aside and spun me around to face the examining table. I wanted to scream in frustration, but the gag made it pointless to try. Even in her current state, the lady knew exactly how to take me to the edge and keep me there for hours on end.

"The boy is hiding ... a red-haired boy hides, pulls out a gun ... Sahir counts the till..."

Christ, could she just shut up about Sahir? Nadine grabbed me by the neck and bent me over the table. I heard the snap of latex and felt a cold dollop of lube hit between my ass cheeks. My third-worst fear and all-time favorite kink—anal penetration—kicked into play as Nadine's slender gloved fingers spread the lube around my clenched hole.

Heart pounding, I wriggled and bucked, desperate to break free. Hell if I was going to let some woman finger-fuck me! I was the guy, *I* was supposed to do the penetrating. No way was I going to stand there, dressed up like fucking Shirley Temple, and take it up the ass from some bitch!

Nadine grabbed me by the scruff of the neck and shoved me back down on the table. With my hands cuffed and my ankles hobbled by those damn ruffled panties, there wasn't much I could do except whimper into my gag. Then Nadine slipped a couple fingers inside my sphincter and I just melted. Waves of pleasure rippled through my body as she eased them in and out of my hole. I couldn't fight her. I didn't want to. It felt good when she fingered me, calling me her sweet boy, playing with my cock while she stretched my hole wide. I wanted her to fuck me. I wanted her to bend me over and make me cry. Most of all, I just wanted to hear her say my name.

"Sahir looks up ... he sees the gun ... Sahir..."

God dammit! I started struggling again. I didn't want to hear about Sahir and some stupid robbery. I wanted Nadine to focus on *me*.

"Sahir sees the gun ... the boy with the gun..."

Nadine forced me back down on the table and slipped a third finger inside me. My knees started to shake. I'd never taken more than two before. Now I was stretched impossibly wide. A million different feelings flooded my brain—fear, pleasure, shock, shame, excitement, relief... I had Nadine's attention, all right. That one extra finger had put me into orbit, and she knew it. If she did anything else...

"The boy pulls out the gun ... puts his finger on the trigger..."

I was so excited I could barely hear the words anymore. Nadine grabbed my hair and pulled me upright as she continued to work my ass. As soon as I was standing, her hand snaked around my waist and gripped my cock. I forgot all about Sahir and Nadine's vision. I rocked my hips back and forth, thrusting into her clenched fist and then back onto the fingers of her other hand. I started to moan and shiver, all my senses focused on my throbbing dick and my aching hole. The buildup inside me grew and grew and grew...

"Sahir sees the gun ... the boy pulls the trigger ... the boy pulls... Oh god, Aaron... Aaron... Aaron!"

My name at last. The sweetest sound in the world issued forth from my lover's lips as I shot my load all over the examining table. Behind me, I felt Nadine stiffen and shudder. Her hand tightened on my cock, squeezing

151

the life out of it along with the last drops of cum. Completely exhausted, my knees gave out. Nadine and I sank to the floor.

Nadine pulled the gag out of my mouth. I turned to curl up against her, burying my face in her neck. "Oh Nadine, oh god I love you," I whimpered.

Panting, she stripped off the latex glove and tossed it aside, then held me tight to stroke my hair. "It's all right, baby. Mama's got you."

I wriggled closer for a kiss. She gave me a squeeze, then straightened up.

"Honey, we got to get moving." She pushed me away and struggled to her feet. "Come on, get up. We've got to go."

"Nadine, please!" But she was already pulling me up after her. With a quick tug, Nadine undid the restraints from my wrists. She tore the electrodes off her face and scalp and grabbed the coat she'd left hanging on a nearby wall hook. Then she snatched my clothes off the floor and shoved them into my arms.

"Don't just stand there, Aaron, we've got to go. Sahir's in trouble."

"What, you saw him getting robbed again?" I snapped. "He gets held up all the time. Why the hell are we running out to help him tonight?"

"Because tonight he gets shot and killed!"

Nadine glared at me, her grey eyes sparking. Shamefaced, I dropped my gaze to my patent leather shoes.

"Can't we just call the police?"

"They won't get there in time. Now come on, we're leaving."

She spun on her heel and raced out of the lab, pulling on her coat as she went. I yanked up my panties and ran after her. I prayed no one would see me stumble outside to the car. The engine was already running by the time I slid into the passenger seat. As Nadine tore off down street, I struggled into my clothes. Oh well, at least she said my name when she came.

*　　　*　　　*

I first met Nadine Edwards Walker at the Westside National Bank. She was a scientist and inventor preparing to start her own business. I was the loan officer handling her application for a commercial loan. Back then, she couldn't see the future, but when she walked into my office, I had a feeling my entire world was about to be turned on its head.

It was her suit, I think, that I noticed first. It was a power suit, but not in the traditional sense of the word. The black silk jacket and pants clung to her trim figure the way an exotic perfume clings to the skin. Though conservatively tailored, the garments hugged her delicate curves, showing off every detail of the body beneath. I caught my breath at the hint of her nipples pressing through her jacket, and the absence of any panty lines beneath her slacks. No undergarments, then. On another woman, that might have seemed obscene. On her, it was simply stunning.

The epitome of feline grace, Nadine reclined in a leather chair before my desk, patiently allowing me to gawk at her. I spent several moments admiring her soft brown skin, slim hips, and small firm breasts before I finally looked up into her luminous gray eyes. The moment our gazes met, I felt a wave of vertigo so strong it almost knocked me out of my seat and onto my knees. I didn't realize it then, but at that moment, I had surrendered my will to her completely.

I jumped when she finally cleared her throat and took charge of our meeting.

"You're Mr. Friedman, I presume?"

I lurched out of my chair to offer her a trembling, damp hand. "Call me Aaron, please. Uh, may I call you Nadine?"

"No," she said, a smile tugging at the corners of her full lips. "But you may call me ma'am or Dr. Walker."

I sank back in my chair, my stomach in knots over her gentle rebuff. "You're here for a business loan?"

She nodded slightly.

"What, uh, sort of business are you hoping to start?"

"You didn't bother to read my application, young man?"

The tone of her voice, patient but chiding, sent a hot flush creeping up the back of my neck. "I did read it, actually."

"Then you should already know the answer to your question."

"Oh." The flush passed my neck and flooded my face. I dropped my gaze down to the document on the desk before me and started thumbing through it.

"Try the first page," she suggested.

"Yes, ma'am," I mumbled, nearly dropping her application in my haste to comply. "Uh, it says here 'health technologies—research, development, and sales.'" I dared to glance up. "That's a bit vague. What sort of research are we talking about here?"

"I'm a clinical scientist, specializing in certain aspects of human health. I create therapeutic products designed to enhance well-being and improve quality of life."

"You mean like medical equipment?"

"Not exactly."

"Well, what sort of products, exactly?"

"I suppose you would call them sex toys."

The clock in my office ticked loudly as I sat with my mouth hanging open. The corners of Nadine's mouth curved a bit more as she waited.

"You want a loan," I began, "to research and develop ... sex toys?"

"Specifically clitoral stimulators, anal vibrators, dildos, masturbation sleeves, lubricants, restraints, paddles..."

The list went on and on, and the more she spoke, the more discomfited I became. We were in a bank, of all places, discussing a business loan, yet here she was rattling off a list of obscene novelties and marital aids. Listening to her made my cock swell until it felt like it was about to burst the zipper of my pants. I squirmed in my seat, on the brink of embarrassing myself, when I finally interrupted.

"Dr. Walker!" I gasped. "Please stop."

She arched an eyebrow at me. "You did ask for specifics."

I bit my lower lip. "Look, I'm sure making and selling sex toys would be a profitable business, but Westside National Bank is a respected commercial institution. We can't approve a loan for that sort of thing."

"Why not?"

"Well, for starters, sex toys are..."

"Obscene? Dirty? They're not illegal, in case you're wondering. I checked the state and local laws."

Completely flustered, I buried my face in my hands. "Whatever they are," I said in a muffled voice, "sex toys are not 'health technologies'. They don't improve anybody's well-being or quality of life."

"Really?" She arched an eyebrow at me. "Scientific studies have shown that a healthy sex life can boost the immune system, relieve stress and anxiety, reduce cholesterol levels, increase blood circulation..." She ticked off the benefits on her fingers. "It might even slow the aging process."

"That's very interesting but—"

"Conversely, sexual inhibition has the opposite effect. A person who has trouble engaging in fulfilling sexual encounters frequently suffers from long-term stress, and we all know what that leads to—headaches, sleep disorders, gastrointestinal problems, a suppressed immune response, poor work performance, memory loss, heart disease, and worst of all, sexual dysfunction which leads to further inhibition which leads to even more stress. It's a vicious cycle."

"Fine," I said. I gripped her loan application tightly to keep my hands from shaking. "Sex is good, inhibition is bad. But I still don't see how selling someone a vibrator is going to improve their health."

"You've never used one before, have you?"

My face turned beet-red. "I don't need one. Vibrators are for lonely old women who can't get a date."

"You might think differently after you've tried one out."

I opened and closed my mouth a few times, but couldn't get any words to come out. Nadine chuckled and stood.

"Here's my address," she said, handing me a card. "Come by tonight and take a look at what I'm working on before you decide to reject my application. I'll see you at eight."

Then she left. I spent the rest of the afternoon locked in my office. I didn't come out until a quarter of eight to avoid running into anyone who might question the wet stains on the front of my pants. When I pulled out of the bank parking lot, I turned left instead of right. It was a fifteen-minute drive to Nadine's place, and the start of our affair.

*   *   *

Nadine sped down the road as I fought to pull on my jeans. The problem with Nadine's epiphany orgasms was that she always had to act on whatever it was she saw. I had nothing against doing good, but some of the things Nadine did to change the future scared the hell out of me. Like driving to a convenience store in the middle of the night to face off against an armed thug who was going to kill someone. That didn't make sense to me.

"I still think we should call the police," I argued. I pulled off the pink baby-doll dress and tossed it into the back seat, then shrugged into my leather jacket.

"So call them."

She tossed her cell phone to me. It slipped through my hands and slid under the seat. "What the hell am I supposed to say?" I said, scrabbling to find the phone.

"Tell them you saw a man, about twenty years old, with red hair, enter the Stop-N-Go on Granby Street. You thought you saw him pull a gun out of his pocket when he went in."

She spun the wheel and the car careened around a corner. The cell phone skidded away from my fingers as I cracked my head on the dash.

"Ow! Crap, Nadine, slow down. I can't find the damn phone."

"Too late, lover. We're already here."

The car screeched to a halt. Nadine killed the engine and jumped out. I snagged the phone and stumbled after her.

"Ah, Miss Nadine, Mr. Aaron. My favorite customers!" Sahir greeted us as we entered the store, his round face splitting into a wide grin. "Are you getting married yet? You know, you make a very lovely couple."

Personally, I thought we made a very odd couple—Nadine the sleek black lioness and me, her pasty-white slump-shouldered boyfriend—but I didn't bother saying so. Sahir continued beaming at us from behind the register, his dark head bobbing in time with the frenzied beat of Bollywood pop music. An altar stood on the counter beside him, its small brass statue of Ganesh obscured by a cloud of blue smoke. Between the thumping music and the perfumed fog that enveloped the counter, I wasn't surprised Sahir never noticed a robber until it was too late.

"Sorry, Sahir, no wedding plans just yet!" Nadine had to shout to be heard over the music. "Is that a new scent you're burning?"

"Oh yes, very nice, isn't it? Jasmine and honeysuckle, perfect for young lovers such as you two. My sister's husband imports it straight from Mumbai. A dollar fifty-nine a pack, aisle number four."

Nadine smiled and wandered over to the incense, pretending to pick some out. All the while, her eyes darted up and down the aisles, searching. When she noticed I hadn't moved from the front door, she hissed at me and pointed to the back of the store. I scowled, but shambled past her to look for a redheaded gunman. I hoped he wouldn't shoot me when I found him.

He wasn't anywhere to be seen, though. Aside from Nadine, Sahir, and myself, the only other person in the Stop-N-Go was a paunchy, middle-aged suit browsing through the magazines. I couldn't see the guy's face, but I was pretty certain he wasn't Nadine's would-be murderer. I started to head back to the front of the store when the suit reached for a magazine and saw me.

"Friedman?"

I froze. I knew that voice.

"Friedman, is that you?"

Slowly, I turned, the blood draining from my face. "Mr. Smythe, what a surprise."

Horace Winston Smythe III, vice president of commercial lending at Westside National Bank, stared at me. "What are you doing here? You're supposed to be at the bank working on the Henderson account."

"Ah, the Henderson account," I stammered. "Well, sir, the risk assessment report still isn't back from the underwriters, so I couldn't finish the paperwork today. And uh, it is rather late—almost midnight, in fact. I thought I would finish up on the Henderson account tomorrow morning."

Smythe scowled. "Need I remind you, Friedman, that our customers expect us to handle their applications in a timely fashion?"

"No sir, I understand we need to process this loan quickly. Henderson Jewelers is anxious to expand their business and we don't want them going to our competitors."

"Hmph. Make sure you get that risk assessment report first thing tomorrow, Friedman. I want to see the completed loan package on my desk by Friday."

"Yes, sir."

"One more thing, Friedman." Smythe gave a desultory sniff as he eyed my faded jeans and leather jacket. "We may not be in the office right now, but you are still expected to dress to a certain standard. You never know when you might bump into a client. Is that clear?"

I bit my lip. "Yes, sir. Perfectly clear."

Smythe abandoned his magazine and marched out of the store. When he was gone, I rushed back to Nadine. "We have to go," I whispered. "Now!"

"We can't. If we leave, Sahir will get killed."

"No he won't! Your gunman isn't here."

"He will be."

"How do you know? Maybe he shows up tomorrow night."

"I saw the date on the calendar by the register."

I squinted. "How the hell could you see anything through all that smoke?"

"I *saw* it, Aaron." She glared at me. "If the guy isn't here yet, he will be. We just have to wai—There he is!"

Nadine dragged me down behind a rack of Sugarbaker's Donuts. We crouched there, peeking around the corner as the front doors swung open. A greasy kid with red hair and a grungy oversized army jacket shuffled in. One of his pockets sagged suspiciously, as though it contained something heavy, like a gun. The door to Sahir's office swung open and the kid darted down an aisle, out of sight.

"I told you," Nadine said. "Let's go."

I pulled out Nadine's phone. "No, I'm calling the cops. Don't—"

But she was already up and moving. I checked the counter. Sahir stood at the register, his head still bobbing to the Bollywood beat. Oblivious to his impending demise, he opened the register and pulled out the till.

"Fuck!" I flipped open the phone and dialed 911. The dispatcher picked up on the first ring and I started babbling. "I need help. I'm at the Stop-N-Go on Granby Street. There's a kid in here, he's got a gun. Uh, red hair, maybe about twenty? You gotta hurry, my girlfriend's back there—"

"I know your mother!"

I dropped the phone as Nadine's voice sang out, loud and clear, over Sahir's music. Scrambling to my feet, I spotted her at the back of the store. She had the red-haired kid backed up against a SnakPak display. I watched in horror as she chattered at him brightly.

"Your mom and I used to hang out together, you know that?"

"Nah, lady, you don't know my mom."

He shuffled from side to side, refusing to look her in the eye. She stepped closer and kept talking.

"Sure I do! We used to see each other at Heber's Market all the time. My gosh, I haven't seen her in years. How is she?"

"I don't, uh, I mean, no, you got the wrong guy!"

"Oh no, I know you, young man. Your mother talked about you all the time. So what have you been up to lately?"

Pale and sweating now, the kid tried to push past Nadine, but she matched him move for move, blocking his escape. I stood stock-still as they seemed to dance together in the aisle of the Stop-N-Go. Then the shriek of a siren split the air. The kid snarled and grabbed Nadine.

"No!" I shouted.

As soon as I spoke, all the sound cut out like I'd suddenly gone deaf. Mouth dry, I watched the boy shove Nadine hard. She fell backward in slow motion, her head slamming into the shelves behind her. Bags of pork rinds and salted nuts flew into the air. The kid bolted for the front door. It slammed shut behind him. The sound came back with a vengeance as I let out a blood-curdling scream.

158

"Nadine!"

In the distance, sirens continued to wail.

*   *   *

About four months into our relationship, Nadine had a nosebleed.

It happened on product-testing night. We were in the lab on the first floor of her house, a big white room, brilliantly lit and overflowing with computers and scientific instruments. The place vaguely reminded me of the college lab where I'd barely scraped through Intro to Chemistry with a C-minus. Nadine's lab, however, lacked the stinging scent of antiseptic that had always turned my stomach. Instead, it smelled of oranges and mint with an undertone of sandalwood. In other words, it smelled like her.

For the evening's session, Nadine had chosen to wear a formfitting bodysuit of stretchy material that changed colors according to her mood. It was one of her latest inventions, something she called "biofeedback fashion." When she was relaxed, the bodysuit was pale blue; when she became aroused, it turned bright red; and when she was about to come, it darkened to a velvet black. Right now, its color was a medium violet, with patches of scarlet around the breasts and groin.

By contrast, I wore nothing but a set of nipple clamps connected by a silver chain. The chain itself was nothing special, but the clamps did interesting things. Like Nadine's suit, they also worked on biofeedback, but instead of changing color, they changed temperature, growing colder as my nipples grew harder.

"Too few people realize how erotic thermal stimulation can be," Nadine purred as she tugged gently on the chain. I sucked in a sharp breath. My nipples, which she had already teased into tight little knots, tingled as the clamps gave off a perceptible chill.

"Very good," she murmured as she touched one of the clamps. "That feels nice and cold. What do you think, Aaron? Do you enjoy it?"

"Oh god, Nadine, oh please..."

For me, nipple play was one of the ultimate forms of sexual torment. Nadine liked to tease my nipples for hours, setting up an endless circuit of buzzing electricity that ran from my aching nubs to my cock and back again. My dick would stand straight up and beg to be touched. Nadine would deliberately ignore it, leaving me to helplessly hump the empty air while she continued to pinch and tease my nipples and, in general, drive me crazy.

159

"Hmm. Subject seems to enjoy the product," Nadine noted on a clipboard. She set the clipboard aside and turned back to me with a smile. Her suit, I noticed, had turned a vibrant shade of vermillion.

"Please, Nadine?" I whined. I stood with my hands clasped behind my head and waggled my hips, hoping to brush my dick against her thigh. With a soft chuckle, she sidestepped me.

"Poor baby, does that naughty cock of yours need some attention? Well I have just the thing. Climb up onto the examining table so Mama can show you what she's been cooking up in the kitchen."

I scrambled onto the table to sit facing her, my ass slipping over the cool vinyl surface. She spread my knees wide apart to expose my cock, balls, and anus. Then she picked up a small jar from a nearby medicine cart, dipped her fingers inside it, and scooped out a dab of thick white cream.

"What is it?" I asked, teeth chattering as the nipple clamps emitted another chilly vibe.

"You'll see. So how was work today?"

I groaned. Another of Nadine's favorite ways to torment me was to ask me about my job while she worked me into a frenzy.

"Terrible." I could barely grunt out an answer. Nadine had reached between my legs and was smearing the cream over my balls and around the base of my cock. It felt cold and smelled faintly of lemongrass.

"Spread your legs wider," she ordered. I complied and she smeared more cream behind my balls and over my prostate. "What happened at work that was so terrible?"

"Smythe ... keeps hassling me, oh god ... about the Steinway ... paperwork. Wanted me to stay late again... Nadine!"

Her fingers slipped over and around my balls, massaging the cream into them. I writhed on the table, trying to rub against her hand and relieve my growing need, but everything was too slippery. Without friction, I couldn't gain any satisfaction.

"Stand up," she ordered. "Turn around. Bend over and spread your ass with both hands."

I whimpered as she spread more cream between my cheeks. "Sounds like you had a rough day," she continued. "Did you try any of the stress relief techniques we talked about?" I nodded. "Which one?"

"The vibrator..."

Nadine's idea of stress relief was a good orgasm, and she'd given me a number of techniques, and toys, for achieving one when work became too aggravating.

"Tell me exactly what you did."

She turned me around and wiped my crotch with a towel. I stared in shock as a patch of pubic hair came away with the cream. Nadine spared me a glance.

"It's my new depilatory cream. Removes hair almost instantly without causing any chemical burns. Smells a lot nicer than anything currently on the market, too. Now answer my question."

In short, halting phrases, I described the half-hour I'd spent locked in my office, sitting at my desk with my pants around my ankles. The vibe I had used was a small, flexible finger-sized device, and I had applied it to my prostate with one hand while I stroked my cock with the other. Nadine prodded me for specific details, like how long it took me to come, whether or not I used lube, what had I fantasized about while jerking off, and did I prefer that particular vibrator over any of the others she had given me. All the while, she continued wiping away my pubic hair. By the time I'd finished relating how I'd climaxed all over my desk, my groin was as smooth and pink as a baby's behind.

"You should have inserted that vibe inside your ass," she chided me. "That way, you could have given yourself a buzz anytime you needed during the day, rather than wait for lunch to lock yourself in your office."

I was too stunned by my freshly denuded pubis to respond.

"Very nice," she said as she stroked the now bare skin. "Very smooth and very sexy. I may never let you grow out your pubic hair again."

"I can't believe you did that. It's just gone, all of it!"

"Oh don't fret, honey." She stepped back and unzipped her bodysuit, pulling open the now reddish-black fabric to reveal the naked body underneath. My heart skipped a beat when I saw her pussy was just as hairless as my cock. "Remember, what's good for the goose is good for the gander."

I didn't bother to ask for permission. I simply dropped to my knees in front of her and began nuzzling her smooth cunt. With one hand, she parted her bare lips while grabbing me by the hair with the other. The nipple clamps turned ice cold, and no longer restrained, I was finally free to rub my aching, frustrated cock against Nadine. I humped her leg, shivering at the touch of cloth against my hairless ball sack, and cradled her ass with both hands. Nadine didn't like sloppy work. She'd trained me to use light,

161

delicate strokes of my tongue, all the better to extend her enjoyment. But she was already wet when my tongue touched her slick folds, her clit peeking out of its hood. I applied myself with eager delight, matching the rhythm of my licking to the pumping of my hips against her leg.

"Good boy," she crooned. "You're so good ... the light is green, green, the traffic light is green..."

My ears perked up. When Nadine gave instructions, I had to be quick to follow them. Otherwise, she'd turn me over her knee and paddle my ass hard. But saying the light was green? What exactly did that mean?

I dismissed what she said the moment she pushed my face into her pussy. That was a direction I could follow, and I did, lapping at her more quickly than before. She kept talking, though, about a green light, saying things that made no sense. Then I heard something that stopped me cold.

"The light is green... Chavez crosses the street, Ernesto Chavez walks across..."

Why the hell was she talking about someone named Ernesto Chavez when she was with me?

I didn't have a chance to ask. Nadine started riding my face, pushing hard against my mouth until she was almost suffocating me. Part of me wanted to shove her away and scream at her for calling out another man's name. Another part was already too far gone to care. My hips moved of their own free will, rubbing my cock raw against Nadine's shin. I couldn't stop myself. Believe me, I tried.

"Ernesto Chavez crosses the street ... the light is green ... a car turns the corner ... yellow car ... too fast, turns the corner... Ernesto Chavez goes to work, goes to the bank, the light is green, the yellow car turns the corner too fast too fast too fast—Oh god, Aaron! Aaron!"

I came just before she did, my screams of rapture muffled by her pussy. With her cunt pressed into my mouth, I caught every drop of wetness when she came. For a few, brief moments, I clung to her, squeezing her lower half tight against me as I made small animal noises of gratitude and relief. Then I remembered her calling out another man's name, and with a snarl, I struggled to my feet.

"What the hell was that about?" I shouted. "Who the fuck is Ernesto Chavez? Nadine?"

She swayed before me, eyes glazed, blood pouring from her nose. Her mouth opened as though she wanted to speak. Then she toppled forward. I caught her just before she hit the floor.

"Nadine, wake up!" I clutched her shoulders and gave her a shake. "Christ, you're bleeding. Please, wake up!"

"Aaron?" Her eyes fluttered, locked briefly with mine.

I was almost ready to faint myself, but I forced myself to stay calm. "I'm right here. You're gonna be okay."

"Who's Ernesto Chavez?"

I sat back, dumbfounded. She'd said his name over and over as I licked her pussy, and she didn't even know who the hell he was? What was this, some kind of stroke?

"He goes to the bank, Aaron. Westside National. I saw it..."

Something clicked inside my brain. Ernesto Chavez, short, balding, a wife and two kids who were very active in extracurricular sports. He was a loan counselor at the bank where I worked. Every quarter he hit me up for the kids' latest fundraiser.

"Who is he?" she muttered to herself. Then she shook her head and struggled to sit up. She wiped a hand across her face. It came away sticky with blood.

"We need to get you to a hospital," I said numbly. Why the hell was she talking about Ernesto Chavez?

"No, baby, I'm fine. It's nothing. I've already seen a doctor."

I blinked. "What? You mean this isn't the first nosebleed you've had?"

She shrugged and tried to stand, then sank back to the floor. "Well, it's the first nosebleed, but I've been having headaches for a couple of weeks now, so this isn't a big surprise. Weather's been kind of dry lately. It's just a little sinus trouble, that's all."

"Headaches," I repeated, shaking. "For the last few weeks. Why the hell didn't you tell me about them?"

She waved me off. "It's nothing, okay? I just need to get a humidifier in here. It's winter and the air in the lab is too dry."

"Fine. Headaches. Whatever you say."

I got up and grabbed my clothes from a hook on the wall. I could feel Nadine watching me, her eyes boring into the back of my head.

"Something wrong with me having a headache?" she asked.

"No."

"Don't lie to me. This is bothering you and I want to know why."

"You mean aside from the fact that the lower half of your face is completely covered in blood? Aside from the fact that I just spent the last fifteen minutes with my face in your cunt, listening to you yell about some

163

other man?" I threw my clothes down. "Why don't *you* try telling *me* the truth, huh, Nadine?"

"I am telling the truth," she said through gritted teeth. She rolled over onto her hands and knees and used the examining table to pull herself up. "It's headaches and that's all, and I don't know why the hell I started talking about that guy. Maybe it has something to do with the headaches, maybe not. Fuck, Aaron, I've been to a doctor. I had a CAT scan done and everything. There's no sign of brain tumors, no sign of stroke or injury. Maybe I had a mild seizure and that's why I started talking about what's-his-name."

"Ernesto Chavez."

"Whatever! I don't know. I'll go back to the fucking doctor if you want, have them check for epilepsy. But all I know right now is it's just a damn headache!"

"Do you get one every time we make love?"

She froze. "No," she answered slowly. "Not every time."

"But you're only getting them *when* we make love."

"How the hell do you know that?"

I pushed the heels of my palms into my eyes to keep from crying. "Because," I choked out, "that's what happens. Every single time."

Nadine tottered over to me and put her arms around my waist. "Baby, talk to me. I don't understand what's going on."

The tears came in spite of my best efforts. "It's just... Fuck, every girl I ever cared about came down with headaches. Every single fucking one! I'd meet someone really attractive, someone who I thought understood and cared about me, and then two or three weeks into the relationship they'd start complaining about getting headaches whenever we had sex. I mean, how cliché is that? Sorry, honey, no sex tonight. I've got a fucking headache!"

Nadine snorted. "Didn't any of these stupid bitches ever hear of aspirin?"

"They weren't stupid," I hiccuped. "That was just ... just the nicest way they could figure out to get rid of me. They kept having headaches and turning me down until I finally figured out it was time to go."

"Why would anyone want to get rid of you?"

"Because I'm a filthy pervert! Because I want... I want..."

I broke down sobbing and we were back on the floor again, Nadine cradling me this time. "You want," she murmured to me, "to be loved, as you are, kinks and all, and there's nothing wrong with that, baby."

Then she rocked me back and forth and told me she loved me over and over until I finally believed her. I didn't mention Ernesto Chavez again, and neither did she. I didn't even think about him until two days later, when I saw him crossing the street on his way into Westside National Bank. He broke his right femur and six ribs when a taxi came tearing around a blind corner and hit him, and the only reason he wasn't outright killed was because I saw the green traffic light and managed to shout out a warning.

*   *   *

"Ma'am, are you sure you don't want to go to a hospital?"

Nadine and I sat on the curb outside the Stop-N-Go. A cop stood over her, a concerned frown on his face. Sahir knelt behind her, pressing an ice pack to the back of her head.

"For the last time, I'm fine. Sahir, will you relax?" She snatched the ice pack from him and winced. "Any word yet on the kid?"

The cop straightened up. "No, ma'am. He was long gone by the time we got here. You gave us a pretty good description, though. We'll keep an eye out for him. Meanwhile, why don't you head home and get some rest."

"Yeah, I'll do that."

The cop ambled back to his partner waiting by the squad car. They talked for a moment and then one of them smirked and pointed at me. I stared back, perplexed. Grinning, they climbed into the car.

"Nice shoes," one of them called to me as they drove off.

I looked down at my feet. "Oh fuck!"

Nadine glanced down and noticed my patent leather shoes. "Honey, it's not a big deal."

"Easy for you to say. You're not the idiot wearing pink Mary Janes and getting laughed at."

"Actually, Mr. Aaron," Sahir piped up, "I think your shoes look very nice. They match your fancy shirt."

He pointed at the bit of ruffled lace poking out beneath the bottom of my jacket.

"Fuck me..." I muttered, yanking my jacket down to cover my waist. What Sahir had thought was a shirt was actually the pair of stupid ruffled panties I was still wearing.

"Sahir, I think Aaron and I will go home now."

"Yes, yes, Miss Nadine. You take good care of yourself, please?"

I slunk back to the car, blushing furiously. "Dammit, you could have at least let me change!"

Nadine slid into the driver's seat. "I'm sorry, but there wasn't time."

"There wasn't time? My boss was in the store. He saw me!"

She started the engine and pulled out of the parking lot. "You mean the old guy checking out the porno mags?"

"Smythe doesn't look at porno mags. In case I haven't mentioned it, he's a tad *conservative*. He doesn't approve of things like porn, or extramarital sex, or bondage, or—"

Nadine shrugged. "Okay, I get the point. But so what if he saw you in the Stop-N-Go? For all he knew, you were there to get coffee."

"He made a comment about how I was dressed. Said jeans and a leather jacket weren't professional. What if he'd seen these stupid shoes?" I kicked them off and held them up to her. "I could have lost my job!"

"Will you just calm down? You're not going to lose your job because of your footwear."

"You got that right!"

We were driving past a local park. I rolled down the window and threw out the shoes. They flew past a streetlamp and disappeared into the night. Nadine stomped on the brakes and the car screeched to a halt.

"Aaron Joseph Friedman, you get out right now and find those god-damned shoes!"

"No!"

"No? *No?*"

Suddenly, it was a race to see who could get out of the car the fastest—me, so I could find the shoes, or Nadine, so she could fetch a leather paddle from the trunk and give me the spanking I knew I'd just earned. I made it out first, but that didn't stop Nadine from coming after me. Paddle in hand, she chased me toward the streetlight where I'd last seen the shoes. The first blow landed on my ass before I reached it. Even through my jeans, it stung.

"Ow, ow! I'm sorry!"

"Not as sorry as you're going to be if you don't find those shoes!"

Nadine's warning sent me scrambling into the park. She came striding after, wielding her paddle with alarming accuracy. Beyond the limits of the streetlight it was pitch dark. I couldn't see a damn thing. Frantic, I dropped to my knees and felt around for the shoes in the grass.

"You found them yet, young man?"

I shook my head. "No, ma'am!"

The paddle slammed into my ass, driving me forward several inches. My balls tightened. My pulse beat faster than Sahir's dance music. Oh god, she was pissed with me.

"Keep looking!"

I fumbled around in the dark, straining to catch a glimpse of pink patent leather. Nadine stayed right behind me, prodding me on with the paddle. Long minutes passed, punctuated by the recurring slap of leather on denim. My ass felt hot and swollen before I finally blundered across the shoes.

"Found them, ma'am!"

"Put them on."

As I squeezed my feet into the shoes, Nadine strolled over to a nearby bench. The park was empty, I noticed with relief. No one, not even a wino, had witnessed the humiliating consequences of my temper tantrum. But Nadine wasn't done with me yet and I knew it. Shivering with dread, I crawled over to where she sat.

"Up on my lap, young man."

I stood up and straddled Nadine's leather-clad legs, lowering myself to sit facing her. Hot pain shot through my buttocks as I settled on her thighs. I felt like a naughty child waiting for Nadine to scold me. Instead, she unbuttoned my jacket, exposing my bare chest to the cool night air.

"Why did you fight me in the lab earlier?"

The question caught me off guard. I had expected her to berate me for tossing away the shoes. I had almost forgotten our session in the lab.

"I just... I don't know."

She said nothing. In the dark, I could barely make out her face, but I could feel her gaze fixed squarely on me, demanding a better answer. I ducked my head and fumbled for something to say.

"I guess ... it was the panties maybe, or the dress. And we've never done more than two fingers before." My face went hot as I lied. Anal penetration scared me just as much as being dressed like a girl, but it never failed to make me come, and Nadine knew it. She clucked me under the chin.

"Come on, Aaron. You got rock hard the moment you saw those panties you claim to hate so much. As for how many fingers I had inside you, you started struggling before I'd even gotten started." She held up an index finger as though to emphasize her point. "You sure calmed down though once I slipped inside you."

I shifted uncomfortably on her lap. My ass throbbed from being paddled, but that wasn't what made me fidget. Our conversation was headed into dangerous territory.

"I've been your domme for months now," Nadine continued. "I know the difference between what turns you on and what really scares the hell out of you. What we were doing tonight should have put you on cloud nine. Instead, you started fighting me. So tell me the truth. Why?"

Her warm hands slid up my bare chest. The tips of her fingers traced small circles around my nipples, slowly spiraling inward until they brushed against my stiffening nubs. I shivered as she gently pinched one.

"I didn't want you to come," I whispered at last.

"Because of the vision I was having?"

I nodded. Then I shook my head.

"It's not the visions," I said in a shaky voice. "It's what happens afterwards. You could have been killed tonight. Why the hell did you corner that kid in the store?"

"I had to distract him so he wouldn't shoot Sahir."

"You could have been shot instead!"

"But I wasn't," she said calmly. "Because you called the police and the kid ran when they showed up."

"You still got hurt," I went on. My hands started to shake along with my voice. "Why do you always do these crazy things? You can't even be certain the future you're trying to prevent is even going to happen."

"First of all, if I see something, it's going to happen," she insisted. "We've collected enough data in this department to know that. And second, what I do to prevent what I see isn't crazy. It's responsible."

I stared at her. "Responsible? Like what you did when you had a vision about a bomb being planted in the Mega-Mall? Remember what you did to prevent that?"

"I called the police," she answered calmly.

"You called in a bomb threat to the police!"

"Well, I wanted them to take the threat seriously, and they did. They cleared the building, they sent in a bomb squad, the bomb squad found the bomb and defused it, and nobody got hurt."

168

I put my hands over my face and groaned. "And if the police had ever traced the phone call back to you, you would have been arrested for calling in the threat. You might have even been accused of planting the bomb yourself."

"That didn't happen, though. We took precautions remember? You said, 'Don't call from home', so instead we went to a public payphone. You even insisted I wear gloves so I didn't leave any fingerprints on the receiver. No one ever figured out I made that call."

She went back to playing with my nipples, kneading them between her fingers until a slow sweet ache spread from my chest to my groin and I squirmed in her lap. Her hands dropped to the fly of my jeans and I squirmed some more.

"Baby, I know what I do scares you sometimes, but we saved a man's life tonight."

She eased the zipper open and pulled down the ruffled panties to reveal the head of my cock. I put my arms around her neck and rocked back and forth on her leg while she teased the swollen tip. I wanted so badly to quit arguing with her and just enjoy what she was doing, but part of me couldn't quite let it go.

"One of these days," I whispered, "you're going to get in trouble."

"Not as long as I've got you around to help me."

With that, she placed her mouth over mine and silenced any further arguments I might have had.

*   *   *

When I was in college, I had a string of girlfriends, none of whom lasted very long. I had no problems meeting women in those days. In fact, no sooner did one relationship end than another would begin. My problem was none of them ever lasted more than three months. Headaches ruined them all.

I tried not to take it personally at first. Headaches are the oldest excuse in the book for avoiding sex, and I didn't expect women at that age to be savvy enough to know how to tactfully say, "Sorry, this just isn't working for me."

But when girlfriend number four began complaining about migraines every time we made love, I grew suspicious. The pattern was too obvious. I'd meet a girl—beautiful, charming, intelligent, and shall we say, "sexually adventurous"—fall in love, and spend several sweaty nights fumbling my way into her heart. For a couple months, things would go well. I wasn't the greatest catch in the world, but I worshipped each and every one of my girlfriends, and they didn't seem to mind dating a guy who wouldn't hesitate to drop to his knees and lap at their cunts until they came screaming.

About two months into the romance, when I was certain that this girl was *the one*, I'd suggest trying something different in the bedroom—a mild spanking perhaps. I wanted to be on the receiving end, of course. Even back then, I knew what I was. None of my girlfriends ever said no and more than a few seemed delighted to try. Thus I'd spend a few blissful weeks bent over the knee of a gorgeous coed as she eagerly blistered my bottom.

Then the headaches would start.

Toward the end of my sophomore year, I was dating a petite blonde sorority girl named Lila Snedeker. We'd been dating for almost four months, longer than I'd ever dated anyone else. She never complained about headaches, never said no when I wanted to make love, and when I cautiously broached the idea of her tying me up and spanking me, she pulled a set of handcuffs out of her purse and told me to strip. Lila was everything I'd ever hoped for and more. Then one evening when I tried to kiss her, she simply got up and walked out of the apartment.

"Where are you going?" I demanded, running down the steps of my apartment building after her.

"I've got a headache, okay?"

The word *headache* hit me like a punch in the gut. "No, it's not okay! You don't just get up and leave because you've got a headache. Why can't you take a fucking aspirin or something?"

"Because!"

"Because what?" I shouted. "Look, if you don't want see me anymore, fine. At least have the decency to say so, instead of marching out like some fucking uber-bitch on the rag!"

The insult reverberated through the hallway. Lila turned on me, hissing like a cat. Some of the other residents cracked open their doors to hear her response.

"You want to know why I'm leaving? I'll tell you. It's because you're a fucking pervert, and I don't do perverts, okay? You wanna get off, go pay someone to beat your ass, you freak! I never should have gotten involved with you. Everybody knows you're nothing but a sick queer. Marcy Chang said you asked her to finger-fuck your ass. Ann Southfield said you wanted her to shave your balls and then use a damn dildo on you. Well, I'm not doing that, you hear? Nobody in their right mind would date a faggot like you!"

We stood there, staring at each other, in a state of shock. The cement floor of the hallway fell away and I sort of hung there in mid-air, unable to walk without something solid beneath my feet. Lila put her hand to her mouth, either to hold back anything else she might say or to keep from being sick. I couldn't tell. Somewhere, from one of the apartments, I heard a snicker. Voices whispered, "Daaaaaaaamn," and, "What a sick fuck!"

"Aaron, I... I'm sorry," Lila whispered. "It's the headaches. I've been having them for weeks. I just can't take it anymore." Tears streamed down her face as she turned and ran away.

Lila never returned my calls, and I never saw her again. Whether or not everyone knew about me before our fight, they certainly knew afterwards. I didn't think I'd ever have another girlfriend as long as I lived, so I swore off dating, but it didn't last. A week after Lila left, I met another girl—sly, dark, and eager to see if the rumors were true. I didn't want to go out with someone who was hoping to prove I was a pervert, but for some reason, I felt compelled. Her name was Roxanne, she was abusive, and she lasted six weeks before the headaches got to her too.

There were other girls after that. Sometimes they were nice like Lila. Sometimes they were like Roxanne. They all came to me and whether I liked them or not, I couldn't turn any of them down. As girlfriend after girlfriend left me, the rumors about me spread. Eventually, I became a campus joke—Aaron "The Freak" Friedman. Spank his ass and watch him go. Bend him over, he won't say no.

*   *   *

I woke up in Nadine's bed the next morning. My nipples felt raw and sweetly sore. Welts on my ass sent sharp jolts of delicious pain shooting through my body. My semi-erect cock was still cupped in Nadine's hand. I'd fallen asleep as she'd lovingly jerked me off, but had spent the night embroiled in nightmares I could only half recall.

"Morning, lover," she murmured as she opened her eyes and sat up slowly. "You sleep okay?"

Staring at the ceiling, I shrugged. "Nadine, when you have a vision, what's it like?"

She pursed her lips, thinking. "It's like a dream, maybe, only without the weird warping of time and place that dreams always seem to have. It's like I'm standing there, watching events unfold in real time. In fact, the only thing dreamlike about it is that I'm watching myself watch what's going on around me."

"Do you see me when you have a vision?"

She leaned over for a kiss. "Always, baby. You're right there in front of me. I can see you, hear you, touch you. No vision's going to stop me from making love to my beautiful boy."

"That's not what I meant. I meant, do you ever see me in your visions."

"Why? You think something bad is going to happen to you?"

Nadine began to nibble at my neck. I sat up abruptly, pushing her away. She flopped back on the bed and sighed.

"You're not still upset about last night, are you?"

I picked at a wrinkle in the sheets. "You saw Sahir in your vision last night, right?"

"Obviously."

"And the kid who was going to shoot him."

"Uh-huh."

"You saw yourself in the Stop-N-Go?"

"Clear as day. I was there in the store, but I didn't know what was going to happen yet."

"What about a heavy-set, balding guy in a suit? You see him?"

"Your boss? I guess."

"Yes or no, Nadine. Did you see him?"

"Yeah, I saw him, flipping through the magazines."

"Did you see me?"

She paused, thinking. "I saw a lot of things. I guess..." she trailed off.

"Did you see me?"

"No," she answered at last. "But I couldn't see the whole store. You were in there somewhere, probably standing by the front door. I'm certain of it."

"What about in your other visions? Have you ever seen me?"

"I don't keep track of something like that, Aaron."

"Bull." I turned to look at her. "You record every single vision, every detail you see, and how things turn out when you intervene. It's all in the red notebook in your nightstand."

She sat up beside me. "All right, I've never seen you in a vision. So what are you getting at?"

I shook my head. "I don't know. I just wanted to know, I guess."

"You sure that's all?" she asked, rubbing my back.

"Yeah." I threw the sheets back and climbed out of bed. "I told Smythe I'd be in early this morning. I've got a client he's desperate to push through for a loan."

"You got time for breakfast?"

"No. I'll eat on the way."

We didn't say anything else. I showered, dressed, and got out the door in less than twenty minutes. Nadine gave me a kiss and a worried look as I left. During the drive to the bank, fragments of my dreams kept floating through my head. Images of Lila Snedeker screaming at me about her bleeding nose as she slowly morphed into Nadine. Smythe flipping through magazines at the Stop-N-Go, whispering about how I'd lost the Henderson account because I couldn't work without a vibrator shoved up my ass. A redheaded gunman singing, "Spank his ass and watch him go. Bend him over, he won't say no." The whole thing had been set to a Bollywood pop soundtrack.

Nadine saw the future. It always turned out the way she said. So what did it mean if she didn't see me?

Maybe I didn't have a future with her at all.

*   *   *

Nadine never had another nosebleed again. In fact, her headaches stopped soon after she had the vision of Ernesto Chavez being hit by a taxi. That was when mine began, however. I had always known Nadine was intent on saving the world, but I thought she'd do it by building better orgasms through modern technology. Until the visions started, I'd never realized how strongly she felt about things like personal responsibility and the need to do what's right.

"If we know someone's going to suffer a catastrophe before it actually happens," she once explained, "then we have an obligation to prevent it."

"Since when did other people's problems become ours?" I remember asking. The stern look I got in response was enough to shut me up on that subject for a while.

In spite of the troubles Nadine's visions caused, I knew I should consider myself lucky. For instance, at least she didn't attribute her visions to God. Being a scientist and a rationalist had long ago led her to atheism, and was I ever thankful for that. Bad enough Nadine was seeing the future and acting on it. I don't think I could have handled it if she had gone all religious on me too. Although, I did appreciate it when she wore her leather nun outfit and made me play the naughty altar boy.

No, Nadine did not look to God for answers. Instead, she turned to science. She observed, recorded, tested, and tried to predict the circumstances under which the visions occurred, and quickly came to two conclusions. The first was that the more intense her orgasm, the more vivid and detailed the vision she received. The second was that the best way to achieve such orgasms was to indulge in her favorite sexual pastime—namely, dominating me. Simple masturbation wouldn't do the trick, unless I was watching and she was doing it to drive me crazy. Thus, it became crucial that I participate in all her experimentation. This had led to a year and a half of the best sex I'd ever had.

It also led to a year and a half of me wondering when I was going to get caught with my pants down, so to speak. Four years of being known as Aaron "The Freak" Friedman had definitely left its mark on me. The name, the rumors, and the reputation hounded me through my last two years of college and into grad school. The day I finished my MBA, I fled all the way across the country to escape the constant staring, pointing, snickering, and gossiping that followed me everywhere I went on campus.

I took a job at the first place I interviewed, Westside National Bank. From day one, I threw myself into my work and quickly rose through the ranks to become one of Westside's top loan officers. I worked eighty hours a week, thus ensuring I never had time to indulge my sexual perversions. Even on weekends, I woke up at six, drove to work, put my nose to the grindstone until ten p.m., then went home and collapsed in bed. On holidays, when the bank was closed, I brought work home.

I thought my dick would shrivel up and die from lack of attention, but I was too afraid of my own desires to even masturbate when I was alone. I had a high-paying job with no social life and no hope of sexual gratification, but at least I was safe from the never-ending cycle of headaches and heartbreak that had plagued me for years. For a time, my life was copasetic.

Then Nadine came along and blew everything out of the water.

I couldn't say I wasn't a willing accomplice. I was. Six years of abstinence and fear had taken a brutal toll on me. When Nadine and I first met, I'd just hit the ripe old age of thirty. I had almost as much gray in my hair as black. My desk was stocked with antacids, blood pressure medications, and the ultimate irony, prescription drugs for migraines. My cholesterol level was okay, but my blood pressure was through the roof and, more than once, my doctor told me I was likely to have a heart attack before I hit thirty-five. I suffered from half a dozen stress-related health problems and if I didn't find an outlet for that stress soon, one day I'd likely have an aneurism and die.

Nadine was the cure for what ailed me. She captured my cock and my heart, forced me to confess my darkest desires, and then ordered me to give in to them. If I balked at acting out one of my intimate fantasies, she'd tie me up and "force" me to perform the deed, leaving me free to enjoy without guilt.

I could stop her, if I wanted, by using the safe word she made me choose. It was supposed to be something completely unrelated to our sexual relationship, but I cheated a little. I chose "Lakshmi," the Hindu goddess of fortune. Sahir kept a small figurine of her in his store behind the register, next to Ganesh. I noticed it the day I first met Nadine, when I went into the Stop-N-Go to pick up a package of condoms. I told myself dourly that I'd probably never get to use them, and I was right, but not for the reasons I'd predicted. Nadine had developed several brands of her own contraceptives, and we tested them all our first night together.

Lakshmi. In the two years we'd been together, that safe word had never passed my lips. For some reason now, it was always on the tip of my tongue.

*   *   *

I sat in my office and stared blankly at the ceiling fan slowly turning overhead. Things were starting to spin out of control. I loved Nadine—needed her, in fact—but I wasn't sure how much she loved me anymore. Changing the future had become her top priority. Her visions were putting my job and the safe little façade of my life at risk.

These thoughts twirled around in my head, keeping time with the blades of the fan. A small tic started beneath my left eye, a nervous symptom I hadn't experienced since before I hooked up with Nadine. My heart pounded a little too loudly in my ears, a sure sign my blood pressure was up. I glanced at the clock on the wall. It was only nine a.m. Still three hours until lunch.

"Fuck it," I muttered. I pulled out my briefcase, opened up a hidden pocket within, and fished out a cock ring—a special toy Nadine had invented just for me. With a sigh, I settled back in my chair and unzipped my pants. Then I put the cock ring down on the desk and stared at it. What the hell was I doing?

I picked up the ring again and twirled it around my fingers. It warmed to my touch and contracted a bit before beginning to vibrate soundlessly. My cock twitched as I handled the device then set it back on the desk again. Freed of my touch, the ring went dead.

"Just use it," I muttered to myself, staring at the ring. "Use it and blow off some steam. You'll feel better afterwards."

My hand crept toward the ring and closed around it. With a sigh, I leaned back in my chair, prepared to slip the ring over my hardening cock. Then a knock came at the door.

"Aaron? Are you in?"

The door cracked open. Shit, I'd forgotten to lock it! I sat up, hastily tucking my shirt back into my pants, and dropped the cock ring into my jacket pocket. Scooting up to my desk to hide my growing erection, I picked up a random file and began reading.

"Come in," I said.

"Aaron?" a woman's voice spoke. "I have the Henderson risk assessment ready for you."

I didn't look up. "Thanks. Just leave it in my inbox, okay?"

I heard a rustle of paper as the report slid neatly into the tray. There was a moment of silence, followed by a slight cough. Reluctantly, I looked up.

"Yes ... Francine?" I guessed that was the name of the woman standing before me, but I couldn't be sure. Her face was pretty, but not enough to stand out in my mind. All I remembered was that she worked in the underwriters' office a few doors down the hall from me.

She smiled as she leaned against my desk, displaying two even rows of bleached white teeth. "My name's Felicity," she corrected me.

"Sorry." My fingers tapped rapidly on the desk. I flattened my palm to silence them.

"I overheard some interesting gossip about you this morning," Felicity said.

My fingers went back to tapping out a rapid staccato beat. I swallowed hard. "Gossip?"

"In the break room. Smythe was doing his usual morning rant about us slacker employees. Apparently he saw you last night at some trashy little convenience store. He said you looked like a punk kid, ready to tear up the town and paint graffiti all over the sidewalks."

"Aaaaah ... well, we did run into each other last night. I was on my way to a party. Smythe didn't approve of my casual dress."

Felicity laughed, a sharp little noise that grated on my ears. "Must have been some party. He said you were wearing ripped jeans, no shirt, and a pair of nipple rings."

"Mr. Smythe was exaggerating," I replied with a forced smile. "I was wearing jeans and a leather jacket, but no nipple rings."

"And no shirt?"

She trailed a finger along the edge of my blotter, watching me with hooded eyes. The hairs on my neck stood up with a nervous prickle. When I finally spoke, I had to work to keep my voice steady.

"Is there something you want, Felicity?"

"Maybe," she answered with a coy smile. "I'll let you know."

With another bark of laughter, she sauntered out of my office. As the door closed behind her, I broke into a cold sweat. What did she know? What was she after? I put my head in my hands and began to hyperventilate. I was too scared to contemplate the answers.

*   *   *

"Mmmm, baby, you are way too tense."

I lay naked on the bed, face down and trying to relax. Nadine sat astride my hips, massaging oil into my back. It was quite a switch from the previous evening, when she'd dressed me up as Little Lady Fauntleroy and tormented the hell out of me. But Nadine claimed she felt the need to pamper her boy, so tonight I was getting the royal treatment. Too bad I couldn't seem to enjoy it.

Something about the whole scenario struck a false note with me. It wasn't out of character for her to coddle me—there'd been times before when I'd shown up from work, frustrated and tired, and Nadine had simply undressed me, made love to me, and tucked me into bed—but tonight she was being too nice, too considerate. Instead of taking charge and telling me what to do, she acted uncertain, like she didn't want to push me for fear I

177

might break. That worried me. People tended to get rid of things that broke.

"I swear, you've got knots in your back that even a sailor couldn't untie," she declared as she kneaded my shoulders. "You have a bad day at work today?"

I shook my head. I didn't want to talk about work. Work reminded me of Felicity and her creepy overture. After our initial conversation, she had continued to hit on me every time I stepped out of my office. In the break room at lunch, she cornered me by the microwave, surreptitiously sliding her hand over my ass as she pretended to make small talk. When I left work, she tailed me to the parking lot. I had to duck behind a minivan and hide for half an hour before she finally gave up looking for me and went home. Just thinking about her made the muscle below my eye twitch.

Nadine sighed. "Not work, huh? Maybe something else is bothering you, then?"

I grunted as she pulled and twisted handfuls of rigid muscle. "Just tired, that's all."

"Hmmm. Well, you just lie there and relax. After last night, I'm thinking maybe we ought to spend a quiet evening at home, have a little cuddle time. Nothing too intense."

"Why is that?" I asked, face pressed deep into the pillow. I wondered if it muffled the hint of fear in my voice. "I could go for something intense right now."

"I don't know, baby. We've been at it pretty hard lately. I figure it's time for a change of pace."

"You're afraid I can't handle it anymore, aren't you?"

She left off massaging my back. I waited for an answer.

"Aaron, I just don't want you to be unhappy," she said at last. "But you are unhappy. Downright miserable, in fact."

I pushed up off the bed, twisting around to look at her. "I'm not miserable, I'm fine. Pull out the paddle and the cuffs. I'm up to doing anything you want to do."

"No, you aren't. Look, last night you tried to talk to me about the visions and I sort of blew it off. This morning I realized I should have listened to you more, but now you've clammed up. I just..." She raised her hands in a helpless shrug. "If the visions are upsetting you, then maybe we should take a break from them for a while and focus on each other instead."

"Wow. Take a break from seeing the future? Can you actually do that?"

Nadine frowned at my sarcasm. "We know intense orgasms trigger the visions, right? So I was thinking we could just stick to plain ol' vanilla sex for a while. That way, we can be intimate without setting anything off."

"So you're going to sacrifice all your enjoyment just to baby me."

"Damn, you are so set on being passive aggressive tonight." She rubbed her forehead, inadvertently smearing massage oil across her face. When she looked back at me, there was a glint in her eyes. "Look, I love you and I know you love me, but we've obviously got some problems going on here, so we're gonna fuck like ordinary folks for a while until we can figure things out, okay? Or do you have a problem with that?"

I slumped back on the bed with a laugh. Nadine was no longer walking on eggshells with me. She was taking charge of her boy again, and I could finally relax. "No, ma'am. I don't have a problem with that. Just one question, though."

"What's that?"

"Do you even know how to have vanilla sex?"

She narrowed her eyes in mock indignation. "Just you watch, young man."

With a sigh, I settled down into the bed and let Nadine work her magic on me. Her hands glided over me in long, soothing strokes. She worked slowly, starting at my neck and gradually making her way down to my ass. The knots in my back slowly loosened and I began to drift, the bed beneath me morphing into a cloudbank that carried me far away from my troubles. Nothing could disrupt the peaceful easy feeling that settled over me like a blanket. Nadine loved me. All my earlier doubts and worries about our relationship evaporated as she began to rain gentle kisses on my neck and shoulders.

Nadine gave me a gentle nudge and I rolled over. The kisses continued down my chest and along both arms. When she reached my hands, she sucked on my fingers, and then worked her way back to my nipples. My cock hardened, trained like Pavlov's dog to respond to any stimulation of my tight pink nubs. Instead of making me whine and hump the air in frustration, though, Nadine slipped a hand between my legs and stroked my swollen shaft. By the time she wrapped her lips around the head of my leaking cock, I was well on my way to Nirvana.

Long slow sucks alternating with a flickering tongue kept me moaning on the bed. When she sheathed my cock in her hot wet mouth and began sucking in earnest, I whimpered. Her hands squeezed my ass, holding me still as her mouth slid up and down the length of my dick. My eyes rolled into the back of my head as she started to hum.

"Oh, Nadine, I'm so close. God, I'm so close..."

The humming deepened, changed, and took on a strange rhythm. The vibrations of her voice sent chills through my balls and up and down my spine. My orgasm began to roll through me in slow ripples of pleasure, followed by a creeping tide of dread.

"Sahir comes ... comes ... to the register..."

Even with her mouth full of cock, I could make out the whispered words. My whimpers turned into groans of despair. This wasn't supposed to happen. Nadine said it wouldn't. Safe, vanilla sex was supposed to keep the visions at bay.

"Sahir comes ... comes ... sees the gun... Sahir comes..."

Every word resonated down the length of my cock and into me. My orgasm kept coming, slowly, surely like the swell of a tidal wave. I wanted to scream at Nadine to stop, but she was blind and deaf to me now. She kept sucking and humming, relaying the vision as it came to her. I thought of grabbing her by the hair and pulling her off me, but my arms seemed trapped in the bed sheets. Even if I could move, I knew I couldn't stop what was coming. It was already here.

"Sahir sees the gun ... sees the boy, sees the gun ... the gun ... the gun... Aaron, the gun!"

Like a shot, my cock exploded, spraying hard over Nadine's face. I felt the bed shudder beneath us as the orgasm passed in a wave from me to her. With a low moan, she convulsed between my legs as though she was having a fit. This wasn't supposed to happen, I thought again. She said it wouldn't. She promised.

"Aaron?" Nadine looked up at me with glazed eyes. She shook her head. "We have to go, baby. It's happening again..."

Her voice sounded distant, hollow, and confused. I watched in stunned silence as she stumbled from the bed, wiping her face with the back of her hand. I prayed she'd stop and climb back into bed, but within moments she was gaining speed, pulling on clothes as her mind came back to the present.

"Get up, baby. We've got to go back to the Stop-N-Go. Sahir is still in trouble. That boy is coming back."

"Don't," I pleaded even as she handed me my clothes. "Nadine, please don't do this."

"I have to!" she hissed. "That kid's going to kill him."

With hands of clay, I began pulling on my things. When I didn't move fast enough, Nadine grabbed my shirt and pulled it over my head. She shoved my legs into my jeans, forced my shoes on, and dragged me out of the bed. It was like the previous night all over again, except worse.

When we pulled into the parking lot of the Stop-N-Go, Nadine didn't say a word. She just bolted out of the car and ran into the store. I followed because I knew I couldn't stop what was going to happen.

Like a recurrent dream, Nadine blew past Sahir, who stood behind his counter still bopping to the Bollywood beat. She combed the aisles, hunting for the redheaded kid with the gun. A little voice of caution whispered in the back of my mind about how I should call the police now, before Nadine found the kid and got her head blown off. Dully, I reached for the cell phone in my pocket, and felt a cold shock as history repeated itself.

"Friedman? What are you doing here?"

A monster in a nightmare, Smythe loomed up by the magazine rack, a handful of periodicals scattered at his feet. Fuming, he bent to pick them up and stuffed them back into the rack. He glared at me as he straightened.

"Did you hear me, Friedman? I said, what are you doing here?"

"I'm sorry, Mr. Smythe. I just came in to get some coffee." My voice was as weak as my excuse.

"What about the Henderson account?" A thin sheen of sweat covered his balding pate as he ranted at me. "I thought I told you I wanted that done by Friday. Today is Wednesday. Are you actually so ahead on your work that you can afford to loaf around in the evenings? Because, if you are, maybe I should expect to see that loan package on my desk first thing tomorrow morning."

Nadine's voice floated to me from the front of the store. I glanced around and saw her talking to Sahir, her face drawn into a serious expression. Sahir listened to her, head bouncing in time with his damned music. There was no sign of the redheaded gunman.

"Well, Friedman? Are you going to hand me the Henderson loan tomorrow or not?"

I turned back to Smythe. "No, sir, the paperwork isn't quite finished yet. I've got a few things left to do. It's just..." Nadine's voice washed over me. Sahir was at the register. Where was that fucking kid with the gun? "It's late sir, and I needed a break. I thought maybe some coffee, a change of clothes ... just a break, sir."

Smythe glared at me, then looked past me and frowned. "Who's that woman at the register?"

My heart skipped a beat. I turned to look at Nadine. "Her? I, uh, I think—"

"She's a customer at our bank, isn't she?"

"Yes, sir," I answered. "Dr. Walker. She has a business loan with us."

"You came in with her." A cold, disapproving frown settled on Smythe's face. "In fact, I seem to remember seeing her here last night, when I saw you. Is there something going on between the two of you, Friedman?"

"I—no, sir. That wouldn't be appropriate. She's a client—"

"Isn't she black?"

His frown turned into a sneer of disgust. I stared at him, watching the wheels turn in his narrow-minded, fascist little brain. What was worse to him, the idea that I might be sleeping with a client, or the idea that I might be sleeping with a black woman? A hysterical giggle threatened to spill from my mouth. What would he think if he knew the real story about our relationship? I could tell him, I realized. Stop hiding and just blurt out that I was Nadine's fuck toy; that I liked to be tied up and spanked, that she depilated my balls every week because she preferred the little-lost-boy look, and that I lived to feel her fingers inside my ass. I could tell him everything right then and there. It was so clear to me, the way killing one's self must seem clear to the suicidal.

"I don't recall what she put down on her application," I said finally. My mouth grew dry as I spun out the lie. "She may have qualified for our minority loan program. I can check, if you like."

"You do that, Friedman. Then come see me in my office first thing tomorrow morning."

"Yes, sir." This time, I was the one who walked away. I stumbled past Nadine on legs that felt like wet noodles. She broke off from her conversation with Sahir to call after me.

"Baby? Aaron, where are you going?"

I didn't answer. I just kept walking, out of the parking lot of the Stop-N-Go and onto the sidewalk. I turned right instead of left, heading away from Nadine's place. Traffic blew past me as I ambled mindlessly toward my own house. By car, the trip would have taken fifteen minutes. On foot, it would take an hour. I should have headed back to Nadine's place, I realized. It was closer, and I could have picked up my own car and

182

driven home. Then I remembered Smythe. What if he followed me to her house? I kept walking to my place.

About ten minutes later, a car pulled up beside me. The window came down. Nadine called out to me.

"Baby, get in the car. We're going home, okay?"

I shook my head. "You lied to me, Nadine."

"Honey, I didn't lie. I had no idea that vision was going to happen. Just get in the car and we'll go home and talk this out."

"No."

The car crawled along beside me, Nadine refusing to give up. "Aaron, I saw your boss. I know why you're upset. Please, let's just talk, okay?"

"He asked me if you were black."

"What!"

I stopped walking. The car stopped too. "He asked me if you were black, Nadine. Right after he asked me if we were seeing each other."

"Why that lousy fat fuck! He's a damn racist?"

I started walking again, faster this time. Nadine followed.

"Aaron, why are you running away? Just because your boss is a bigot?"

"He knows I've been seeing you. He knows something's going on. The only thing he hasn't figured out yet is what we've really been doing."

"What do you care if he figures it out?"

"I could lose my damn job!"

"So you lose your job. You hate it anyway!"

"Easy for you to say, Nadine. It's not your livelihood on the line here, is it? If I get fired, what does it matter to you? You get to keep on making your damn sex toys and having your damn visions and saving the whole fucking world. What does my job matter compared to all that?"

Nadine hit the brakes. The car's engine died and she jumped out of the front seat to come after me.

"That's not what this is about!" she shouted. "You're not afraid of losing your job, you're afraid of being found out. You're so scared of what you are, and what people might think, that you've got to hide behind your safe little banker persona, working yourself to death because you don't dare try to enjoy yourself."

I rounded on her and started shouting myself. "How the hell can I enjoy myself when you keep running off every time we fuck? Our sex life isn't about making love anymore. It's about you seeing the future so you can play hero and rush off to save someone. Only there wasn't anybody who needed saving this time, was there? Your precious visions lied to you, just like you lied to me!"

"I didn't lie. I told you, this wasn't supposed happen this evening. We were gonna stay home and spend time together—"

"Then why didn't we stay home? Why did we have to run off and save Sahir again? Shit, Nadine, the kid wasn't even there! You had a fucking rerun. You didn't see the future, you saw the past!"

"It wasn't a rerun!"

"Then why wasn't the kid there?"

"I don't know!" she exploded. "He should have been there. Maybe it was the wrong night. I didn't get a clear picture this time, okay? Dammit, you know how this works. You know I don't see anything unless I'm having a fucking multiple-orgasm, which I might point out, I didn't have tonight!"

"Well, I'm so sorry you didn't get off the way you wanted to tonight!"

"You son of a bitch!" she snarled. "Why the hell are you doing this?"

"Why did you have to get up and leave?"

"Because I have to. Because, if I know someone's going to be hurt, I have to stop it!"

"No, you don't. Christ, can't you just let the future take care of itself for once?"

"No. I have to do something."

"Then from now on you'll have to do it without me."

I bolted down the street before she could stop me. Her angry shouts chased me all the way down the block. I had to fight the urge to turn back, to beg for her forgiveness and a chance to lie over her knee. I had to keep going. I had to escape. I couldn't deal with the visions anymore. I just couldn't.

*   *   *

I had a dream that night, after I ran all the way home. I dreamt that I was at work, heading into Smythe's office to discuss my future with Westside National Bank. Only, when I opened the door to his office, I found he'd redecorated it to look like the Stop-N-Go. His desk stood smack dab in front of the glass doors, with the rest of the store spread out

184

to infinity behind him. For some reason, Smythe's chair was a toilet, and he sat on it with his pinstripe pants down around his feet as he flipped through the files on the Henderson account while I tried to explain to him why Nadine wasn't really black.

I'd worn my Sunday best for the occasion—a pink taffeta baby-doll dress with ruffled panties and shiny Mary Janes. Smythe slowly turned the pages of the loan report, occasionally stopping to stroke his cock, while I rambled on about how Nadine could see the future, and nothing was black or white there, but grey, just like her eyes.

Meanwhile, Felicity from the underwriters' office stood behind me, her hands sliding over my body like greasy dead things. When she pulled down my panties, my cock sprang out rock hard, but not because of her. I could see Nadine, far off in the distance, waiting at the register for Sahir. He sat at the desk next to Smythe, humming along to his music as he counted his till. The redheaded gunman walked around the desk in circles, pointing the gun at Sahir's head and shouting *Bang!* every few seconds. I wasn't worried, though, because I knew the gunman was shooting blanks. But then Smythe looked up at me and said Nadine was ruining my performance at work, so she would have to go.

The gunman took his cue and headed for the register where Nadine waited. I tried to scream a warning to her, because I knew the gunman was out of blanks and he only had real bullets left, but she was too far away to hear me. So I started to run, only I tripped over the panties tangled around my feet. Felicity pulled me back up, but she wouldn't let me go, and when I screamed again, she put a cock gag in my mouth.

"She can't hear you if you don't speak up," Felicity said, and she started running her hands all over my naked cock and balls.

I tried to reach for Nadine, but Smythe leaned over his desk and took away my arms. Finally, I resorted to the only means I had left to contact her—my cock. I pumped my hips into empty air, getting harder and harder, willing my dick to grow huge enough to send a message in her direction. When I finally blew, I sprayed a ton of jism all over Smythe and the Henderson account, but the farthest drop fell a million miles short of Nadine. The gunman was still walking toward her, so I thought I could try again, but then Felicity reached around and grabbed my dick. "You need to point that thing at me," she said.

I started to cry then, because I knew the gunman would reach Nadine long before I would. I was still crying when I woke up, tangled in sticky sheets that reeked of sweat and semen. It was the most miserable wet dream I'd ever had.

*　　*　　*

I took the bus to work the next morning. I had no idea how I was going to get my car back. Frankly, I didn't care. The damn thing could sit in Nadine's driveway and rust. I wasn't going back to her house.

As soon as I got into the office, I pulled the file for Dr. Nadine Edwards Walker and tromped over to Smythe's office, where I was interrogated for an hour.

Was I dating Dr. Walker? No, I answered—at least not anymore, I added silently.

Did I do anything untoward to help her in procuring her loan? No, I did not. When I realized I was in love with Nadine, I made damned sure she got her loan via the proper channels and procedures—and quite frankly, she never would have tolerated anything less.

What was the purpose of her business? I pulled out the loan application and read off the description—research, development, and sales of health technologies.

Did she have any relevant background for such a business? I showed Smythe her resume. Prior to starting her own business, Dr. Walker had worked for ViaTech Labs, where she'd specialized in developing therapies for the treatment of disease related chronic pain using neurostimulation and biofeedback. This had led to a stint at the CDC, where she'd furthered her research in biofeedback symptom management and developed new treatments for people suffering from AIDS and other autoimmune related diseases. Her work at the CDC eventually turned to an interest in the prevention and treatment of sexually transmitted diseases, and she was currently applying for a patent for a new home test kit for HIV. She was a doctor and a scientist, through and through, and a regular humanitarian to boot, dedicated to helping those in need.

By the way, I added, she did list herself as African American and had qualified for Westside's minority loan program. Her payments were up to date, her business was thriving, and her prospects for the future looked good.

Smythe huffed and puffed for a while longer before finally releasing me to finish up work on the Henderson account. I walked out of his office and returned to my desk, operating on full autopilot, which is why I failed

186

to notice Felicity from the underwriters' department prowling after me until we reached my door.

Her hand closed over mine when I grabbed the knob. "Got a minute?" she asked.

"Not really," I answered, but she had already shouldered her way past me and into my office.

Taking a deep breath, I followed. Felicity had taken the chair behind my desk, propping her feet up on the blotter, on top of the Henderson file. I stood to one side, trying to figure out how to make her leave. She smiled at me, parted her legs a bit, and adjusted her skirt to give me a view that went all the way past her thigh-high stockings to her exposed cunt.

"See something you like?" she asked.

"No. Get out of my office." Her gross behavior was a complete turn-off.

She narrowed her eyes. "Don't be too hasty. I overheard Smythe talking in the break room again this morning."

"So what?"

"He thinks you've been screwing around with a client. Dr. Nadine Walker?"

"Dr. Walker is a client of mine, but we are not involved in any sort of romantic relationship."

"Liar." She dropped her feet to the floor and leaned forward, like a jackal getting ready to feed. "I've been through Dr. Walker's file. I know who she is and what she does."

I tried to look bored. "She's a research scientist, working on health technologies."

"Now that's an interesting euphemism for cock rings and dildos. Who came up with that bullshit description? You or her?"

The jackal loomed closer, and like any small animal about to be devoured, I froze. "What are you talking about?"

"Oh don't play stupid with me. It's an underwriter's job to research clients, and it wasn't all that hard to find out the truth about Dr. Nadine Edwards Walker. Unlike you, she doesn't hide her perversions. Her *health technologies* business popped right up on my first web search."

Felicity stood up and circled behind me to breathe down the back of my neck. "Quite an interesting inventory she sells on her website—collars, restraints, vibrators, nipple clamps, anal toys... Tell me, did she ever let you try out any of her wares?"

My fight or flight instinct kicked in, sending my thudding heart into overdrive. The urge to flee was overwhelming, but there was no way I could outrun this. My mind cast about desperately for a weapon, any means of fending off the predator at my back. Then, suddenly, it hit me. Felicity had already handed me one.

"You've seen this ... website of Dr. Walker's?"

"Oh yeah, I went through every page. She had some lovely product *placement* pictures."

I turned to face her, eyebrow cocked at a quizzical angle. "So what you're telling me is that you've been visiting a pornographic website to ogle sex toys, during work hours and on the bank's computers? I wonder what Mr. Smythe would think of that? Perhaps we should go ask him."

She hesitated. "Is that a threat?"

I glanced at the door. "Care to find out?"

It was a bluff, a big one. My whole defense was nothing but a bristling of fur, a baring of teeth, and a shitload of attitude. I had no idea if Felicity had used her computer at work to check out Nadine or not. If she hadn't, all she had to do was head straight for Smythe's office and I was as good as dead.

Fortunately, the bluff worked. Licking her lips, the jackal backed away. "Looks like we're at an impasse. Too bad. I thought we could have some fun."

"I'm not interested in your idea of fun."

"Maybe you'll change your mind." She picked up a pen and sticky note from my desk and pressed a note with her phone number to my jacket lapel, letting her hand linger a moment too long.

"Get out my office," I said again. She slunk away, giving me a sly, cagy look as she slipped out the door. I pulled the sticky note off my lapel. Don't ask me why I put it in my pocket and not the trash.

*   *   *

By five p.m., the Henderson loan application was finished, all the *i*'s dotted and the *t*'s crossed. I stopped by Smythe's office to hand it in, only to discover he'd left half an hour earlier.

"Fucking hypocrite," I muttered as I tossed the file onto his desk. "Must be nice to leave early and not have to answer to your own little neo-Nazi boss."

188

I tried to walk home from work, but only made it as far as the corner outside the bank when Ernesto Chavez drove up and insisted on giving me a ride. It was the least he could do, he said with a laugh, seeing as he owed me his life. As he drove me to my house, I thought about what Nadine would say about that. Then I remembered she wouldn't say anything, because I wasn't ever going to see her again.

At home, I pulled off my jacket and slumped on the couch to stare at the bare walls and floor. Before meeting Nadine, I'd never been home from work long enough to bother decorating the place. After we got together, I spent all my free time at her house. With a groan, I realized more of my stuff was at her place than at mine, including most of my suits. They could stay there, I decided, with the car. Maybe Nadine would throw them in the trash. More likely she'd give them to charity. She always tried to help people in need.

An hour passed, maybe longer, and I just sat there in my empty house, contemplating my empty life. My stomach grumbled. I considered making dinner, only to recall that there was nothing in the fridge because I always ate at Nadine's. So I sat a little while longer. I decided if I were still sitting there in the morning, I'd go to work. Or maybe not. My job didn't seem to matter anymore, which struck me as funny because my job was the reason why I'd left Nadine. Wasn't it?

I didn't notice the message light on the phone until the sky outside grew dark. I hadn't bothered to turn on the lights and in the deepening shadows of the house, the blinking red light fluttered like a heartbeat. I thought about ignoring it, but the more I tried, the more urgently the light seemed to flicker. At last, I dragged myself over to the end table to check it out. It was probably Smythe, calling to harass me about the Henderson account. I hit the replay button and got a surprise.

"Aaron, are you there? It's Nadine. Please pick up."

I gawked at the phone. How could she possibly have called me after the argument we'd had the night before?

"Baby, I know you're upset," she went on. Her voice was a soft caress that sent a shiver through me. "I'm sorry about last night, I really am. I didn't mean for things to turn out the way they did. You have to believe me. I know I promised we'd stay home and spend some time together, and I'm sorry it didn't work out that way. And what I said about you quitting your job, that was out of line. It's your job and if you want to keep it, then that's your call not mine."

There was a pause. I wrapped my arms around myself, dumbfounded by her words. Nadine was apologizing. Did dommes actually do that? I didn't know, but if she had called to say she was sorry, that meant something. It meant that she did care about me, after all. My cock had gone rock hard at the sound of her voice, so hard it almost hurt, and my nipples had tightened into knots the size of gumdrops. I squeezed myself, overwhelmed by a rush of adrenaline that left me giddy with relief. I had to call Nadine back. I loved her. I needed her. She was the only woman who'd ever stuck with me, the only one who'd ever truly loved me and accepted me. I reached for the phone. We'd talk. We'd work things out. We'd make love. Everything was going to be okay.

"There's just one thing you've got to understand though, Aaron," she continued. All my warm fuzzy feelings suddenly evaporated. "I love you, but I can't ignore these visions. After you left, I started thinking that maybe you were right. Maybe what I saw last night was some sort of rerun. I hit my head pretty hard when that kid knocked me down. That could have caused a repeat, I guess. But when I went to sleep last night, I had a dream about Sahir and that stupid kid with the gun. It was all distorted and crazy, but it felt just like the other visions. Even your boss was there, flipping through the porno mags again.

"Something's going on. I think when we chased that kid off we didn't stop what was going to happen. We just delayed it. I love you, Aaron, but until I figure this out, I have to keep acting like that vision was real. I don't know what else to say. I can't take the risk that what I saw was just a repeat, not when a man's life is on the line. I know you're not going to be happy about this, and I'm sorry. Can we at least talk about it, though? Call me on my cell phone. We'll figure something out. I promise."

The message clicked off and silence flooded the house. I flopped back down on the couch, hot tears threatening to spill from my eyes. I grabbed the phone and threw it against the wall. It hit with a jangling clatter and left an ugly black mark on the blank plaster.

So Nadine was sorry. Big fucking deal. She cared about me, but not enough to choose me over her precious visions. And if I wanted proof of that, all I had to do was call her on her cell phone, because she wasn't at home. She was at the Stop-N-Go, playing guardian angel to stupid Sahir and waiting for a kid with a gun who was never going to show. Well, if she could wait for him, she could wait for me too. She could wait until Hell froze over, because I was tired of playing second fiddle to her crazy premonitions.

I threw the couch cushions after the phone until I was sitting on the bare frame. Anger poured over me in waves. Furious as I was, though, my cock still throbbed and now it really was getting painful. I tugged open my fly and slipped a hand down my shorts, anxious for some relief. I didn't need Nadine to get off. I could handle this myself. But twenty minutes later I was still stroking my dick and getting no results. My balls felt ready to burst and I was about to curl up in the fetal position and die when I was struck by a mad impulse.

I rolled off the couch and crawled to the phone, but not to call Nadine. I retrieved the yellow sticky note from the pocket of my discarded jacket and dialed the number written on it. Felicity answered after three rings.

"Hello?"

Even over the phone, her voice creeped me out. The sound was husky, almost hoarse, like a monster trying too hard to sound sexy instead of scary. I wanted to hang up as soon as I heard it, but wounded pride and my aching cock wouldn't let me.

"Felicity?" I choked out. "It's Aaron."

She growled. "Are you calling to make more threats?"

"No. No, ma'am." I flicked a dry tongue over my lips before rushing on. "Actually, I was hoping you'd make the threats this time. And then carry them out."

∗   ∗   ∗

Once upon a time, back in my days at college, I had a girlfriend who asked me why I wanted to be spanked. I can't remember her name. It was Katie, I think, or maybe Kathy. She hadn't lasted long, I remember that, but before she'd handed me the usual line about having headaches and needing to leave, she'd been pretty nice. At least, nice enough to ask why I wanted what I wanted.

I'd tried to explain to her, although back then I didn't really understand it myself. There was just something about being turned over a woman's knee, feeling helpless and excited as she paddled my ass until it glowed bright rosy red. Every single smack brought a jolt of pain and pleasure, the sting on my behind a salty-sweet contrast to the wicked feel of my cock rubbing against her thigh. The soreness of a really good spanking could linger for days afterward, forcing me to sit with care and cover up my lap as the resulting pain brought my cock to attention.

191

Stranger still was the longing I felt to be penetrated, to have a woman slip her fingers inside me and play with my anus while I wriggled and moaned in shameful delight. Maybe it was the fact that it was dirty and forbidden. Maybe it was me trying to cast off my orthodox upbringing by any means possible. I didn't know. It was never something I could put into words and I never did make it plain to Katie, or Kathy, or whatever her name was.

Nadine understood, though. I'd never needed to explain anything to her. She'd always been able to look at me and just know what I needed. It was more than simple spankings and ass-play. She showed me things that I'd never known about, had me try things I never even dreamed of, tormented me in ways I never could have imagined. But she always gave me what I wanted and, no matter what she did, she always left me feeling safe, secure, and loved.

I didn't have those feelings as I stood outside Felicity's apartment. I felt scared and a little sick as I raised my hand to knock on the door. Felicity had already proved herself to be a vicious, scheming predator. So why was I here? It wasn't for love or even desire. This was strictly revenge, to get back at Nadine for abandoning me in favor of her precious visions. It was a petty, stupid thing to do, especially with someone like Felicity, who would just as soon ruin me as look at me. I wanted to walk away. I dropped my hand without hitting the door and took a step back.

The door swung open on its own. Felicity slouched against the jamb.

"What's wrong? You too afraid to even knock?"

"Uh..." I stared at her, disconcerted by her appearance. At work, she had looked every inch the professional banker, starched into her tailored suit with hair and makeup sensibly styled. Attractive but nondescript, she blended in perfectly with the sheep at Westside. Only her behavior toward me had marked her as a predator.

Now, in her own territory, Felicity had abandoned the disguise. She still wore her work clothes, but the tailored skirt was rumpled and the silk blouse was unbuttoned to reveal the flimsy black bra beneath. Her polished makeup had melted, mascara bleeding into dark rings around her eyes and dabs of lipstick congealed at the corners of her mouth to look like blood.

"Well, Aaron? Are you here to play or not?"

She offered me a feral grin. I shuddered at the sight of her teeth streaked by more bloody lipstick. Her eyes, I noticed, were bloodshot and

192

bleary. Was she drunk? Hell if I was going to submit to a woman who wasn't completely sober. Even I wasn't that hard up, I decided.

But when I tried to walk away, I found out otherwise. On the first step, my dick spasmed so painfully that I couldn't move. I sucked in a sharp breath and fell against the wall, paralyzed by the nastiest case of blue balls I'd ever experienced.

"Problem?" Felicity asked. She grinned at my rigid cock, plainly visible beneath my pants.

"No," I hissed. "No problem. Can we go inside?"

She moved aside and gestured for me to enter. I shuffled into her apartment, wincing as the door slammed shut behind me. I heard the rattle of the chain being drawn, the *thunk* of the lock being turned.

"Come into my parlor," she drawled as she pushed me ahead.

I stumbled into a small, sparsely furnished living room. A thick pall of smoke hung in the air, bitter acrid stuff that stung my sinuses and made my eyes water. It wafted up from an overflowing ashtray on the coffee table. Felicity shoved past me and dropped onto the couch. She plucked a still-smoldering joint from the pile of burned-out stubs and sucked on it, then offered it to me.

"You want a hit?"

"No thanks."

"Suit yourself."

She kicked her feet up on the coffee table, sending an empty beer can rolling across its surface. So she was drunk. High too. More and more, this looked like a bad idea. Nadine never used drugs or alcohol. Whenever we had sex, she stayed in complete control—of herself and me. She was always fully aware of what was going on.

But was she really? asked a nasty little voice inside my head. With all the visions she had, could I really say that Nadine was there when we made love?

"Maybe I'll have a hit, after all," I said, and took the joint from Felicity.

I put it to my lips and choked on the first few inhalations, but finally managed to take a big enough toke to feel an effect. Swirling blue smoke clouded my mind. I slumped on the couch next to Felicity. She handed me a beer and I downed it. More beers followed, along with another joint. The edges of room blurred. Felicity blurred too. Pot did not improve her appearance, I decided. If anything, she looked even more beastly. Not at all like Nadine who always looked like a goddess. A cool, distant goddess who was now forever beyond my reach...

Thinking of Nadine made my cock hurt. I smoked another joint to ease the pain. The sharp throbbing turned into a dull leaden ache. Felicity reached over to unbutton my shirt. I sank into the cushions while she felt me up, a little bothered by her clumsy fumbling. Her hands were cold and damp, not at all sexy. Still, as long as they did the job, I wouldn't complain.

I wished she wouldn't be so brutal about it, though. She kept twisting my nipples between her fingers until they felt raw and irritated. When she started pinching them, I pulled away.

"Don't," I said. "That hurts."

Felicity laughed. "I thought you liked to play rough."

"Not like that."

"Shut up and finish your joint."

She put the blunt to my lips and I took a long, deep drag. My head was swimming. Felicity went back to abusing my nubs for while. When she got bored with that, she tugged my fly open and yanked my pants down to my knees.

"Nice." She leered at my hairless groin. "I see Dr. Walker likes her boys pretty and smooth."

She pawed at my cock with her clammy hands. I groaned and gave an involuntary thrust my hips. My heart ached for Nadine. My dick didn't seem to care.

"You want it, don't you, bitch?" she muttered. "Say, 'please.'"

"Please, Felicity. I want it."

The room dissolved around us as she pulled off the rest of my clothes. My joint dissolved too, in a big puffy cloud. I felt as though I was watching the whole scene from far, far away, through a filter of dense smog. Even the touch of Felicity's hands on my body felt muffled and remote. Only my cock responded to her, indiscriminate in its need. The rest of me was long gone.

I closed my eyes as she wrapped a hand around my dick and squeezed. Nadine would be so pissed with me if she found out about this, but I couldn't stop. The one-eyed monster had to be appeased. Too bad Felicity was so trashy and ham-handed. It really ruined the mood. Maybe if I kept my eyes closed, I could pretend I was really with Nadine. I was high enough. It might work.

I drifted off into a dream about a lovely goddess with gray eyes, brown skin, and four arms. In one hand she held a sacred paddle, in

194

another a ball gag, in the third a birch switch, and in the fourth, a shiny set of handcuffs.

An audible click brought me out of the dream. I opened my eyes and saw the metal bracelet locked around my wrist. The other, open cuff rested in Felicity's hand.

"Get up and turn around, bitch. I'm gonna lock you up."

"Oh noooooooo..."

The word seemed to stretch out forever as I pushed Felicity away from me. She fell on the floor with a yell. I staggered up from the couch and tried to run. Something hit me right below the knees. I crashed down on top of the coffee table, burning myself as the ashtray went flying and hot sparks rained down. The table collapsed into a pile of splintered wood. I lay there on top of it, too stunned to figure out which way was up. By the time I realized I was face down on the floor, Felicity managed to lock the second cuff around the leg of the couch.

"I don't take 'no' for an answer, you little fuck." She sat on the carpet panting, a rabid gleam in her eyes. "You pissed me off this afternoon with all that shit about going to Smythe and telling him I've been looking at porn at work. That was a nasty little threat."

"Sorry," I mumbled. I pulled feebly at the cuff locked around my wrist.

"Sorry don't cut it, little boy. You deserve a beating for what you did today."

Her words cut through the haze of pot smoke, chilling me to the bone. Felicity snatched my pants off the floor and whipped the belt free from the waistband. I gave a low moan as she forced me into a kneeling position, my head down on the floor between my arms, my ass pointing up toward the ceiling. I closed my eyes and gritted my teeth. I was so fucking stupid. Why, oh why did I come running to this slut for relief? I should have called Nadine. Even when she was obsessing over her visions, she still treated me way better than this.

The first blow of the belt cut right across both cheeks. I howled.

"Shut up!" Felicity snapped. She grabbed one of my socks and stuffed it into my mouth. Then she delivered two more searing strikes. I bellowed into my makeshift gag. Oh god was I stupid! The ache in my cock flared into agony, fueled by the shock of raw pain. Again and again, the belt connected with my ass until one blow landed so hard I felt it slice through the skin.

"That'll teach you to threaten me." Felicity tossed the belt away and pushed me onto my back. She hiked up her skirt and climbed on top. Her hips ground against my outraged dick. Oh please God, I prayed she wouldn't actually try to fuck me. I had no idea what sort of diseases she might be carrying.

Fortunately, she was too stoned to bother with putting my cock into her hole. Instead, she seemed content to rub against me. I squirmed beneath, retching against the sock stuffed in my mouth. The realization that I had one free hand only slowly wormed its way into my pot-addled brain. I pulled the sock out of my mouth and started hitting Felicity.

"Get off me, you crazy bitch!"

She grabbed my flailing arm and pinned it to the floor. A strand of drool stretched from the corner of her mouth. "Shut up, shut up... don't take no for an answer ... don't take no... Sahir doesn't know..."

I stiffened beneath. What the hell did she just say?

"Not funny, Felicity. Get the fuck off me!"

"The boy is there... Sahir doesn't know... Sahir comes ... comes to the register... Sahir doesn't know..."

Oh fuck.

"Sahir comes to the register ... the boy hides ... hides with the gun... Nadine waits ... waits ... waits at the register ... the boy comes to the register..."

Her head lolled back and she started to twitch, small tremors at first, then violent shakes that jerked her whole body. The first drops of blood fell from her nose onto my face. More drool leaked from her mouth. Her sightless eyes rolled back into her skull as she kept talking.

"Nadine waits ... the boy comes to the register... Nadine doesn't see, can't see, I see, the boy comes, the boy with the gun, with the gun, he pulls out the gun gun gun gun gun gun!"

Felicity started to shriek. Blood spouted from her nose, spraying me across the face and chest. She stiffened and went into a full-blown seizure as my cock erupted beneath her.

"Nadine! Nadine!" she screamed. Then with one last jerk, she keeled over on top of me.

Shaking, I rolled her onto the floor and started slapping her. "Come on, wake up!" I said. "What did you see? Tell me!"

Felicity groaned. The bottom half of her face was painted with blood. Her eyes fluttered open and focused on me.

"What did you do to me?"

"Tell me what you saw," I demanded. "What happens to Nadine?"

"You lousy fuck, you hit me..."

"Tell me what you saw!"

She shook her head feebly, and muttered Nadine's name again. "The gun. Some redhead kid shoots her with the gun." She touched her face and felt the blood. "Is this mine or hers?"

Panic-stricken, I backed away as far as the cuffs would let me. How could there be two of them, two women who saw the future when they came? Impossible. But what if it were true? Did that mean Nadine was about to die?

I tried to get up. The handcuffs yanked me back down. Furious, I shoved against the couch, trying to lift the front legs off the ground. Felicity pulled up to sitting and sneered.

"No you don't. We're not done yet."

"Fuck you!"

I pushed harder, putting my back into it. The damned thing was heavy, a huge monster of cheap upholstery and particleboard. Felicity struggled to her knees. "You're going nowhere," she threatened.

The couch came up, just an inch. I yanked the cuff off the leg and let it crash to the floor. Before Felicity could stand, I threw myself against her. We went down in a tangle of limbs, rolling over her demolished coffee table and toward the door. I jumped to my feet and ran.

"You can't get away from me!" she screamed as I streaked down the hallway to the front door.

"Want to make a bet?"

On a table by the door, I spotted Felicity's purse. I snatched it, dumped the contents, and found the keys to my escape, or at least to Felicity's car. I grabbed them, threw open the bolt, broke the chain as I yanked open the door, and raced out of the apartment. In the parking lot, I ran to the first car I saw and pressed the key remote to unlock the door. No luck. I jumped over the hood to the second car. Again, no luck. It took me four more tries before I found her car, a two-door coupe painted cherry red. I slipped into the front seat, jammed the keys into the ignition, and roared out of the parking lot, headed for the Stop-N-Go.

Pot no more improved my driving than it had Felicity's looks. I wove back and forth across the road, doing my best to stay on the asphalt while my head spun out of control. Twice, I cut across the sidewalk as I turned a corner. After running a few red lights, I noticed flashing blue lights in the rearview mirror accompanied by a strange wailing noise that I recognized from when Nadine hit her head on the shelves of the Stop-N-Go. I couldn't remember what that sound meant, but it set my heart racing in my chest and I mashed my bare foot down on the accelerator to go even faster.

I swerved and dodged through the late evening traffic like a kid playing some wild video game. Fortunately, there weren't many cars ahead of me on the road. There was a whole pack of those flashing blue lights behind me, but as long as they were back there, I didn't care. I just didn't want something to pop up in front of me, because I knew I'd run its ass over to get to Nadine.

I took a wrong turn, and then another. I hauled on the wheel and sent the car screeching around the corner, over a median, and through a strip mall, leaving the blue lights and wailing sirens way behind. The Stop-N-Go sign loomed up on the other side of the highway like a bright red and green homing beacon, and I aimed the coupe straight at it. I had just enough presence of mind to hit the horn as I tore across the four-lane road and into the parking lot, where I smashed Felicity's car into a sleek silver sedan that I recognized as soon as I crunched the back end. It belonged to Nadine. She was there, but was I in time?

I swung open the car door and fell out onto the pavement. I saw Nadine through the windows, standing by the register.

"Nadine!" I shouted as I struggled to my feet and ran toward the store. "I'm here!" I smacked into the glass front door before I remembered it was there, then wrenched it open and barreled inside.

Nadine spun around as I rushed in, hands held out as though to ward me off. Sahir stood behind her, his hands raised high above his head like he was a character in an old western about a bank robbery. Perhaps that was because it was a robbery. I saw the open till resting on the counter, and the villain was a kid who stood beside them. I thought I recognized him—bright red hair, grungy army jacket, holding something black and heavy in his hand. He whirled around as I skidded to a halt.

"What the fuck is this?" he shouted. He raised his hand as though to point at me. Nadine screamed and leapt at him.

"Aaron, get down!"

Nadine landed on top of the guy, knocking him over. A loud bang split the air as they landed on the floor. The heavy black thing flew out of the kid's hand and skidded away beneath Sahir's incense display. Still a dollar fifty-nine, according to the sign, I noticed, imported from Mumbai.

The guy rolled over, sprang to his feet, and took a swing at Nadine. When his fist connected with her jaw, I went berserk.

There was a lot of screaming and yelling after that, most of it coming from the kid who hit Nadine. Somehow, he ended up back on the floor, this time beneath me. His face quickly turned to hamburger beneath my fists. In the back of my mind, I noted that the flashing blue lights had returned, bringing a shitload of police with them. They poured through the doors, shouting and waving their guns. It took four of them to pull me off the kid and hold me down.

"Stop it!" I heard Nadine yell. "You've got the wrong man!"

Minutes later, I was back on my feet, a pair of handcuffs locked around my wrists, but not too badly damaged thanks to Nadine. Two officers cuffed the redheaded kid who lay moaning on the floor. Another helped Nadine to her feet while a weary fifth tried to calm Sahir, who ranted and raved about how he was always getting robbed, and if it hadn't been for Nadine and I, this time he would have been killed because the cops certainly never bothered to patrol his store—even though his doughnuts were at least five cents cheaper than the place across the street. It was madness, pure and simple, enough to make my head pound, but even though I hurt, nothing could erase the big goofy smile from my face as I watched Nadine argue with the police to let me go. Who cared if I went to jail? She was alive. That was all that mattered.

More police arrived, and an ambulance. The chaos in the Stop-N-Go subsided. I was being herded out the door, Nadine still demanding my release, when without warning the men's room door swung open. The cops all turned as one and pulled out their guns.

"Freeze! Come out with your hands up!"

That's when the most bizarre and unexpected sight of the night came shuffling out to greet us. Horace Winston Smythe III waddled out of the men's room, pants around his ankles, clutching a copy of *Hustler* to his chest. The look of shock on his face was matched only by the one on Sahir's, who shouted at the poor guy as he tried to hide behind the magazine.

"You sir, what are you doing? Customers are not allowed to jerk off in my store. You will pay for that magazine. You have made it all sticky now and I cannot sell a sticky magazine!"

I never laughed so hard in my entire life.

*   *   *

I was sober by the time Nadine sprung me out of the clink, and possessed enough common sense to know I was damned lucky she'd decided to spend that much of her time and money to bail me out. When I was brought out of the holding cell wearing borrowed sweats and a "Just Say No" t-shirt, I offered her a very quiet *thank you*, then kept my mouth shut as we walked to her car.

She didn't say a word about how the back half of her sedan looked like an accordion. She just held open the passenger door and glared at me until I got inside.

"What happened to your clothes?" she asked as she slipped into her side of the car.

I plucked at the t-shirt. "I, uh, sort of left them at someone's apartment."

"Would this be the same someone whose car you stole last night?"

"Yes, ma'am." I knew better than to offer any excuses about extenuating circumstances and the need for a ride. There would be time for that later, I hoped.

I gave Nadine Felicity's address. We drove over in silence. The car made a weird rattling noise every time we turned left. When we got to Felicity's apartment building, I slipped off the seat belt and reached for the door handle.

"Oh no," Nadine said. "*You* stay here. I'll get your things for you."

"Yes, ma'am."

She got out of the car and strode through the predawn mist to Felicity's apartment. I watched her rap on the door, then push her way inside the moment it opened. The door shut behind her. I waited for several minutes, sweating. When she came back out again, she carried my clothes in her arms. Felicity followed her to the car, snapping at her heels like a rabid Chihuahua. I rolled down the window to hear her screech.

"You think you're tough, you little black bitch? You think you can just bust in like that and push me around? I had your slut boyfriend. He was begging at my feet, saying you couldn't give him a good fuck if your life depended on it!"

Nadine turned so suddenly that Felicity tripped and fell. She started talking, very low and quiet, pointing once to me in the car. I did my best to look contrite, but I couldn't keep myself from grinning as Felicity backed away from Nadine, visibly shaken by whatever my domme had said. When

Nadine finally walked away, Felicity ran back to her apartment and slammed the door.

"Thank you," I said as she got back into the car and dumped my clothes in my lap.

"Wipe that smile off your face, young man. You're in a hell of a lot of trouble."

When we reached Nadine's place, she got out of the car and headed straight for the door. I ran after her, relieved to finally be home. She stopped me before I could set foot on the porch.

"And where do you think you're going?"

I shrank back. "Inside with you?"

"What makes you think I'm going to let you into my house?" Her eyes narrowed to razor-thin slits, giving me a look sharp enough to cut straight to the bone. I took a deep breath and prayed.

"I'll leave if you want me to, but please let me talk first. I may not be able to explain everything I've done, but at least give me a chance. *Please.*"

"The way you gave me a chance before you went begging to that two-bit whore?"

I sagged, defeated by my own hypocrisy. What could I say to her? It was all over. I'd never see Nadine again.

"Get your ass in here, boy," she said as I turned to shamble away. "You're not getting away without answering my questions."

Heart pounding like a trip-hammer, I followed her into the house. We went straight to the lab. Nadine grabbed a chair and sat. I stripped off my shirt.

"What are you doing?" she demanded.

"Getting ready for my punishment." It was chilly in the lab. My cock shrank as I stepped out of the sweats.

She glanced at the black and blue marks on my backside. In a withering voice she said, "I think you've had enough for one night. Don't you?"

"Yes, ma'am." I didn't dare say no.

"Then put your clothes back on."

I got dressed then stood there, wondering what to do. If Nadine wouldn't punish me, how could I make things right? Twice, I tried to speak, to say I was sorry and that I would do anything she wanted if only she'd give me another chance. Both times, she shook her head. She didn't want to hear it. She just sat there, the muscles in her jaw twitching as she

201

glared at me. I kept my head bowed, eyes on the toes of her black leather boots. A paddle, a crop, a cock cage, even being paraded naked through Westside National Bank on a collar and leash would have been preferable to waiting in silence. My knees started to shake. Sweat poured down my face and back. Just when I thought I would collapse on the floor, she finally spoke.

"I don't even know where to begin, you know that? I called you last night to say I was sorry, that I wanted to talk. Did you get the message?"

"Yes, ma'am."

"Did you even consider calling me back?"

"Yes, ma'am."

"But you didn't."

"No, ma'am."

She let out a deep breath. "Well then, what did you do?"

Keeping my eyes fixed on her boots, I told her. Everything. Up until I got to the point where Felicity had me on the floor, handcuffed to the couch and my belt in her hands.

"She, um, she said I deserved it ... for saying no..."

The lab did a funny little slide sideways and tilted up. At about the same time the lights went out. When they came back on, I was on the floor, my head in Nadine's lap.

"Baby? Baby, wake up. It's okay. Mama's got you, it's okay."

"Nadine? I think I'm gonna be sick."

She found a trashcan and held me while I puked. When I was done, she wiped my mouth with her shirtsleeve.

"Oh honey, why did you ever go to that nasty woman? She could have hurt you. She *did* hurt you."

"I didn't want to," I said. "Not after I got there. Things just sort of got out of control."

Nadine hugged me to her. "It's over now. She's never going touch you again. I'll put that bitch in jail if she even so much as looks at you! No wonder you stole her car and came running to Sahir's."

"Actually," I said slowly, "that wasn't the reason why. Something else happened."

"What do you mean?"

"Felicity had a vision."

Nadine blinked. "A vision?"

"After she beat me with the belt. She climbed on top of me and started dry-humping." I shuddered as I remembered it. "She started saying stuff about Sahir and the kid with the gun, and then her nose started bleeding and she kept saying your name. Then she screamed and had some sort of fit."

"She had a vision?" she asked again.

"Just like one of yours. Happened when she came. She had a nose bleed too, a bad one, just like you did when you saw Chavez getting hit by the car."

Nadine let out a shaky breath. "Oh you sneaky son of a bitch."

"I'm sorry, Nadine. I didn't mean to have sex with her. I wanted to leave—"

"She didn't have a vision."

"But she did," I said. "She saw you at the Stop-N-Go."

"She never had a vision. And neither did I."

I shook my head, confused. "I don't understand."

"You said she came, right?" I nodded. "Did you come first, or did she?"

"I didn't mean to," I said in a small voice. "I didn't want to, not after what she did."

"But you came, and then she came."

"Yes, ma'am. I'm sorry."

Nadine stroked my face. "It's okay, honey. If you hadn't, I'd probably be dead now. Don't you see? The visions come from you."

"Huh?"

She took me through it slowly. "Remember how you asked me if I ever saw you in the visions, and I said no, but I was sure you were there? I could see myself, I could see where we were and what was happening, I just couldn't see you? That's because the visions come from your point of view, Aaron. I only see what you show me. That girl last night saw what you showed her. I don't know how, but when you come, you transmit a message, and when I come, when she came, we receive it."

I closed my eyes, trying to wrap my head around what she was saying. "How do you know that?"

"I don't. It's just a theory that fits all the evidence. All your girlfriends in college kept leaving you, complaining about headaches. Even I had headaches, but I stayed longer than any of the others, right?"

"Yeah. None of the others ever made it past four months."

"And four months into our relationship, I had a nosebleed, and the first vision."

"The one about Chavez..." The puzzle pieces began to fit together in my mind. "Felicity had a nosebleed when she saw you being shot. But what do headaches and nosebleeds have to do with the visions?"

Nadine shrugged. "Maybe our brains don't come readymade to receive the visions. Maybe the signals you're sending have to keep pounding away at a receiver until they finally punch through and that causes the nosebleeds. Once they've created a way in, the headaches and the nosebleeds stop."

"But I didn't have a four-month relationship with Felicity, I swear it. It was just one night, because I was mad at you and desperate to get off. She never even had time for a headache."

"But she did have one hell of a nosebleed, didn't she? Maybe you knew what was going to happen in your subconscious and you were so desperate to transmit that vision, to prevent the future and keep me from being killed..."

"That I forced her to see it so I could rescue you," I finished. "It's crazy."

"It's a theory. Theories always sound crazy until they're tested and proved."

Nadine helped me sit up. I put my head on her shoulder. "If I had called you last night, would you still have gone to the Stop-N-Go?"

"Yes. But then maybe you would have been on the phone with me when the gunman showed up. Maybe you would have called the cops and saved me that way."

"Or maybe we would have made up and I would have joined you there," I said. "I didn't necessarily save your life by going to Felicity, did I? I could have saved you just by calling you on the phone."

"Probably. It seems to me like you were going to be at the Stop-N-Go last night no matter what."

I heaved a sigh. "Then I guess I'm still in trouble for what I did last night."

"You better believe it, honey. You had options, and you didn't pick the best one. As soon as those bruises on your ass heal up, you're going to get some serious corporal punishment. Between now and then, I've got other ways of disciplining you, and you'd better jump at every opportunity I give you to earn my forgiveness.

"But that's for later," she said, kissing the top of my head. "For now, let's go upstairs and get some sleep. We'll see what the future brings tomorrow.

The Lonely Farmer

The lonely farmer loved the good earth.

In the spring, he plowed her fields and planted his seed. All summer, he bowed to her demands. Come fall, she bore him a fine crop of sons.

The lonely farmer loved the good earth.

About the Author

Helen E. H. Madden is a writer and artist who quit her lucrative day job years ago to tell dirty stories for fun and profit. Her published works have appeared in various anthologies, including *Cream: The Best of the Erotica Readers and Writers Association* and the charity anthology *Coming Together: With Pride*. Helen also writes and produces the *Heat Flash* erotica podcast, a free online audio program of erotic short fiction. In her spare time, she draws *The Adventures of Cynical Woman*, a web comic about life as a stay-at-home mom and erotica writer. When she's not working, Helen likes to think about sex. A lot.

Website: http://www.helenehmadden.com
Heat Flash erotica podcast: http://www.heatflash.libsyn.com
The Adventures of Cynical Woman:
http://www.theadventuresofcynicalwoman.blogspot.com

Other books by Logical-Lust

Messalina – Devourer of Men
by Zetta Brown

When life imitates art...

Eva Cavell is a woman with an embarrassing secret.

She is sexually frustrated and is convinced that her size and race intimidates men.

In an attempt to relieve her sexual tension, every Thursday Eva goes to a local movie theater and allows desperate strangers to fondle her in the dark. She allows no eye contact, no phone numbers—and definitely no names.

During one of her escapades, renowned artist, Jared Delaney, a smooth Southern gentleman with irresistible violet eyes, has Eva breaking her own rules. He has been watching Eva on her weekly visits and sees through her icy defence and straight through to the hot passion burning underneath.

...expect to be framed

Messing about in dark theaters isn't a good pastime for Eva. She is a tenure-track instructor at a private Denver college that is currently embroiled in a sex scandal and she is the youngest child of a prominent black family.

To add to her turmoil, Neil Hollister, Eva's classroom aide and former student, is a handsome, barely-legal frat brat whose interest in her is carnal rather than academic—and she's tempted.

Despite desperate attempts to maintain control, Eva's world is spiralling into chaos. As emotional pressures build inside her, an explosion is imminent. Will she ever be able to live her life how she wants and without shame?

The answer may lie with a woman who is bold and unashamed in her sexuality.

Can Eva be more like her? What would happen if she even tried?

Messalina - Devourer of Men is available worldwide in paperback and digital (ebook) formats, direct from www.logical-lust.com, or from Amazon, Barnes & Noble, and all good retailers!

Swing!

Adventures in Swinging by Today's Top Erotica Writers
Edited by Jolie du Pré

SWING! is a stunning anthology of swinging adventure stories from some of the world's top erotica writers, compiled and edited by Jolie Du Pré.

Being edited by Jolie Du Pré, you can expect some hot, sizzling sex stories, both well written and highly creative. We don't pull any punches when we say we expect **SWING!** to be one of *the* top erotica releases of 2009!

ABOUT THE EDITOR

Jolie Du Pré is an author of erotica and erotic romance. Her stories have appeared on numerous Web sites, in e-books and in print. Jolie is also the editor of **Iridescence: Sensuous Shades of Lesbian Erotica**, published by Alyson Books, and is the founder of GLBT Promo, a promotional group for GLBT erotica and erotic romance.

SWING! is available from Spring 2009, and is published in digital (ebook) formats. Get your copy direct from <u>www.logical-lust.com</u>, or from Amazon (Kindle) and other worldwide online retailers!

Bittersweet

Stories of tainted desire

by Amber Hipple

Not all sex is romance or fun. Sometimes there's desperation there. Explore the deeper, darker aspects of love and want in "Bittersweet", Amber Hipple's intensely emotive debut collection of tainted erotica. Be moved by the cycle of wanting to be wanted and the pain of wanting too much. "Bittersweet" is a lesson in reality; it's what love and desire can be. Expect no "happy ever after" in these stories, but expect to be left wanting more.

Jim Brown, owner of Logical-Lust, says; *"Amber Hipple has come up with something quite out of the ordinary in 'Bittersweet'. Gone is the sugary-sweet romanticism and the happy-ever-after, to be replaced by the profound emotions and outpourings that are real in love and sex. You'll find your heart being wrenched apart by the yearnings and the despair of the characters, yet still be stirred and aroused by the sheer passion in the erotica she produces."*

BITTERSWEET by Amber Hipple, will be released on 30th March 2009, in both digital (ebook) and print formats, and will be available worldwide through www.logical-lust.com, Amazon, Barnes and Noble, and all good online retailers.

Crimson Succubus: The Demon Chronicles

by Carmine

"*A few years back, I began receiving emailed submissions to the erotic literary ezine* Sauce*Box *from a writer known to me only as* 'Carmine'. *These submissions were short pieces* ('flash-fiction', *if you will*) *detailing yet another* 'Tale of the Crimson Succubus'. *Each was a stand-alone jewel, horrible, cruel, fantastically, outrageously, graphically sexual, but also somehow (dare I say it . . . forgive me, Carmine) charming. I liked them very much and published every one that was sent.*

"*Now I find that some these short tales along with longer pieces concerning the* 'adventures' *of the Crimson Succubus, and a third section concerning a mythical nymph Mytoessa who also becomes involved with the succubus have been collected together in one place—a delightfully, tastefully disgusting book,* **Tales of the Crimson Succubus, The Demon Chronicles** *by Carmine.*

"*This person, Carmine, is one sick puppy, but one with adorable eyes and floppy ears. The tales involve much blood- and semen-letting, murder, torture, deception and pain, but at the same time, I often want to laugh and wish that the creatures would appear for real, in front of me, so that I could see with my own eyes and even touch (very, very carefully, mind you) these monsters formed from the primordial slime of all of our great cultural myths.*

"*And of course, like all myths, these tales speak to our deepest fears, and hopes and fantasies . . . perhaps to archetypes from times before even the written word, times long forgotten in consciousness but remembered in the collective genetic code. I don't know. Whatever. They're a great read, an exciting read and one that will tickle your nightmares and daydreams long after you've put this book down.*"

Guillermo Bosch, Editor: *Sauce*Box*, Ezine of Literary Erotica
Author of **Rain** and **The Passion of Muhammad Shakir**

<u>Crimson Succubus: The Demon Chronicles</u> is available worldwide in paperback and digital (ebook) formats, direct from <u>www.logical-lust.com</u>, or from Amazon, Barnes & Noble, and all good retailers!

www.ingramcontent.com/pod-product-compliance
Lightning Source LLC
Chambersburg PA
CBHW031333170626
46807CB00002B/681